THE FRAGRANCE OF VIOLETS

Faces of Courage Book Two

SUSAN K. BEATTY

ISBN: 978-1-951839-59-8

Celebrate Lit Publishing

304 S. Jones Blvd #754

Las Vegas, NV, 89107

http://www.celebratelitpublishing.com/

*To my parents, Jack and Jenny Denapole, who always told me
I could do whatever I set my mind to and encouraged my reading and
writing.
I wish you could have lived long enough to see me realize the dream.
I love and miss you.*

Forgiveness is the fragrance
that the violet sheds on the heel
that has crushed it.

Chapter One

Fiona's bare feet slapped the wet sand as she raced along the beach beyond the grasping waves. Lungs already close to bursting, she ramped up her speed.

Faster, Fiona. Faster.

But there it was. The proverbial runner's wall. Smack in her face.

Bending at the waist, she grasped her knees. Her lungs heaved and her legs shook. She had not outrun the anger, the depression that crept up the back of her skull.

She eased to standing, fisted her hips, and turned slowly. The swoosh of the waves and the briny-scent of the ocean registered, but not enough to reduce her anxiety. At 6 am, few people were on the beach even in late August, although a handful of diehards rode the waves. How far had she come? The shore curved so she could just make out the gate she'd passed through only minutes ago. A mile?

Today, she'd lost her head. Instead of mapping a circular route and keeping to the private beach belonging to the resort where she worked, she just ran. She needed space, and lots of it. Now she had to go back the way she came and having hit the runner's wall meant she'd probably have to walk it.

Still, the rage burned deep in her gut.

Tentative steps to test her strength proved she could at least walk. Focusing on the resort's gate, she moved toward it, her steps intensifying up to jogging speed.

But her mind kept moving, too. Why had she been skipped over for the promotion? Hadn't it been promised to her? She deserved it. In fact, had been counting on it. And the much-needed raise.

She reached the wrought-iron gate and swiped her Princessa del Mar Resort employee card. The job had its perks. A private beach, luxurious surroundings, gourmet food. The downside was the cost of living nearby. Even sharing a teeny apartment with her best friend was costly, and it was going to get even more expensive soon when she'd have to foot the bill alone.

The path, lined with a profusion of lush bougainvillea, wound around beside the Mediterranean-style building, past the check-in lot and circular drive, bringing her to Ocean Avenue. She teetered on the curb waiting for the walk sign to let her cross. Didn't people in Southern California beach towns ever stay home?

Fiona flicked her wrist to see her smart watch better, 6:45 am She'd have to hustle in order to show up before everyone else so she could confront her boss.

Finally, she crossed the street and trudged uphill toward her apartment building, the warm pavement scratching her soles. She was already sorry she hadn't worn shoes.

Would Lottie still be asleep? Just in case, she eased open the front door and tiptoed in. She needn't have bothered. In what passed as their kitchen, Lottie hummed while monitoring the ancient coffeemaker as it trickled into the carafe. It wasn't really a kitchen, only a little nook with a curtain to hide it from the main room. Couldn't Lottie have chosen a curtain without frills? Her irritation grew as her mind criticized the room.

"One of these days, we really need to buy a new coffeepot." Except it wouldn't be we. Her best friend, her rock, was leaving her to get married.

Lottie swung around, her waist-length blonde hair flying. "Oh, for pity's sake. You scared me. Why are you sneaking in?"

"I was trying not to wake you." Fiona grabbed a towel from the rack next to the front door and wiped the sand from her feet.

"So. What are you going to do?"

"Take a shower."

"Ahem." Lottie could be really loud when she tried. She handed Fiona a mug of fragrant brew.

"I'm going to tell boss lady off." Fiona dropped into the bistro chair and cradled her steaming coffee.

"Fi—o—na." Lottie drew out her name so far, Fiona thought it was going to land on the sidewalk outside their front door.

"What?"

"Seriously."

Fiona gulped the coffee and scalded her tongue and throat. "Argh."

"Serves you right."

"Hey, whose side are you on anyway?" Fiona fanned her mouth as if that would help.

"Here." Lottie handed her a glass of water. "Although I don't know why I bother."

Gulping the water, Fiona battled the irritations and the rising tide of anxiety. She needed to tamp it down now. *Think of something else.* She looked off through the curtain-free window, her gaze on the cloudless blue sky floating above the ocean. A perk of living so close to the beach. Of course, they could only see a small slice of the vista. The resort commanded most of the view.

Nothing was helping. Not her run, not the view. Her leg jiggled, and panic began an ever-tightening vise on her mind.

"Fiona." Lottie stood in front of her and gripped her arms. "Look at me. You will not give in to the panic. Please. Look at me."

Fiona willed her gaze up to her friend's eyes, strength seeming to flow from Lottie's deep walnut-colored eyes to her own amber ones.

"Breathe. Breathe deeply."

After several deep, cleansing breaths, Fiona's heart rate settled down and her leg stopped its rhythmic movement. "Thanks. I'm okay now." She dropped to the couch.

Lottie knelt in front of her. "What brought this on?" Her voice was a whisper. "Was it my wedding?"

She couldn't always figure out the source of her anxiety attacks, but today it was absolutely clear. "That promotion was mine. The director had no right to give it to Heather."

"Maybe not. But it's her *right* as the director to decide. Pray. Let the Lord help you figure out how to accept this." Lottie stood and shoved a hank of hair behind her ear. "Now. I have to wrangle this mop so we can get to work."

A rank odor almost knocked Fiona out. *Oh, man, gotta shower.* She set her mug in the sink and suppressed a sigh. "I'm going to need a lot of help doing that." *And you won't be here.*

As she hurried to the bathroom, a whispered lie in her ear told her she hadn't deserved the promotion anyway.

———

Thick carpeting muted the already hushed tones of the business office. A resort like the Princessa del Mar, that charged as much as one month of Fiona's salary for one night, could afford such luxuries. It beat the tile floors of the cut-rate hotels she'd worked in before coming here. To say nothing of the many tawdry registration desks she'd stood behind.

Fiona shuddered.

The director sat sheltered behind the glass windows of her office, an executive's perk, while the rest of them shared double-desked cubbies in the vast room.

Fiona's gaze wandered to Lottie three spaces down and across the aisle from her own. How had Lottie fashioned a sophisticated up-do so quickly this morning? Her own pixie cut paled in comparison. She paled in comparison. Lottie was so good, so strong. She'd rightly talked Fiona out of confronting their director.

The intra-office messaging system on her computer and her smart watch dinged. Nothing like being tied to your job. *Meeting, conference room, five minutes.*

Gathering her notebook and files, Fiona stood, struggling with the anger that was again trying to claw its way out of her throat. Heather's promotion would surely be announced. The director would announce Fiona's failure.

Lottie appeared at her side. "Stuff it, Fiona."

Her best friend knew her so well. With her free hand, Fiona smoothed her consignment store silk blouse over her hip.

Settled in the conference room, Fiona inhaled the scent of sugary donuts and gourmet coffee as it wafted from the center of the table. Everyone seemed tight-lipped. No chattering about who got what donut or passing the carafe.

Their boss didn't bother to sit, but merely stood to her considerable height at the head of the table. She pulled off imposing well. Maybe this meant a short meeting. One could only hope.

"With the departure of my assistant director—who left us for the Pacifica Resort," her mouth puckered as if she were sucking a lemon when she named their competition. "I have appointed Heather as the new assistant director. Also, since two of our largest clients have elected to take their business to the Pacifica, I'll be reassigning accounts."

When she mentioned Heather's promotion, all eyes had turned toward Fiona. See. Everyone else expected her to get it, too. It was getting more difficult to resist the anger.

In a monotone voice, almost as if she were reciting a grocery list, the director re-assigned clients to sales associates.

"Fiona, take the Optometrist's Society."

Oh, great. Small conference, and their budget allowed few frills.

"Heather, you take the Skinner-Williams Wedding in January, since you've already worked a lot with the planning. In fact, I understand the bride and groom's parents are coming for a site visit next week."

Fiona flinched. Williams? But there must be hundreds, if not thousands, of people with the last name Williams. Nevertheless, she squirmed in her chair.

"Client files are on the back table. Pick up those applicable to you as you go out. That'll be all." The woman's gaze swept the room and fell on Fiona. "Fiona, would you stay behind a moment?"

What excuse would she give for denying her the promotion? Fiona stayed seated at the opposite end of the table, and the director strode toward her, the abundant scent of far east spices leading the way.

"I know you were expecting the promotion, Fiona, but you're not quite ready. You often seem insecure in your decisions." She moved toward the door but turned back. "Plus, there's a little spark of rebellion in you that needs to be quenched."

As the director strode from the room, Fiona's face flamed. Insecure? Rebellion? Shame piled up in her chest. The director was right. She wasn't worthy. The name Williams echoed in her mind. No, of course she wasn't worthy.

But if she worked harder, perhaps she could prove herself. Move beyond her past. She'd done well with previous jobs, until shadows of her past threatened to overwhelm her and destroy her confidence, her relationships. Lottie was always telling her to trust her business-trained mind and her decisions. She also told her to let others into her life. Yet, they never stayed. They abandoned her. Just like her mother. Her father, who wasn't her father. She couldn't think about him.

Charlotte, her Lottie, had inexplicably stuck by her. A best friend, a wise and trusted counselor since high school, always telling her the truth in love and expecting the impossible from her. And now she was leaving her, too. Lottie promised Fiona getting married wouldn't change anything but their living arrangements, and that she'd always be there for her. Besides, they'd see each other at the Princessa del Mar every day for work.

What would Lottie say about the director calling her insecure and rebellious?

———

"You've been a rebel since I've known you. I bet you've always had that wild streak." Lottie pulled two slices of pizza from the greasy delivery box and settled wedges on a paper plate. The pungent aroma of pepperoni, cheese, and tomatoes mingled with the yeast from the crust, filled their apartment. She handed the plate to Fiona and filled another plate for herself.

"Why would you say that? I think I'm pretty much a follow-the-rules kind of gal. By the way, thanks for ordering tonight's pizza." Fiona bit off a chunk and savored the gooey goodness.

Lottie chortled and raised the pizza to her mouth. "Yeah, right," she mumbled around her mouthful of food.

"You agree with the director? How can I be both weak and insubordinate?" Fiona threw her napkin down and huffed, her irritation rising.

"I didn't say that. But you have to admit your anxiety

issues occasionally, only occasionally, make you hesitate and question yourself."

As twilight descended outside their window, lights snapped on in the distance. Darkness threatened to shroud Fiona's mind. She could shake it off. Would shake it off.

"When does your wedding dress come in for your fitting?" Lottie's wedding was not really a safer subject, but it was all that came to her.

"Next month. You'll go with me, won't you?"

"Mmf, corse," she mumbled around the much-too-large bite of pizza in her mouth. After swallowing, she continued. "Ya know, I don't even know why I got into this business."

"I've always been afraid it was just because of me."

Lottie was partly right. At the point she had to finally declare a college major, she'd thought what her friend was doing in her hospitality classes looked fun. She liked the sound of the word "hospitality," but she'd had a different idea of what that meant in real life. How juvenile was she to pick her major because she liked the sound of a word? On the other hand, she discovered she was good at the details and had the organizational skills needed. Even her people skills were good. Most of the time.

So, why didn't she get the promotion? Was what her boss said that she wasn't ready, was insecure and rebellious, the real reasons?

Fiona grinned at Lottie. "It's always just because of you. And look how we ended up at the same hotel."

"Truly a blessing of God." Lottie pushed away her plate and wiped her fingers on several puny napkins from the pizza place.

Must be why I'm in this business. Thank you, Lord.

Chapter Two

Nason Williams' keys clattered as he dropped them into the marble bowl on the entry table, echoing in the otherwise silent house. His briefcase thudded against the wood-planked floor, and he tossed his jacket toward the coat rack.

An empty house for a change. Good thing after such a pitiful day.

He grabbed a Dr. Pepper from the refrigerator and sank onto the couch, propping his feet on the coffee table. Irina would nag him about that. Well, she wasn't home. He popped the tab and took a long swig, savoring the cold sweetness as it bubbled over his tongue.

If one more person wanted a piece of him, he would scream. The entire office seemed to stand in front of his desk thrusting important decisions at him today. Couldn't people figure things out on their own?

After another long drink, he set the can on the end table, slid down, and propped his head against the beige linen fabric.

"Nason. I've asked you a hundred times not to put your feet on that glass coffee table."

He opened one eye and peered at his wife standing over him with her hands fisted on her hips. For such a petite woman, she sure had a loud voice. And where had she come from, anyway? He closed his eye but slid his feet from the table to the carpet with a thump. "Happy now?"

"Humph."

Although he couldn't see her, and the carpet was well-padded, he knew she stomped away. Because that was Irina's MO.

"Hey, Dad. You asleep?"

Nason slid his eyelid open again. Now his son loomed over him.

"Nope. Your mother already made sure of that." Nason finally opened both eyes and sat up. People said Rick favored him. Tall, sandy blond hair. But Rick was more muscled. Lifted weights, whereas Nason prided himself on being a lean runner. "What's up?"

"Yeah. Look. I know you said you and Mom would help out with the wedding since Rainbow's parents have zero money...But, um. Well, we're going to need more money."

"What? I'm not—"

"Made of money. Yeah, I know." Rick was one of those rare guys who couldn't hide his feelings well. Maybe he'd outgrow it, but right now his face had regret written all over it.

Nason tried to dial back his attitude. "How much and what for?"

Rick plopped onto the matching sectional opposite his father and leaned forward, his arms resting on his thighs. "The resort's original estimate was for just the basic room rental. Didn't include stuff like microphones and the PA system, tablecloths."

"How much?" The attitude crept back into Nason's tone.

"Don't know yet. But we'll find out when we visit the resort next week—"

"Well, of course, darling." Irina inserted herself into the setting and the conversation. "Anything you need. Right, dear?" She delivered the last two words as a threat.

Nason held back a sigh. "Irina, we'll have to see. As I said, I'm not made of money."

"Dear." She elongated the word and infused it with venom. "Anything they need." She turned on her heel and marched out of the room.

Irina was going to make him pay for his predicament for the rest of his life. Then it wasn't her fault, was it? Even if most of it had been before they were married, what happened later hurt her, and for that he was sorry. For her sake, he'd cut off ties fifteen years ago.

Not that Maeve got the message. She seemed to think that just because they'd had a brief fling, he owed her something. She still kept asking him for money. For drugs he assumed. But he had supported her and the child for twelve years until he'd found out the child wasn't his. No, he wasn't about to give her any more. And he sure as heck wasn't going to let Irina know she'd tried to contact him today.

Thoughts of the child, well, adult now, stabbed at him. Since he had accepted Christ into his life last year, he couldn't shake the feeling he had to somehow make up for his wrong.

"Sorry, Dad. Didn't mean to start trouble." Rick's mouth drooped. "If there was any other way…"

"I know. I know. We'll work it out." He slid back down and again dropped his head against the couch. "What *are* the Skinners contributing? I assume they're contributing something?"

"Not much." Rick examined his hands. "Most of what you and Mom aren't paying, Rainbow and I will have to come up with."

Nason stifled a groan. "Considering you're just getting your engineering career started and Rainbow is still in college, how are you guys coming up with anything?" He stood and stretched.

Still not looking up, Rick said, "Um…I cashed in the insurance policy you gave me when I started high school."

"You what?" The bellow was out before Nason could grab

it. His gaze swiveled around the room. He needed to make sure his wife hadn't come back. He sank back onto the couch, and a little more quietly, said, "Rick. Rick. Why didn't you talk to me first?"

"I didn't want to be any more of a burden."

"Well, for goodness' sakes, don't tell your mother."

Rick chuckled. "Yeah, no way. I tried to talk Rainbow into a much smaller wedding. She would have agreed, but you know Mom. She had her heart set on the Princessa del Mar Resort and talked Rainbow into it."

"Yes, I know your mom." But the truth was, Nason was just as eager for Rick and Rainbow to have a show-stopper wedding. It would be good for his successful attorney's image. That meant he'd have to pay. "Don't worry. We'll work it out, son. Anything else? Can I just rest now?" He resumed his slumped posture and put his feet back on the table.

"Did you invite the Skinners out to dinner after the resort visit next week? You know, you said it was a good idea for the four of you to get more acquainted." Youthful hope and eagerness played across Rick's features.

Nason had heard people call Rick classically handsome, but when asked recently by a co-worker, he hesitated to describe him that way. They did look alike, and he didn't want to seem *too* vain.

He chuckled.

"What?" His son raised an eyebrow at him.

"Nothing." He closed his eyes again. "Yeah, yeah. Check with your mom."

"Thanks, Dad." Rick strolled from the room as he called out. "Mom?"

Sleep eluded him. Although his eyes were closed, his thoughts somersaulted through his mind. *Who in the world named their child Rainbow? Could he convince that big company to retain his and his firm's legal services? He'd really need the new client and the billable hours to pay the wedding bills now.*

Then somehow his reverie turned a corner. During the rare times Maeve contacted him, she no longer spoke of Fiona, which for the most part was for the best. But what did Fiona think of him? Did she even think of him at all? Where was she? At...what? Rick was twenty-three, so she must be twenty-seven. She might be married. Should he have been there for that? He knew the answer, and guilt tightened his chest.

"Nason. How many times do I have to tell you to keep your feet off the table?"

———

The next morning, Selena, his legal assistant, slipped a file in front of him.

"Beltway Corps?"

She nodded. "But you're not gonna like it. Two new plaintiffs have been added to the suit against them." Crease lines dominated her forehead.

Nason flipped open the report and allowed his gaze to skim the words and numbers. "Not a problem. Get me their complete deposition transcripts as soon as possible."

"Sure, Boss. Oh, and here's a phone message from a Heather Faulkner at the Princessa del Mar Resort. Since when do we handle cases for the resort?"

"What? No. Must be about Rick's wedding." He clenched his jaw.

As Selena went back to her own office, Nason slapped the folder closed and picked up the message slip. Why was she calling him at work? He didn't have time for this stuff. He dialed the number and almost hung up after the third ring.

"Heather Faulkner, Assistant Director of Sales." The voice was monotone, almost bored.

"Nason Williams here. I'm returning your call. How's your day going?" He'd just turn on the charm and cheer her up.

"Oh, yes, Mr. Williams. Apparently, we need a credit card from you to complete the contract for your son's wedding."

"Ms. Faulkner, we don't even know the charges yet."

"Yes, sir, I understand. I am sorry, but our policy is to have a credit card on file to hold a date. May I have your credit card number, please?" Ms. Faulkner's voice warmed up just a tad.

Who was this woman? His irritation increased the twitchy feeling in his legs. He reluctantly gave her his credit card number and hung up. Time to get back to earning the money to pay that credit card bill.

A rap on the door and Selena stuck her head in. "Nason, Jim Longstreet called and wondered if you could meet him in his office right away."

"Longstreet?"

When the division head summoned a junior partner like Nason, you went.

Selena nodded, made a face, and withdrew.

Coward.

Now what? He shot from his chair and hurried out of his office. Electricity crackled through his body. This was going to be good or bad. No neutral. Which way would it go?

He entered the elevator and rode two floors above, a floor specifically for senior partners. He stepped out into a reception area larger and more opulent than the main floor lobby. Law apparently was a very lucrative business. If you were part of the in-crowd executives anyway.

Not that Nason could complain. He'd done well here at The McArthur Group, achieving a comfortable existence, if you didn't count the stress levels. Making junior partner six months ago added to his sense of accomplishment.

A receptionist who appeared to be fifteen immediately ushered him into another office where he was met by the woman who had been Longstreet's secretary since the beginning of time, or so it seemed.

He finally reached the inner sanctum, where the man stood behind a desk that looked to be the size of Nason's entire office.

"Williams. Have a seat." The man's high voice contrasted the size of his girth. "One of my clients is being sued by several former employees for under payments. I've another matter I'm handling for them. Plus, several other hot cases. Since corporate finance and HR issues are more your expertise than mine, I want you to take over this case. You can make it a priority in your schedule."

It was not a question. Getting asked by the new division head to take over a case would be good for his track record, even if he had to share the accolades with Longstreet. The man was still a mystery to him, having only been transferred to Orange County a few months ago.

But he had more important things to consider than figuring out the new boss. Could he focus on this case with the other ones he already juggled? Keep everyone happy and maintain his reputation? A slight quivering in his stomach didn't leave him reassured.

"Williams?"

"Yes, sir."

"BioTech is a longtime client and the board of directors are friends. Don't blow it. You do well, and I'll see you get included in larger cases on a regular basis."

Longstreet was about his own age, probably early fifties, but with a full head of blinding white hair.

Longstreet reviewed the suit with Nason and asked him to look at the client's pay records and related finances, while he, Longstreet, attended to the other legal matter for BioTech.

"Get me a preliminary report by Monday a.m. We have a lunch meeting with the client."

"A day and a half. Not much time." Nason looked at his watch. It was already the lunch hour.

"There's always the weekend." Longstreet stood up and reached out a hand. "Thanks for coming on board."

He guessed that was a dismissal.

Longstreet waved him off and turned his attention to his paper-strewn desktop.

"I won't let you down."

Dude, what did you just do? This was a great opportunity for him, and he didn't have a choice, did he? His father had trained him in business matters to always meet the task head on and failure was not an option. The training had done well for him, getting him through law school, moving him up from a minuscule private practice to the huge law firm of The MacArthur Group.

On his own, he'd never been too much bothered by a strict adherence to ethics. Until he left his own practice and became a Christian. Of course, being an attorney, he'd always been careful, but not always careful enough.

The past was the past. He wasn't that guy anymore. When he gave his life to God, he'd vowed to be meticulous in his ethics.

Could he trust Longstreet? They hadn't worked together before, but those rumors made Nason skittish.

Scuttlebutt was that Jim Longstreet played on the edge. That he was a little too laid back, forcing other attorneys to pick up the slack. He'd also heard Longstreet played fast and loose with the truth at times. Well, that just couldn't happen with Nason on the case. Not on his watch. Anyway, maybe the rumors were false.

How the man maintained his job and reputation was beyond him. Unless the brass condoned it. No. The McArthur Group would not be as successful if the higher ups looked the other way. And they certainly hadn't when Nason's past had been in the crosshairs. No one wanted to be brought up before the State Bar Association accused of misconduct.

No. It all had to be unfounded rumors.

Indulging in Sunday brunch, the glutton's favorite meal, had been high on his much-loved list, too. He enjoyed eating out in restaurants that offered everything from breakfast to lunch to dinner, and every decadent treat imaginable. In truth, he still liked the special meal that spanned breakfast and lunch, but since becoming a Christian, it interfered with going to church. Irina hadn't been thrilled with his conversion and was even less excited about him going to church on Sundays instead of taking her out.

Some Sundays they went to brunch right after he got home from services, but Irina always complained that by that time it was lunch. Why did the time matter to her? The restaurants and the food were the same.

Irina was happy today to be seated at Jim Longstreet's table at the Orange County Mining Company, high in the hills overlooking the region. He guessed it wasn't so much who they were eating with, but she was finally getting brunch at a decent time. She might even be glad he wasn't able to go to church.

Nason shoveled a forkful of lox and capers into his mouth, wishing he had turned down the invitation. That wouldn't have been wise. He didn't want to start out offending the new division head, and the bonus was, it would cement their relationship.

Next to him, Irina giggled at something said by the man on the other side of her. While Irina had her faults, unfaithfulness was not one of them. Nason knew he could trust her. Why had that thought come up? Just because she seemed to enjoy herself with a strange man?

Get a life, dude.

"Nason?"

Stopping mid-chew, he looked up at Longstreet. Apparently, he'd missed something in the conversation.

He swallowed the bite of omelet. "Sorry?"

"You ready for the client meeting tomorrow?"

"I have done an overall review and have some preliminary questions ready."

"Over-all review? I can't help think that won't be good enough."

"Sorry, sir. I've only had access to the records for a short time. After I get the answers to my questions tomorrow, I'll be able to dive deeper."

"Hmm. I suggest you do another 'overall review' tomorrow morning just to be on top of your game."

"Sure." Nason sipped his coffee. Great. He'd have to get into the office early tomorrow to review his review. Such nonsense. But he'd follow through.

Soft tones chirped from the cell phone in his suit jacket. Plucking the phone out of his pocket, he rose, murmured his apologies, and moved away from the table.

"Rick? What's up?" He continued walking toward the lobby.

"Hey, Dad. Am I interrupting?"

"We're having brunch with one of my colleagues."

"Oh, sorry about that. Just reminding you about the resort visit tomorrow. Oh, and dinner with the Skinners after."

"Thanks. I haven't forgotten."

Rick apologized again and hung up.

Truth was he had forgotten. Well, not forgotten, but it wasn't at the top of his mind either, and now with meeting the big-wig from BioTech tomorrow, his head was crowded. How had both events ended up on the same day? He fished around in his brain for the time of the visit. Of course, he could have asked his son, but then Rick would think he had forgotten. Three p.m. That was it. Plenty of time to complete the client meeting and make it to the resort.

Tableware tinkled and clanked as he returned to his seat.

"Don't forget we have lunch scheduled with the client right after the meeting."

Prime rib caught in his throat. Gulping water as fast as he could, he dislodged the knot of beef. It finally went down but left his throat sore. Great. Would he be finished with lunch in time to get from Irvine to Dana Point? Irina would have to meet him at the resort.

"I…I may have to cut lunch short. We have an appointment for my son's wedding." Nason gulped down more water.

Although Nason couldn't actually see it, he knew Longstreet's stink eye bore into him.

He hated inconvenient situations where he'd be running from here to there. Steady, life should be steady. Usually, if he was in control, life as an attorney was good. Satisfaction from delving into computer records, wrangling figures and time-lines, pulling out the right evidence to straighten out the client's woes drew him out of bed each morning. Tomorrow would definitely be tiresome.

What a drag.

Chapter Three

The resort hallways buzzed with activity. Conference attendees stood in knots, chattering and laughing as Fiona strolled by, monitoring the servers. The ambient energy could be overwhelming. Conference organizers, stressing out over making their conference the best ever, passed on that stress to her.

"Fiona. I've been looking for you." Speaking of stressed conference organizers, this client's eyes were as large as the round banquet tables. "No microphones in the workshop rooms yet."

Clinging by a thread to her own sense of peace, Fiona promised to solve the leader's problem and moved on, giving instructions to the server and audiovisual staffs.

Her insides were in a tangle. The last day of an event left her yearning to get it over with. She'd be glad when this conference ended, and everyone moved out of the building tonight. And after three intense days of organizational issues, tomorrow would be a welcome day off.

A shrill voice in her ear caused her to jump. "Heather, you scared me." Why was she on edge?

Heather raised an eyebrow. "Really, Fiona." She cleared

her throat. "I know you're supposed to have a day off tomorrow, but my assistant landed in the hospital, and I need someone to work with me on three site visits. I can authorize overtime." She looked rigid in her black power suit and slicked back mousy brown hair.

The assistant director must really be in a bind for her to offer overtime. So much for a relaxing day off. Well, she could use the money, couldn't she?

"Sure. What time do you need me in? I'm likely to be here until midnight waiting for this group to move out."

"Yeah. Okay. Ten'll be fine. First site visit is at ten-thirty, then two more, one and three o'clock. See you in the morning." Heather turned on her sensible heels and moved on.

Why had Heather received *her* promotion? Fiona didn't buy the "rebel" or "indecisive" labels. She didn't embrace the idea Heather was better suited for the role. In fact, the woman's personality didn't exude grace and warmth to their clients. At least not as far as she had seen. Maybe Heather would show a different side of herself tomorrow when Fiona would have the opportunity to observe firsthand.

Lord, help me accept this.

"Fiona." It was the frantic client again, still in a state of panic.

At last, all event leaders and their materials were out of the ballrooms. The staff had retreated to their various hidey-holes or gone home. Fiona looked at her smart watch. Eleven fifty-five. After three years of working similar events, she'd guessed right about the wrap up time. Actually, it wasn't a guess. It was experience. Experience that should have counted for something.

Back in her office, she grabbed her purse and briefcase. Not that she'd need anything in her case between now and ten the next morning, but she felt naked not carrying her laptop and files with her at all times.

She walked through the silent corridors and made her way

through to the lobby, empty except for registration desk staff chatting quietly. Crystal chandeliers glowed softly, marble columns and floors reflecting a high sheen. Lush green plants and trees sprouted from planters throughout the expansive area. A lone traveler traipsed through the automatic doors and was met by one of the bell staff, who helped him with his bag and escorted him to the desk.

This was how she liked it. Quiet and calm, attentive staff. Of course, if it was like this all the time, she'd be out of a job. Why was she in this job again? She shrugged away the thoughts and hitched her briefcase up on her shoulder as she began her short walk home under a black sky with few stars. She was sure they were there somewhere, but lights from the many resorts blotted out all but the moon, tonight shining fully, unhindered even by clouds.

At the foot of her staircase, she wished they hadn't chosen an upstairs apartment. After trudging up the hill, stairs were the last thing she wanted. But they did have that view, such as it was.

As she let herself in, she was greeted by soft lights flickering in the living room.

"Lottie? You up?" Fiona dropped everything on the floor next to the front door. She didn't need to go looking for it in a few hours.

"Good thing I was, or I wouldn't be now." Lottie giggled as she emerged from her bedroom. "How'd the event go? Lucky you with a day off tomorrow while I slave away."

"No. I'm working with Heather tomorrow. Overtime. Remind me again why Heather got to be assistant director?"

"Ah, leave it alone, Fiona."

"Maybe when you get married and leave me, I should look for another job and a cheaper apartment I can afford by myself." Fiona kicked off her heels and removed her sweater. "I don't want to look for a new roommate."

"I'm sorry. If I didn't love Rex so much, you know I'd never leave you. Besides, we won't be far away. Unless you move to some forsaken place. You won't, will you?" Lottie wrinkled her nose. "Stay at the resort, so I can see you every day."

"Nah. I'm not goin' anywhere but to bed. Gotta be in by ten." She wiggled her fingers in a goodnight.

"Yeah. See you in the office."

Fiona's last view was of Lottie, hands clasped behind her back, staring at her.

———

Three cups of coffee and Fiona still struggled to focus on what Heather was telling her about the site visits they would handle today, the first in just a few moments.

"Okay, so that's our ten-thirty and one appointments. The last is the Skinner-Williams wedding party …"

Fiona was wide awake now.

"They are looking at the Crystal Ballroom. The groom warned me his mother might have some pretty strong ideas about what she wants. Why is it that the mothers always try to take over?"

"No idea…" She could just ask Heather the names of the parties involved. Right? She rubbed her bare forearms.

Besides, who would be getting married? Ricky? He'd be kinda young. Twenty-two, twenty-three? Stop. It had to be someone else.

Easy-peasy site visit number one concluded, Fiona grabbed an egg salad sandwich to go and another coffee—her fourth—from the resort's marketplace and searched for Lottie. She found her in her cubicle fixated on her computer screen. Since her cubby mate was not at her desk, Fiona slipped into the empty chair.

"Hey."

Lottie shot her a glance and went back to the screen. "Hey, yourself. Thought you were doing site visits."

"About that." Fiona unwrapped her sandwich. "Heather briefed me. And...we're handling the Skinner-Williams wedding today." Her throat tightened. She sipped the coffee to make way for the egg filling. As she chewed, she looked up to Lottie staring at her. "What?"

"What do you mean, *what*? You know it's unlikely to be your Williams."

"*My* Williams?" She scoffed. "For sure, not mine."

"There are millions of people named Williams. What are the chances these people have anything to do with you? And, anyway, what if they are?"

"*What if they are?*" She wanted to scream and run away at the thought.

"Fiona." Heather peered over the cubicle wall at her. "Time to head to the lobby and meet our one o'clocks."

She stuffed her uneaten sandwich and coffee cup in the trash can.

Lottie still stared. "One o'clock?"

"No. Three."

"I'll be praying."

Fiona nodded her thanks and came alongside Heather, who frowned at her.

"What was that all about?"

"Just a joke." No way would she tell her assistant director.

The site visit went overtime, and Heather asked Fiona to run back to her office to pick up the Skinner-Williams file and meet her in the Crystal Ballroom. Normally, she'd be irritated to be sent on such an errand, but this would give her the chance to read the file before facing whoever was waiting for her in the ballroom. She speed-walked toward Heather's domain.

The file was not in the center of Heather's desk where she expected to find it. She quickly searched the other neatly stacked files. Not there. Checked the in and out trays. Nothing.

Her smart watch showed it was five after three. Maybe the parties would be late. Panic nearly overwhelmed her. Her cell phone beeped. Heather.

"Sorry, Fiona, I had the file all along. The Skinners and Williamses are here. We'll wait for you in the Crystal Ballroom." Heather clicked off.

Fiona dropped into Heather's chair. *She had it all along?* Could she just choke the woman? Better get going. See where this leads. She stood on wobbly legs but gained strength as she shuffled out of the room.

So, what if it was Nason? Maybe this was God's way of reuniting them. Or at least putting them on the road to some sort of reconciliation. A fantasy played in her head in which Nason apologized and begged for forgiveness. Told her he wanted to be her father again.

Get real. She forced her mind to slam the cover on that fairy tale book. Besides. It couldn't be him, right?

Staff members nodded or waved as she passed. She dipped her head in acknowledgement, but she was sure little sincerity showed.

Drawing up just outside the open Crystal Ballroom doors, she listened, but only Heather's voice droned. She took a deep breath and entered the room.

———

Nason tried to catch his breath. He'd dashed out of the restaurant with profuse apologies to the BioTech CEO. Relieved the man had easily answered all his questions, Nason switched mental gears as he sped toward Dana Point. He'd pulled up to the valet parking with two minutes to spare.

Irina, Rick, and the Skinners congregated in the ornate lobby. Their silence was not a good sign.

"Nason, finally." Irina frowned.

"Dad, thought you wouldn't make it on time." Rick grinned, it appeared, with some relief. "Dad, you remember Rainbow's parents? Red and Vivian?"

He was kidding, right? No wonder they named their daughter Rainbow. "Sure." He extended his hand to Red, who shook it with gusto. "Vivian. And Rainbow. Good to see you."

With a name like Rainbow, one might expect a vivacious and vibrant girl. Not this Rainbow. She was pale from her colorless hair—blonde?—to her ashen complexion. Her personality did little to dispel the bland label. What did Rick see in her? At least she was sweet and seemed to love Rick. That was all that mattered, he supposed.

Rainbow took after her mother, who looked like her twin, just twenty or thirty years older. With identical meek smiles, too. The father made up for his wife and daughter's lack of charisma. Red was surely a nickname after his flaming hair color.

"Glad to see you again, Nason." His voice matched his loud hair. "Gonna be quite an event, right?"

A woman approached them, tucking a cell phone into her pocket. At least he assumed she was a woman, but with slicked-back hair and a slightly masculine black suit, Nason wasn't quite sure. It was a good thing her name was plastered on her badge. Heather. He'd never known a man with that name, so his guess seemed sure. She greeted them and introduced herself. Her voice was feminine, and that reminded him of their phone conversation over his credit card.

The hotel representative prattled on as they moved en masse down wide, luxurious corridors toward a room he'd been told was called the Crystal Ballroom. Sounded expensive. Heather unlocked a set of double doors and led them into a large room devoid of furniture. Not only did it sound expensive, it lived up to its reputation. Extra plush carpet, crown molding with gold filigree, and the eponymous crystal hanging from the chandeliers.

Rainbow clutched Rick's arm and squealed. "Ricky, I love it. It's beautiful. I'm so glad you suggested this hotel, Irina."

Irina asked the representative several questions that went over Nason's head. Thank goodness for his wife who could navigate wedding detail muck.

"My assistant should be here any moment, and she can go over some of those ideas with you. Ah, here she is now."

Everyone in the room turned toward the doorway. A lithe, sandy-blonde woman stood there looking a little like the proverbial deer in the headlights.

"Let me introduce you to Fiona Hanlon. Fiona, this is Mr. and Mrs. Skinner and Mr. and Mrs. Williams." She gestured to each couple. "And the happy couple, Rick and Rainbow."

He stepped back, and Irina, hand over her mouth, gasped.

Red moved forward and extended his hand to Fiona. She moved like a robot as she shook it.

Nason's feet froze in place, and, for a split second, his mind went blank. This was the rep's assistant? This was Fiona? She'd grown into a lovely young woman. At least on the outside, but with a mother like hers, who knew what she was really like.

He stared, and she stared right back. Forcing his gaze from her, he looked quickly at Irina, whose face looked like an ice sculpture. And Rick? He gaped, his mouth forming a perfect "O."

Before anyone could acknowledge what was happening, Heather returned them all to the subject at hand. During the next hour, she deferred to Fiona, who'd come out of her stupor and spoke knowledgeably and with ease about prices and equipment. She also avoided looking at him again the entire meeting.

"Well, then, I will draw up the sales order and forward it to you, Mr. Williams, for your signature. I'll leave my assistant

here to escort you to the lobby. Good day and thank you."
Heather strode off.

That woman was obtuse. Nason just couldn't decide
whether that was, in this case, a good thing or a bad thing.
Probably good. Had she acknowledged any sort of awkward-
ness, she would have embarrassed her clients. Never a good
thing.

"This way, please." Fiona led them down the hall and
carried on a polite conversation with Rainbow, asking about
other plans for the wedding.

They reached the lobby, and Fiona said her goodbyes. As
she appeared poised to leave, Rick put his hand up, palm out.

"Excuse me. They said you were Fiona Hanlon, right?" At
her brief nod, Rick looked back and forth between Fiona and
Nason. "Dad?"

Her face flamed red. Without another word, she turned
and fled.

Nason stepped toward her as if to follow, but thankfully
Irina grabbed his arm.

"Time to go. Now." She dragged him outside.

For once, he was grateful for Irina's interference. What
would he have said to Fiona? He wasn't even sure he wanted
to talk to her. What good would it do after all these years? She
probably hated him and wouldn't talk anyway. On the other
hand, he'd probably have to talk to her during this whole
wedding thing. Maybe they could just keep it to wedding
plans.

Yeah, right. You are such a fool, dude.

Under the resort's awning at valet parking, the Skinners
looked perplexed, but Nason didn't think they could be any
more perplexed than he was.

Chapter Four

Tormented by a roaring in her ears, she fled from the lobby, berating herself for acting like an idiot when she'd seen Nason. Despite anticipating it could be him, she was so shocked her muscles had gone weak and her body wouldn't move. Her eyes must have mimicked Nason's, wide and staring.

Irina's gasp echoed in her mind. And poor Rick. He'd recognized her, although he'd only been eight years old the last time they'd seen each other. Even if Rick hadn't been with Nason and Irina, she would have recognized him. He looked so much like his father. Of course, everyone had said how much she looked like Nason, too, and she'd been so proud of it. Her mother's coloring was the exact opposite. Black hair, deep brown eyes, and an olive complexion. Yet Maeve was her mother, and Nason was not her father. Neither biologically nor in practice since she was twelve.

Escaping into the first set of restrooms, she locked herself in a stall where she sagged against the door and her body shook uncontrollably. She'd dreamed of their reunion, and it looked nothing like this. She pictured him begging her for forgiveness and giving her a big bear hug like he used to.

They hadn't even spoken.

And what did she do when Rick tried to talk to her? She ran away. *You are such a coward, girl.* At least she'd talked with Rick's fiancée. She seemed sweet.

How would they get through the next several months until the wedding? Could she confine her interactions to Rainbow? She groaned. As usual, Irina appeared more in control of the nuptials than Rainbow or her mother. And if she understood Heather's parting comments, Nason was footing the bill.

Maybe she should gather her courage and initiate meeting him. Get this over with now. Perhaps he would apologize like in her daydreams. Her body continued to shake, and she sat on the edge of the toilet seat, teetering a little. *Don't fall in. That's all you'd need to make the day complete.* Why didn't these toilets have lids anyway?

It was coming. She could feel it. Sweat pooled on her lower back. A dizzy haze floated through her mind, and her stomach churned. *Remember the steps. Breathe through your mouth, feeling the air slowly fill your chest and belly and then slowly leave them again.* She breathed in for a count of four, held for a second, and then breathed out for a count of four.

If only she had her lavender oil with her. She patted her pockets, but no little bottle of calming oil hid there. She focused on the graffiti someone had etched into the stall door but ignored the words.

Something resembling calmness settled over her. It was only a faint echo, but at least she could function. Her mind returned to Nason.

No. She would not go to Nason. It would look like she was begging. It was up to him to contact her. Yes, that was it. Fiona stood up, threw her shoulders back, and marched out of the restroom back to her cubbyhole.

Her bravado waned as she wove her way to Lottie's desk. She was on the phone, and she wasn't alone. Her cubby mate occupied the other desk in the minuscule space.

Fiona touched Lottie's shoulder and met her friend's questioning gaze with a grimace. Lottie raised her eyebrows and nodded as Fiona made her way to her own desk.

"Fiona." Heather appeared at her side.

Why must Heather always sound like she was yelling her name?

"I've decided you can handle the paperwork for the Skinner-Williams wedding. I'll forward you the draft I started. Add the details and figures and return to me for review by tomorrow morning."

"Morning?" She heard the tremor in her own voice and cleared her throat. "I was planning to head home now. Besides, I, well…" That was Heather's job on this contract, not hers. How to say that without sounding insubordinate? Sounding like a rebel? "You sure you trust me doing that on your contract?"

The other woman's expression turned from haughty to confused and back to haughty again. "Yes. But you can have until two p.m. tomorrow. No later." With a dismissive wave, she continued beyond Fiona's cubicle, dragging her rolling briefcase toward the hallway door.

Ha. Fiona sniffed. At least someone got to be on her way home.

Lottie sidled up and dropped into the empty chair in Fiona's cubicle. "What is it? You look like death warmed over."

Taking a deep breath, she relayed the CliffsNotes version of the afternoon's events. "I'll tell you more later. I've gotta go home before I can't drag myself up that hill."

Lottie waggled her eyebrows, patted her smooth up do, and stood. "I can't believe this. They just happened to pick this hotel. And Heather just happened to need you for their site visit. Does this mean you're permanently part of their sales team now?"

"Apparently. Heather assigned me to complete the sales order. By tomorrow. But I'm too tired to stay tonight."

"Oh, bother. Okay. Head home. I've got another hour's work at least. Why don't you order us a pizza?"

That girl could eat pizza twenty-four seven. Not that Fiona didn't like it, but occasionally she'd prefer some other sort of takeout or delivery. But Lottie was seldom demanding. In fact, Fiona did most of the demanding with her panic attacks, Bible questions, insecurities. And who could forget her *rebelliousness*?

"Sure. See you at home."

Sometimes she wished she lived farther away from her job so she could use the driving time to chill or just think. At least she'd have the apartment to herself for a while until Lottie got home. Soon, she'd have the apartment all to herself. Lottie's wedding was in December. What would she do then? At least they'd still be working together at the resort.

As she slogged toward home, her mind swung toward the other wedding, Rick and Rainbow's. January 5. Four months to deal—or not—with Nason. And Irina. She shuddered thinking of Irina's hard face when she realized she was in Fiona's presence after all these years. Irina hadn't changed at all. She'd always looked pinched.

Although the August sun beat down despite the five o'clock hour, the sea breeze cooled her skin and ruffled the palm fronds sparkling in the bright sun. If she moved, she'd lose this feeling of being in paradise. When she wasn't dealing with Lottie's upcoming desertion and Nason's past aban-donment.

The ringing of her cell phone cut into her pity party. Mom. The last straw for today.

"Hey, Mom. How are you?" She waited for the crossing light.

"I'm just terrible." The whine hurt Fiona's ears. "You wouldn't believe the day I've had. A lady at the thrift shop was so rude. There were no empty machines at the laundromat, so

I had to walk all the way home with a basket of dirty laundry, then go back again. I'm exhausted. Can you loan me a hundred?"

No hello, how are you, how was your day? That was probably just as well. She couldn't tell her mom about running into Nason anyway.

"I gave you a hundred four days ago. What'd you do with that?" Fiona stifled the anger.

"Oh, sweetheart. I had to spend that on food."

"What do you need more money for?"

"Bus fare and what not. Spent the last of it on the laundromat. You know it doesn't go far these days. And my rent will be due again soon."

"Mom, what about your salary at the thrift store?"

"I don't get paid for two more weeks." She ramped up the whine.

"Then you just got paid. What happened to your paycheck?

"You know. It's always spent before I get it."

"Mom, I can only spare fifty right now."

"That'll just have to do, won't it, pet? Can you drop it by tonight?"

Maeve had settled for less awfully fast. If she was spending the money she gave her on drugs, she'd just...just...Well, she didn't know what. It wasn't like this was new. Fiona had been dealing with Maeve's problems on her own since Nason had chosen not to be her father anymore.

Thanks to her mom, she'd have to rush through the pizza, then rush to mom's place, then rush back to get a few hours' sleep. No rest. Maybe Lottie would go with her and they could at least have a good talk.

———

Nason had expected a quiet ride home, but he hadn't figured on Irina riding to the resort with Rick and Rainbow. Now he'd have to listen to Irina the whole way home. Her voice was already droning in his ear, and they hadn't even left the parking lot.

"You knew she worked there, didn't you? How could you do that to me?"

"You're the one who insisted on having the wedding at the Princessa del Mar, not me. Remember?" His turmoil at seeing Fiona was boiling into anger. He hated being put in the position of unexpectedly facing her and then being accused by his wife of orchestrating something. If he were going to orchestrate a meeting, it surely wouldn't be in front of strangers and certainly not with Irina present.

"Oh, I wouldn't be surprised if you stuck that idea in my head. And I just bet Maeve is somehow involved. Did she put you up to this? You've seen her, right?" Irina was practically shrieking now, hysteria fueling her fire.

He jammed on his brakes at a light, throwing them forward against their seat belts. He turned to her. "Stop it, Irina. Do you hear yourself?" Seeing her mottled face sickened him, and he looked toward the stoplight again.

"You think I'm going to let this drop? Oh, no. You got another think coming—"

"Shut up. Just shut up." The stoplight turned green, and he punched the accelerator. He'd never hit a woman, not even Maeve who had driven him beyond his limits. But his hands itched to hit Irina right at this moment.

She stilled without another word. Had she sensed she'd pushed him too far?

Guilt washed over him. He had no business even thinking about hitting her. Didn't that mean he'd already committed the sin in his heart? His chest heaved, and he took one hand off the steering wheel to swipe his face from hairline to chin.

You idiot. Sure, she was making ridiculous statements. And, of course, he was agitated over seeing Fiona. But that didn't give him the right to talk to her that way. He cut a glance at her, but she faced the window. His cue that she was giving him the silent treatment. That was infinitely preferable to the shouting match they'd just had.

The vehicle's on-board system chimed with an incoming call. A nasally computer voice greeted him with, "Call from Rick. Answer?" After a quick "Yes," the line crackled.

"Dad, we're waiting at the restaurant. You get lost?"

Nason slapped his forehead. "Oh, man. Sorry, Son. We, uh, got distracted. We'll be there ASAP. Go ahead and order for us. Whatever you're having."

Before he could end the call, Irina was shrieking again. "*We* got distracted? How could you forget we were having dinner with the Skinners? You better get us there fast."

"I didn't hear you reminding me. You didn't notice I was heading home? Too busy berating me for something I didn't do."

"Humph."

Nason inched over to the next lane and took the first exit. It was a good thing the heavy traffic kept them from getting too far. Except now he had to spend the next couple of hours in a crowd. Would Rick bring up seeing Fiona? Would the Skinners ask what was going on back at the resort? More worrisome was what would Irina say. Do. They would be in public. She couldn't do much. Or could she? She'd done the unthinkable in public before.

Fifteen more minutes of thick silence and Nason pulled into the beachside restaurant. They'd driven miles to go the six blocks from the resort to where they were having dinner. If only Irina hadn't gotten so irate, maybe he'd have remembered. Had Rick reminded him before they separated to their own cars?

Something nudged him as he stopped at the valet stand. It

felt almost physical, but that was impossible. Only Irina was there, and she stood three angry feet away.

Nason. It wasn't exactly a voice, but a deep sound in his soul. *Turn to me. My yoke is easy.*

What? Was he hearing God? No, that couldn't be. He shook his head and took the claim check from the young man.

Unbidden, his thoughts told him it had been his fault after all. If he hadn't been distracted from seeing Fiona.

It wasn't Irina's fault.

It went back way further than that, didn't it, Lord?

He slipped up beside Irina and put his arm around her shoulders. "Look, I'm sorry. I honestly didn't know Fiona worked there. You have to believe me."

Irina shrugged him off, looking sideways at him with her signature glare. She clicked her tongue, but something in his face must have satisfied her, because she said, "Yeah, okay. Maybe you didn't."

They reached the hostess stand, and Irina was all smiles as she told the young man their party waited for them. He beamed back and led them to a table by the window that looked out onto the dazzling Pacific. Restaurant ambience shut out the sound of the waves crashing to shore. What Nason wouldn't give to be out there on a surfboard.

"So, Nason." Red took a sip of his wine and shot the first volley. "Where've you been? Get lost?" He guffawed.

"Sorry. Got distracted. So, Rick, what'd you order for us?"

"Tonight's special. Sea bass. Did you know Fiona—"

"Sounds great. Thanks." He snapped his son a stern look and shook his head just enough to indicate he should be quiet, but not enough that others would notice.

"Darling, you didn't let Rick—"

He squeezed Irina's hand. "Sea bass sounds good, right, *darling?*"

She opened her mouth, and he squeezed harder. "Hey." Irina yanked her hand out of his.

"Rainbow, I hope you liked the ballroom." Nason gave his future daughter-in-law an encouraging smile.

"Fantastic. It was just fantastic." She clapped her hands as she gushed. "Irina already has some fantastic ideas for decorating. Don't you, Irina?"

If she said fantastic one more time.

Irina's animated face brought a sparkle to her eyes that he hadn't seen in a long time.

Thank you, Rainbow. Her limited vocabulary notwithstanding, he was grateful she'd moved the conversation on.

That got the women babbling in a way that would have been annoying if it didn't beat the alternative of discussing Fiona.

"Dad." Rick leaned over and whispered. "What about Fiona?"

He shook his head again. "Later." Despite the ladies' chatter, he spoke under his breath. He wasn't about to have this conversation here. "Red, what business did you say you were in?"

"Appliances." Red's joviality evaporated. "Wedding's come at a bad time." He put up his hand. "But we're really happy to get Rick as a son-in-law. Don't get me wrong. It's just that we've already had to dip into our limited savings. I...I'm sorry." His face matched his name.

"Not to worry. We've got it handled." He shouldn't have asked about his business. Red probably thought Nason was fishing for that apology. Time to change the subject. The man was embarrassed enough. "Say, is Red your given name or a nickname?"

Red chuckled. "It's a nickname. But you don't really want to know my real name."

"That bad, huh?"

"Well, all right. It's Orville." He chuckled again.

"Brother named Wilbur?" The three men chuckled while

the women remained engrossed in their own conversation. The rest of the meal was surprisingly pleasant as the women talked wedding and the men covered a variety of topics. Anything but Fiona.

Standing once again at the valet stand, the Skinners and Williamses said their goodbyes.

Just as the valet pulled up in Nason's Mercedes, Red said, "Say, what was all that business at the hotel, Nason? I got the feeling you knew something the rest of us didn't."

———

Pizza and Lottie arrived on the doorstep at the same time. Lottie handed the delivery guy a handful of bills and thanked him.

"I was going to pay. You got it last time." Fiona shut the door behind the pizza-laden Lottie.

"Who's keeping track?" Her friend slid the pizza onto the table, dropped her purse, and grabbed Fiona in a hug. "I'm so sorry this all went down today. You look a wreck."

"Thanks. Whatta friend." Fiona giggled. "I'll feel better after I get some of that in me."

They plopped down and plucked slices of the steaming doughy goodness, nibbling to avoid the cheese burn.

"Whoa. Hot. That's one disadvantage of living so close to the pizza joint." Lottie jumped out of her chair. "Want a Coke?"

Silence reigned as they each devoured two slices. Lottie sat back and wiped her mouth but kept her gaze on the pizza left in the box. "Should I have one more? Okay. Thanks. I will." She grinned around another slice.

Fiona shrugged and joined her. "Can't let you get ahead of me."

Finally, Lottie pushed her empty plate away and tapped

the table with her other hand. "Do you want to tell me the whole story?"

With a hitch in her voice, Fiona relayed the day's events. She got up and paced the room.

"And Nason didn't say anything?"

"No. Ricky started to, but someone cut him off. I don't remember who. Might of even been me. I was petrified."

"You couldn't acknowledge Nason either, huh?"

"Told you I was struck dumb."

"Now what?"

Fiona's pulse quickened, and she shook her head. "I have no idea. What should I do?"

"Contact him and ask him why he's been such a jerk."

"Lottie."

"Okay. Okay. Of course, you can't do that. It wouldn't be Christlike. But, really, don't you want to contact him and ask him what happened? What did happen anyway? I mean, what did your mom tell you? How old were you?"

"I was only twelve, and she just said I wouldn't be seeing Nason anymore. And wouldn't answer when I asked why. I cried for months. But, you know, I have occasional memory flashes of overhearing some conversations between Nason and Irina and Nason and my mom that I don't quite understand. I've never been able to remember enough to make any sense of them."

"Hmmm. How did you find out about the DNA test?"

"I found a copy in the mail that Nason sent my mom. I knew I shouldn't have opened it, and my mom was furious. Even when she was drugged up, she'd never hit me, but I could tell she wanted to."

"And?"

"She told me it was a lie. Nason was my father. She's always maintained he is. She sued him for child support, and we had to do another DNA test. Came back the same. The courts ruled he didn't have to pay. But you know my mom, she insisted, and still insists he's my father."

"Wow. Now I remember you telling me all that a long time ago. I'm so sorry, Fiona."

"Funny, I've been thinking more about him lately." She let her gaze wander to the few houseplants still alive on the windowsill. For some reason, the blue violets were surviving despite the instructions' warning that they needed careful attention. Which they were not getting. Neither she nor Lottie had green thumbs. In fact, Fiona often joked you knew you had a black thumb when you could kill a silk plant.

"Maybe that was the Lord's way of preparing you for today."

"Well, it didn't. Speaking of my mom, I've got to run over to her place. Take her some money. Will you go with me?"

They made quick work of the mess on the table, washed up, and ran out the door.

———

As she drove through the dilapidated Santa Ana neighborhood, Fiona glanced at the graying sky.

"Thank goodness it stays light so late, but it won't be for long." Fiona muttered. "And I want to be outta here before dark."

Apartment complexes with peeling paint hunkered on each side of the narrow street lined with rusted cars, some windowless, some hoisted on jacks. Yards were littered with broken bikes, shopping carts, and trash.

"It doesn't bother your mom to live here?"

Fiona shrugged. "It's all she can afford. Besides, it's probably closer to her dealer."

"Oh, girl. I'm so sorry."

"Hey, it's her choice." Nevertheless, her mother's choices draped a blanket of sadness on Fiona's soul each time she came here. It was hard to watch her mother slip further into this lifestyle. Even if Fiona tried to help her more, Maeve would probably use it for drugs, cigarettes, or alcohol.

Finding a vacant space four buildings down, Fiona parked. Lack of sidewalks caused the two to scurry across yards of brown grass and weeds.

When Maeve answered the door, her thick black hair swirled in disarray around her head. "Ah, Fiona. And Lottie. There you are." Her voice was husky.

She pushed open the listing screen door that squeaked on its hinges. Fiona's shoulders rose to her ears. Fingers on a chalkboard.

"Hi, Maeve. How are you?" Lottie leaned into her and gave her a hug.

Fiona winced from guilt, knowing she should be the one hugging her mother and because she knew what was coming.

"Just terrible, Lottie. Just terrible. What a day I had—"

"Mom, we can't really stay. But I wanted to bring you the money." She thrust a few bills into her mother's hand.

Maeve's face sagged in disappointment. "You drove all this way and can't stay for even a Coke?"

"We need to get home before dark—"

"We can stay for a Coke, can't we, Fiona? We have plenty of time." Lottie moved further into the room that was even tinier than their living room. She relocated one of the many piles of dirty clothes and sat down.

Ashtrays and saucers overflowing with cigarette butts squatted on every possible surface among the dirty dishes, takeout wrappers, and junk mail.

Maeve teetered her way through stacked cardboard boxes, stopped suddenly, then plopped onto a hardback chair. "I'm a bit dizzy. I must have the flu."

The flu. Yeah, right.

"Pet, can you get the drinks?" She looked at Fiona with

rheumy eyes and lifted one corner of her mouth. Today's version of a smile.

Stifling a groan, Fiona bustled about scrubbing glasses, retrieving ice, and a giant bottle from the refrigerator. If only her mother would let her help. Really help. Not a few dollars here and there but allow Fiona to get her into a rehab center. Her mom's refusal to get real help hurt too much to think about.

They sipped and chatted. At least Lottie talked while Fiona brooded over images of seeing Nason earlier in the day. It was almost as if Fiona was supposed to tell her mother about today. She clamped her mouth shut and let Lottie handle the prattle.

"Pet, did you bring me some money?" A whine lingered in the air.

"Mom. I handed you money when I first walked in." Her tone developed an edge. "What did you do with it?"

Maeve shook her head. "No, pet. You didn't. I would have remembered."

Fiona jumped up and checked the table, then she and Lottie pawed through piles of laundry. Her mother's glassy-eyed gaze followed their frantic search. Coming to a stop next to her mother, Fiona frowned at the half-empty bottle of scotch. She reached down and patted Maeve's sweater pockets.

"Mom. It's right here in your pocket."

"See. I knew you hadn't given it to me." Maeve plucked the money from Fiona's fingers and stuffed the bills back in her pocket.

Trying to explain reality to her mother would be useless.

Not bothering to finish the last few inches of her drink, Fiona dumped the contents into the kitchen sink full of food-caked plates and nudged the counter's dirty dishes aside to find room for her glass. "Really. We need to leave." She glanced out of the smudged window at the pinks and gray of the sky.

"Pet, when can you bring me some more money?" Maeve's deep brown eyes pleaded with her.

"Mom. I don't know. Finances are tight right now, and with Lottie getting married soon, I have to save so I can stay in my apartment. Or move."

"Oh, Lottie. You're getting married?" Her face lit up. "How wonderful. If only Fiona would find a nice boy and get married, too."

Boy? Boy or man, he'd be saddled with a mother-in-law to support. Nope, couldn't do that to the guy. Not that she had anyone to turn down. At least the subject of marriage had distracted her mother from asking for more money.

Fiona dragged Lottie out of the apartment with promises to call Maeve soon.

———

Back in the car, Fiona felt dirty from being in her mother's trashed apartment, then berated herself for the feelings. Her embarrassment at Lottie having seen it didn't help. To say nothing of her mother's plea for money. Lottie would figure out what Maeve wanted to use the money for. Why hadn't she thought before asking Lottie to come with her?

"I'm sorry, Lottie."

A car sitting low to the ground and jammed with raucous teenagers crept up close to her car. Cat calls, whistles, and loud banging on the outside of the door from the tattooed hulk in the passenger seat sent chills through her as the vehicle inched past. As soon as the thugs had moved ahead far enough, Fiona pulled the car onto the street and made a U-turn, anxious to be away from the neighborhood.

She inhaled a shaky breath and spoke again. "I'm so sorry."

"Now what for?"

"You know. The neighborhood, the state of my mom's place, the gang-banger car."

"I've seen worse."

"Where? Not at your parents' house."

"My mother's not perfect."

Fiona scoffed.

"If it bothered me, I wouldn't have suggested we stay. Besides, she really wanted us to. Didn't you see how happy she was?"

Unfortunately, Fiona saw and knew she should have been the one to suggest it. She should have wanted to visit awhile. Just to make her mother happy. She sighed.

I'm sorry, Lord. Next time. I promise. If she could escape the dread of seeing the guys in that car.

The sunset had disappeared, and the sky had faded from pinks to gray to black by the time they made it home.

Now, hours later, Fiona stared at her bedroom ceiling. Despite Lottie's commiseration and words of encouragement over the Nason incident, the time with her mother had stolen any solace she may have gained. Was there to be any peace? Obviously, she should have done something differently, both with Nason and her mother. She knew what she had to do about her mother, but what about Nason? What should she do now?

Heartache tormented her as she tried to think about the future, so she allowed her mind to wander back to her child-hood before Nason left. She found a few memories of life before he'd married Irina. A Christmas with her grandparents, well, his parents. Being held against his broad chest as he carried her everywhere, even though she could walk. Some big arguments between him and her mother.

Fiona recognized a few flashes of images from Nason and Irina's wedding when she was three. She also remembered Irina had only been nice to her when Nason was around. Why hadn't he and her mother married? Wasn't that the way it was supposed to be?

While it had been hard being shuttled between Nason's and her mother's, and despite Irina being less than a doting stepmother, it had been the happiest of times for her. She'd been excited over the birth of a little brother. During weekends at Nason's, she felt like she was part of a real family. Loneliness plagued her at her mother's. Not that Maeve hadn't shown her love, but being a single mother, she'd had to work a lot. Too frequently when she wasn't working, her use of drugs or alcohol interfered.

What went wrong? Why did Nason stop loving her? Why did he abandon her?

If she hadn't met Lottie in high school, despair would have consumed her. Lottie's family became her substitute family. And, while she was grateful, it had been second best.

Fiona turned onto her stomach and thrust her head under the pillow.

Lord, I don't understand. I don't know what to do. Basically, I know nothing. I don't even know how to pray. Lottie told me to just tell you what I'm feeling, but I don't even know what I'm feeling.

Was He listening? She couldn't feel it. Had He abandoned her, too?

Lottie had told her it wasn't a feeling. Regardless of how she felt, God was there, listening, caring for her. *Is that true, God?*

When she woke up, the LED clock light glowed three a.m. She didn't remember falling asleep. Perhaps the Lord was there and had made his presence known by allowing her to sleep. She pulled the duvet up around her ears and permitted herself to relax into slumber again.

Chapter Five

Three days since he'd run into Fiona at the hotel, and he still didn't know what to do about it. He only knew he was grateful for a busy work schedule. Examining every pay record and accounting entry, to back it all up and keeping up to date on his existing clients kept him paddling as fast as he could.

If only someone would have warned him when he made the decision to cut Maeve and Fiona out of his life. Foretold the possible future consequences of meeting the child fifteen years later. And feeling like a heel. Would he have listened? At the time, all he wanted was to end Maeve's pleas for him to come back to her. To get her to stop blackmailing him for money. Even after he married someone else. And his wife. Irina had pretty much given him an ultimatum. It was her or Fiona.

What was a man to do?

"Boss?" Selena stood in front of him, and he hadn't even heard her come into his office.

He emerged from his thoughts, heavy with unsolved questions. "What's up?"

"That new clerk has some billing questions about that last client. What do you want to do?" Selena raised one eyebrow.

"Have him talk to the billing boys directly."

"Boys?"

"Boys. Girls."

She looked down at him, a frown deepening.

"Okay, okay. Department. Whatever. Have them work it out."

Selena's only fault, and it wasn't really a fault, was her insistence on politically correct language to avoid gender bias. In truth, he needed her to remind him. He couldn't help it if he was a macho-kind of guy. *Thanks, Dad.* There'd been a few workplace rifts in the past that didn't do much for his career.

"You got it." She turned on her heel, but when she got to the doorway, she turned back. "You okay? You've been kind of distracted this week."

"Me? Distracted? No, I'm fine." He shifted his gaze to his monitor. He'd better get back to dealing with numbers. Dollars and cents. If only his brain had some sense.

His office door clicked shut, and he sagged against his leather executive chair. He rubbed his eyes and tried to focus.

Just as he'd finally found some concentration, a rap on the door pulled him from the numbers.

"Yeah." Nason didn't look up, just continued scanning the spreadsheet.

"Dad?"

Rick stood in the open doorway, looking unsure whether he was invited in.

"Ricky. What are you doing here? Come in." It was always an ego boost when the boy sought him out. Except maybe when he was asking for wedding money. "Sit."

"If you have a minute, I need to talk about what happened." He lowered himself onto the coffee-brown leather visitor's chair.

"What happened? What are you talking about?" A sick feeling in his gut told him he already knew what Ricky meant.

"Please, you know what. Fiona." Accusations colored his words.

Nason raised his hand to run it through his hair but was met by locks stiffened by too much hair gel, so he rubbed his neck instead. "I didn't know Fiona would be there. Did you?"

"What? No. Rainbow only talked to that Heather. Besides, that's not what I mean."

"Well, what then?"

"You know Mom has forbidden us from being in contact with Fiona or Maeve."

His neck muscles stiffened. What right did Irina have to forbid anything? Yet, he had agreed. "Your mom is not the head of the house."

"Oh, so you're going to pull that old-fashioned religious stuff on us?"

Rick had been resistant to Nason's conversion and wasn't hesitant to be vocal about it.

"Has nothing to do with religion. But as it happens, I haven't been in touch with either of them before seeing Fiona at the hotel."

"It was just random? Right." He scoffed.

"Look. I didn't choose that hotel. Your mother and Rainbow did. So drop the attitude."

Rick flushed a pale shade of pink.

At least he had the grace to be embarrassed over his false accusations.

"What are you going to do about it?" He lifted his chin towards his father.

His embarrassment hadn't lasted long.

"Nothing." Was that true? Nason had no idea. But he wasn't ready to talk about it or decide. He knew he should be praying about it. Every time he thought about praying, his stomach felt like it was alive with crawling ants. Like now.

"She and her mother have already disrupted our lives enough. She's not part of our family." Rick stood and adjusted his tie. "I better get back to work. See ya later, Dad."

His son was gone, leaving him in a heap. Without praying, Nason knew it was time he did something about Fiona. God had been pulling at him even before he saw her.

I can't, Lord. I just can't.

After Rick left, he worked late to get caught up. And to avoid thinking about Fiona. Now he sat in The McArthur Group parking garage. Eight-thirty. Irina was going to have his head. He continued to stare at his phone, knowing he had to call Fiona and set up some sort of face-to-face meeting.

Scrolling through his contacts, he realized he didn't have a cell phone number for her. Well, it would be easy to get her through the hotel. Whose number was also not stored in his phone. Relief coursed through his body. He couldn't call. At least not right now.

Coward. Look up the Princessa del Mar's number on the internet. He found the number and dialed before he could chicken out. An operator answered and directed him to the sales and catering department. His heart beat wildly as the extension rang several times before being answered by voicemail.

Nice timing, dude. Of course, no one would be in at this time of night. He didn't bother leaving a message. Was that disappointment or the feeling of a short stay of execution? Maybe Rick was right. She wasn't part of the family, and he owed it to Irina and Rick to put them first. Right?

Then why did he feel so lousy?

He turned on the ignition and wound his way out of the garage. His dashboard pinged with a message.

IRINA: WHERE ARE YOU?

Irina. He should have let her know he was working late. He spoke into the microphone.

NASON: ON MY WAY. HOME IN HALF AN HOUR.

The cavernous exhibit hall, with its concrete columns, echoed with activity as workmen moved equipment around and built three-sided booths out of plastic pipe and drapes. A supervisor shouted, trying to be heard over the din.

Fiona's sensible pumps clacked on the concrete floor, adding very little to the ruckus. She stopped, consulted her iPad list, and hurried toward the supervisor.

"Hi. Are we going to make the two p.m. move in? The show organizer is getting anxious."

The short, stocky man kept his head bent to his work. "Yeah. Yeah. No problem."

"How about the extra pipe and drape? Did that come in?"

"Yeah. Yeah."

It was obvious he wanted to be left alone to get the job done. But she had a job to do, too.

"Sorry, but one more question. The fire marshal said we had to avoid putting a booth in front of that exit." She pointed to the far corner of the space, but she didn't think he watched her. "Can you get the crew to shift everything over?"

Finally, the man looked up, his large mustache quivering. "Shift everything? You're kidding, right? He already approved the floor plan."

"I know. I reminded the inspector, but he wouldn't budge. Sorry."

He grumbled under his breath. Fiona was sure he used a few words she wouldn't like, but she didn't really hear them, so she let it pass.

Teagan, Fiona's cubicle mate, strode toward her.

"You look like you're on a mission, Teagan."

"Someone had to tell you to check your walkie." Although Teagan tended to be direct, her voice was always kind. "Is it on? Heather's been trying to get you for fifteen minutes."

She snatched her walkie talkie off her belt loop. "Oh, my goodness. How'd it get turned off?" Fiona turned it on by positioning the little dial to channel one. "Thanks for the rescue."

"Anytime." Teagan flashed her a smile, then stared into Fiona's eyes. "I know you're usually careful about these things, but be extra diligent. Heather's on the warpath today."

Lottie was her best friend, but if there were a runner up, it would be Teagan. Their busy lives, including Teagan's responsibilities at home, prevented them from spending much time together outside of the office.

Her friend smiled again while patting Fiona on the arm. She turned and walked away as purposefully as she had arrived.

Fiona's walkie talkie crackled. "Calling Fiona. Heather here."

She pressed the talk button. "Go ahead for Fiona. Over."

"Why was your walkie off?" Heather's voice was strident, although that wasn't unusual for her. "You have a call from the client waiting for you. They have changes they want to make. Over."

"Sorry about that. Changes? Good grief. Okay, put 'em through to my cell." Fiona clucked her tongue in frustration at herself and the client.

She couldn't afford to tick her boss off. And any changes by the client would delay the finish. Today, she needed to get out of work on time for dinner with Lottie and her family.

Her cell phone beeped, and she strode out of the exhibit hall to hear better. Standing in the hallway, she dealt with the excitable show coordinator on the phone, convincing her she didn't need the changes and reassuring her all was in hand.

As soon as she hit end, her phone beeped again. At least it was only Lottie. "Hey, girl. What's up?"

"Just checking that you can shake it loose on time. Rex's friend is picking us up at six." Lottie's voice was on high energy.

"Sure. But even if I can't, I can drive myself. Wait. What friend?"

"No way. You're coming with us."

"What friend?"

Lottie's long exhale travelled through the phone. "His name's Trevor. When my fiancé asks me to invite his friend over to a Butler family dinner, you know I just can't refuse. Besides, I think he wants Trevor to spy on me." Now she chuckled.

"Spy on you?" Should she be worried about Lottie? Or her fiancé? Or this friend?

"Just kidding. Look, his family lives in D.C., and has been nice to Rex. So, we just need to return the favor. Now be home on time. Bye."

Fiona pulled the phone away from her ear and looked at the screen. As if that would tell her anything. *Bossy.* She stuffed the phone back in her pocket and headed to the loading dock.

Why did Lottie's fiancé feel the need to orchestrate, all the way from Washington, D.C., this family time for Trevor? And was Lottie up to something? She was always full of surprises. Not all of them welcome.

Still, Lottie and her parents, the Butlers, had adopted her as part of the family, coddling and nurturing her. Being there for her when Maeve wasn't. They were the ones who had pushed her to apply for the college scholarships she'd won. Extra money was often put in her Christmas and birthday cards.

Rex had also been kind to her. Never complaining when Lottie wanted or needed to spend extra time with Fiona. He was a good man. Stands to reason anyone he asked Lottie and the Butlers to be hospitable to would also be worthy.

Were Rex and Lottie up to something?

Probably not. She was just being silly. Too self-absorbed.

It's not all about you, you know.

Of course not. But, then again, it seemed suspicious.

Trevor drove his classic '65 Mustang through the winding hills of Laguna while Fiona fidgeted in the front seat next to him. Lottie had insisted on sitting in the back seat, leaving the front seat for her.

Except Lottie was doing all the talking.

"Trevor, you grew up in Washington, D.C.?"

"Maryland, really. But we spent a lot of time in D.C. My father is an attorney working with several civil liberties groups."

"Interesting. And how long have you been in California?"

Fiona couldn't help cutting sideways glances at Trevor. He had a chiseled face and short, spiky hair with a neatly trimmed mustache and beard. Where the hair on his head was a plain brown, the facial hair was a deep black.

"About a year. I met Rex on a photo shoot right after I moved here. But then, of course, he got transferred to D.C. Ironic, huh?"

Photo shoot? Was he a photographer like Rex? The army had sent Lottie's fiancé to the Pentagon on a short-term assignment to be an official photographer for something or another.

The little red Mustang pulled into the Butler's driveway, leading to a typical sprawling Southern California ranch house, distinguished by its mid-20th century sloping roofline. Fiona felt at home here. Not as upscale as many houses in the Laguna area, it was nevertheless Fiona's ideal family home. It even beat Nason's house, which was too ritzy, too cold to feel comfortable. She preferred the older home he'd lived in before.

Music and merriment had always been part of the Butler's family life, and tonight was no exception. Fifties rock and roll blasted from some iPhone speaker device, and the Butler family and other guests were gyrating and laughing at each other's antics.

Joy bubbled up. How she'd missed this family.

Lottie's mother, Jolene, drew away from the patio dance floor. "Hello, hello, my dears. I'm glad you're here." She had to raise her voice to be heard above "Jailhouse Rock," and she hugged each of them in turn. "Fiona, it's been too long. This must be Trevor. Welcome to our home. Look, kids, food's on the serving tables. Help yourselves. I better go check the dessert in the oven." She hurried off, her sturdy body belying her age.

Jolene had to be about the same age as Maeve, but she looked ten years younger. And that was probably being generous to Maeve.

They wove their way through the crowd to the table loaded with dish after dish. Fiona leaned into Lottie and whispered, "Should we have brought something?"

Her friend shook her head, and they piled their plates high with pork barbecue, baked beans, coleslaw, and more. Finding an empty round table, Fiona and Lottie sat down and dug in while Trevor chatted with Lottie's father a few feet away.

"Well?" Lottie looked at Fiona, her eyebrows making their way to her hairline.

"Well, what?" *Oh, no.* "You aren't. Tell me you aren't."

"But, Fiona, he's so sweet. Be nice to him."

She would throttle Lottie when they got home. No matter how sweet Trevor was, she was not in the market for a date, much less a relationship. *And just why not?* If the thoughts in her head could have a tone, hers would definitely be accusatory. *Because I don't need the hassle. Got enough going on.* Great, she was arguing with herself.

Trevor joined them at the table, sitting in the open chair next to Fiona. His lithe body was more graceful than hers. Was he in on this?

As Trevor unfurled the napkin surrounding his plasticware, he turned to her. "I hear you and Lottie have been friends for a long time."

"Yeah. Since high school. Are you a photographer like Rex?"

The smile faded a little, and he squirmed in his seat. "Actually, I'm a model."

She almost dropped her fork. Of course, there had to be male models. Look at all the catalogs and ads. *Duh.* She'd never thought of them as being real people. Or meeting one.

"Must be interesting." What was she supposed to say? *What are you doing in such a ridiculous job? Get a real man's job.* That wouldn't go over so well. She kept her gaze on her plate and took another bite of barbecue.

"Don't worry. A lot of girls think it's a weird profession."

Had she said something out loud? No, she couldn't have. Was it on her face? She didn't want to offend the poor guy. A lot of girls? He probably had scads of women after him.

"Oh, I didn't—" Her face was getting warm. Now she was blushing?

"It can be. Interesting, that is. And it's a good living."

"What kind of modeling do you do?" There was more than one kind, right?

"Mostly catalog. Men's clothing. Print, but occasionally, video. Stuff like that."

"I see." *I see? What a stupid thing to say.* "Does Rex photograph you much?"

"Yes. Until recently at least. You work with Lottie at a hotel?" He took a long drink of his iced tea.

"The Princessa del Mar Resort. Sales and catering."

He raised an eyebrow. "What does that mean? You cook?" His blue eyes crinkled around the edges again.

Fiona laughed. It was a question she got a lot. "No. It means Lottie and I work with people who want to use our facility for meetings, conferences, exhibits, and the like. We do sell catering to them for their events. But, no, I don't cook."

"At all? Or you mean just at work?"

Now she fidgeted in her chair. Guys usually didn't like girls who didn't cook. But this was a new age. "Not at all. Well, apart from the occasional frozen pizza." She winced, waiting for the shock to appear on his face. "Unfortunately, Lottie doesn't either." If she was going down, so was her roommate.

"So Rex has told me." This time, he chortled. "You gals are pretty busy. I love to cook. A few years ago, I took a gourmet cooking tour of Italy. Ever been?"

"Not on a cooking tour, for sure. Lottie and I traveled to London once for an international hospitality conference."

"Hospitality?"

"That's what our industry is called. Lottie and I have degrees in hospitality." *Hospitality?* And here she was thinking being a male model sounded funny. She waited for the usual smirky remark about hospitality. But it didn't come.

Maybe this guy was as sweet as Lottie said. Maybe. She still wasn't going to let her off the hook. And perhaps she shouldn't judge modeling as a male profession.

The three of them chatted about cooking and travel until they had sopped up all their barbecue sauce with cornbread, cleaning their plates.

"Fiona, next Saturday we're doing a photo shoot in a Temecula winery. It's beautiful country, and the shoot is sponsoring a winery luncheon that is supposed to be spectacular. Would you like to come? Lottie, you're welcome to come, too." Trevor's hazel eyes sparkled under his neat eyebrows.

A date? It had been quite a while since she'd been on one. So long ago she couldn't remember when. But she hated to admit, not only to herself, but to Lottie, that she liked Trevor and watching him in action would be fun. *Don't kid yourself, girl.* Spending time with him sounded tantalizing. Besides, didn't she just say she needed to give his profession a chance? Watching Trevor work would be a great start.

It wouldn't really be a date because Lottie was coming, too. Right?

After Fiona agreed, Lottie snuck in her bombshell. "I wish I could come, but I have previous plans."

Previous plans? Yeah, right. Traitor.

So now this was a date. No guarantees there'd be more than one.

As the little red car sped home, Fiona's thoughts fell into a hole. A black hole. What was she doing accepting a date? What if that date led to something? And then he would abandon her, because everyone did sooner or later. She'd accepted a long time ago that she just wasn't lovable enough.

Her own father—at least he was supposed to be her father—left. After twelve years of being her father, how could he have just rejected their relationship? Just because some stupid DNA test said she wasn't his daughter.

No, better to cancel her date with Trevor. That way no one would get hurt.

An ache of loneliness wrapped around her, squeezing, squeezing and at the same time dropping her farther into the Bermuda Triangle. Too exhausted to struggle, she fell limp against the leather seat of Trevor's car.

Previous relationships had either exploded in the end or melted away. At least with the explosions, she knew it was over and had something to deal with. When her boyfriends disappeared with no explanation, she held onto hope they'd be back. Kind of like her hope Nason would come back and resume his role as her father.

What was the matter with her?

I created you, beloved.

"For it was you who created my inward parts; you knit me together in my mother's womb."

You are remarkably and wondrously made.

"I will praise you because I have been remarkably and

wondrously made. Your works are wondrous, and I know this very well."

Memorized Scripture continued to play through her mind.

She'd heard others say God didn't make mistakes when He created humans. Did that mean He had created her to be an extraordinary being? But that didn't mean there was nothing the matter with her, did it?

"We are the clay, and you are our potter; we all are the work of your hands."

Child, you are precious to me.

"I have loved you with an everlasting love."

Lord, let me feel your love and trust you with all my heart.

Chapter Six

Nason threw his golf clubs into the trunk, withdrew his street shoes, and slammed the lid. Sweat trickled down his face, neck, and to the small of his back. He grabbed a handkerchief from his pocket and mopped his forehead.

As they'd made their way around the course, every tree and bush in the golf course stood still. An absence of the coastal breeze allowed the sun's relentless freedom.

If only the heat were the sole culprit for making him feel like he was at the bottom of Niagara Falls. This should have been a peaceful Sunday golf game with his buddies. But before they could get started, there was a call from Maeve. How many times must he tell her to leave him alone, that he was not giving her money? On the heels of that call, Irina called complaining the air conditioning wasn't working. She could just as easily have called the A/C repair people. Then, Longstreet called. BioTech's CEO had been on the phone grilling him about Nason's progress.

He couldn't help it if the company's records were in bad shape. Tomorrow he'd have to dig further into the financials and follow up on the clerk's billing questions for the other client. Hopefully, the billing boys, er, department had cleared things up. Selena's scolding was making inroads.

Once he'd finally shut off his phone to get their game started, it was too late. He couldn't gain the needed concentration, and his game had gone south. Fourth out of four. Unacceptable.

He changed into his loafers and tossed his golf shoes to the passenger side floor. Then he slid into the front seat, the leather hot through his golf pants. Cranking up the air conditioner, he waited for the cool air to wash over him. And he waited. *No. No.* Not his car A/C as well. He pushed the button to roll down the windows, praying the hot air would blow away and the cold would start flowing from the vents. Finally, the vented air became cool enough to raise the windows.

Basking in the A/C, he sat there, his head cushioned against the headrest. If the air wasn't working at home, he didn't want to be there. He wriggled and fished his phone out of his pants pocket to text Irina.

NASON: GOING INTO OFFICE. DID YOU CALL A/C PEOPLE?

The office would be cool, and he could get a jump start on the deep dive into BioTech's records.

IRINA: AC COMPANY CAN'T COME UNTIL TOMORROW. EARLIEST. GOING TO MY SISTER'S. OVERNIGHT.

Oh, fine. What was he supposed to do? Definitely not going to her sister's. Go stay with Rick? Hotel? He'd figure that out later.

NASON: OKAY. DON'T WANT TO GO TO YOUR SIS. MAYBE I'LL GO TO RICK'S.

IRINA: GOOD. BECAUSE YOU WEREN'T INVITED. :-)

Love you, too, babe.

His head whirling from the communication frenzy, Nason

threw his phone onto the passenger seat, jammed the car into reverse, and headed to the office. The twenty-minute drive gave him a chance to mentally review records that weren't making sense. The case had been too rushed. It was merely a matter of looking more carefully, and it would all fall into place.

He swiped his entry card and stepped into the invigorating cold air. Heaven.

Powering up his computer, he logged in and reviewed the employee time records. Nothing out of the ordinary. So far, it appeared the company had been legally compensating their employees. Just to be sure, he'd again cross reference with their books. He inspected each line item.

Wow. The corporation had paid a hefty deposit fee of $75,000. The other case Longstreet was working on for them must be a doozy. But the more he poked around in other files, the more uneasy Nason became.

Hours of looking at the computer screen dulled his vision, both anatomically and mentally. Tomorrow he'd relax and get a fresh start on Tuesday.

Relax? In a house without air conditioning? He'd almost forgotten.

Time for a shower, a change of clothes, and dinner. He'd have to go home for a shower and change of clothes. Or would he?

Conquering the day's problems gave him a feeling of adventure. More like reckless indulgence. He deserved it, didn't he?

Waving to the security guard, he looked forward to his new plan. He drove to the Irvine Spectrum Center, the biggest and nearest shopping area. His choice of stores was dwindling because of the late Sunday hour. Ah ha. Nordstrom was open. He sailed through the store, finding the perfect shirt and slacks, then underwear and socks, even a pair of light lounging pants and a tee-shirt. He could probably get toiletries from the hotel.

Hotel. His plan was probably foolish, but he made a reservation anyway. She wouldn't be there on a Sunday, and he'd have to check out early in the morning or pay for another day for what was sure to be an expensive venture.

Traffic on the coastal highway was always brutal on a summer Sunday evening, and today was no exception. He should have eaten something hardier at the Spectrum. The cinnamon roll was delicious but had done little to stave off the ache from hunger now growing exponentially in his stomach.

The resort's circular drive finally offered a respite from the traffic. He pulled up to the valet stand and, as he grabbed his shopping bags and briefcase, realized he should have thought to purchase some sort of suitcase, or at least a duffle bag. What was the matter with him? *Oh, molly!* Too late now. He headed across the marble-floored lobby to the registration desk.

The price was ridiculous, but once checked in, he hurried up to his room, craving the cool air, and the bonus, peace and quiet. He glanced around the space, and the ocean view outside his balcony windows spoke to his surfer soul.

Peeling off his sweaty golf clothes, he felt sorry for all he'd come in contact with over the last few hours. He smelled pretty rank.

Showering and dressing in record time—he would never understand why it took women so long—he was out the door looking forward to a decent meal. The steakhouse was a perfect choice, but the menu prices were outrageous. On top of what he was paying just to spend one night. He chastised himself for spending so foolishly. But it was only one night, right? And maybe tomorrow morning he could run into Fiona. Would she be working on Labor Day?

Yeah, and what then, dude?

He ignored the voice in his head and ordered a ribeye steak with mashed potatoes and asparagus.

———

Saturday had been a real pity party. She hadn't gotten dressed, gone for a run, or even showered since Lottie had gone back to her parents' house earlier that morning. Fiona had been invited, too, but it would have been wedding planning on steroids, and she just wasn't up to it.

Now Sunday morning wasn't much better. Eleven a.m. and she was still in bed. How could she even think about going out with Trevor? Even if it wasn't so much a date as accompanying him to watch him as he was photographed.

She pulled herself up in the bed, rearranging every one of her six pillows behind her. Leaning back against the cushy softness, she sighed. Yep, this is why she had so many of the darn things.

Her head propped up on her fist, she had to think of how she was going to get out of going with Trevor. Maybe she'd just call him—no texting would be safer. Seriously? She didn't have his number, and she wasn't about to ask Lottie. Maybe she could get his number from Lottie's fiancé without making her roommate suspicious.

Bother him in D.C.? Silly girl.

Little improved with Fiona's mood or attire over the next hour. Dragging herself out of bed for breakfast or lunch was just too much work.

The front door clunked open and shut and then Lottie towered over her bed. "Girl. It's noon, you're not even dressed, and you missed church? Hey, you didn't stay like this all day yesterday, did you?" Lottie reprimanded her at the top of her lungs. "You're wallowing in self-pity. And for what I'd like to know? And it's not like you to miss church."

Fiona couldn't help thinking the neighbors probably thought a maniac had broken in. Her best friend didn't let her get away with much, and she was calling her on it now. Lottie was usually successful at whatever she did, so it was a good bet Fiona wouldn't get away wallowing anymore today.

"Now get up. Get your running togs on and hit the beach. Don't come back until you've run at least five miles." She stood with her feet wide apart and her fists planted on her hips.

No one argued with Lottie.

Thirty minutes later, after Fiona had gone out for a run, she came back energized, then showered.

"Now that's better," Lottie said when Fiona emerged from her room. "Since we both have paperwork to catch up on, let's head to the office."

While Fiona didn't like working on a Sunday, she did like the quiet when no one else was around. Besides, today she needed the distraction. Tomorrow a new show moved in, and she'd be less stressed if the paperwork was already taken care of.

As they ambled toward the resort, Fiona realized she'd been so self-centered she hadn't even asked Lottie about how the wedding planning went.

"You and your mom get a lot done? You know, with the wedding stuff."

"Yes, lots. Say, my mom has to go out of town and doesn't think she can make it back for my final fitting. So, I thought you could come with me instead. Actually, I was going to ask you anyway, but now I really need you. Can you come?"

"Of course. What's the date?" She was going to get sucked into all these details, regardless of how hard she tried to stay out of it.

"Not until November. The seventeenth. Will that work for you?" Lottie turned toward Fiona, a broad grin lighting up her face.

There was no refusing her when she looked so happy. Fiona took Lottie's arm and squeezed it. "It'll be fun. I should schedule my final fitting for the same time. Gotta look the maid-of-honor part."

"Oooh, let's plan lunch out, too."

They giggled so loudly as they entered the resort, the concierge chuckled and waved.

The more determined Fiona was to enjoy Lottie's wedding plans and the wedding itself, the truer she knew it would be.

———

It seemed only moments later that Lottie peered over the cubby wall. "Hey, girl. I'm finished and wiped out. How about you? Ready to go home?"

Fiona looked at the clock on her monitor. "Seven already?" How could three hours have passed? "Nah, I have about another hour's worth of work to do. You go on home. I'll catch you there."

"Okay. How about a movie and popcorn later?"

"Perfect. See ya." Fiona put her nose back to her monitor, and Lottie's humming faded away.

Eight o'clock. Pretty good guess. She shut her monitor down and locked her desk. Rolling her neck and shoulders to ease the fatigue and stiffness, she berated herself. She knew better than to work for three hours without even getting up to walk around. Now her body was going to pay. Good thing she'd had that run earlier. She stood behind her desk and performed stretches.

She wondered what movie Lottie picked out for tonight. She turned off the lights and locked up. Better not be a romance. She felt lighter than she had since Trevor asked her out. A good run, hanging out with Lottie, and work to keep her mind occupied had been all she needed. Maybe she'd even keep her date with Trevor. Maybe.

The hallways were busy with conference attendees coming and going. Tourists in casuals fancier than her dressed up clothes strolled about. Several languages swirled around, validating the Princessa del Mar's international reputation. The throngs increased as she neared the lobby.

A large group that looked to be on a conference-atmosphere high congregated in the center, forcing her to skirt around the edges near the steakhouse. One day she would splurge and eat there. Even with her employee discount, that would be quite an expense.

As she approached the restaurant entrance, a now achingly familiar figure emerged.

No. No. Her chest beat a bongo drum rhythm as she took in his sandy-colored curls in a perfectly styled disarray. His polo shirt and slacks looked immaculate, brand new even. She skidded to a stop and frantically looked for an escape. Sidling up to the group, she inserted herself, smiling and nodding as if they were all great acquaintances as she exited the far side away from Nason.

She managed two steps.

"Fiona?"

Her stomach dropped, and she turned slowly. "Da—Nason. What are you doing here?" How did he get through the crowd so quickly? And what was he doing here on a Sunday evening? Was Irina here, too? Rick?

"No A/C at home. Needed somewhere to cool off."

His face appeared placid. Wasn't he surprised to see her?

"You working tonight?" Nason rapped his fingers against his thigh.

"As a matter of fact." Her voice went rigid. What? They were just supposed to have a conversation of small talk? After all this time?

"I suppose you wouldn't have time for a coffee?"

"No." *No way. I can't do this now.*

"I see."

Did he? Was he getting the message?

"Could we talk sometime soon?" Apparently, he didn't have a clue.

Fiona drew in a long breath and let it out. "I don't know. Why? It seems you finished talking fifteen years ago."

His neck grew pink. "Yeah. We need to talk about that."

Need to? No, she didn't need to.

Yes, Fiona, you do.

"Maybe. Call me at my office, and I'll look at my schedule." *Translation: I'm not going to find time.*

"I'm staying the night. Maybe I could just drop by your office in the morning?"

The nerve. He was staying the night? Where was Irina? But, of course, she'd never ask.

"I have a show moving in tomorrow. Won't have time."

"I see. All right. I'll call another day. See if we can't set something up." Nason's face sagged as he waved and turned toward the elevators.

Had she been too cold? Well, what did he expect?

The lobby had suddenly emptied, and Nason stood at the elevators watching her. She couldn't walk out the front doors now. He'd know she wasn't working. But she had been working. She hadn't lied. The woman at the concierge desk was an acquaintance and a sweet gal. Fiona crossed the wide-open expanse and greeted her, chatting until Nason disappeared into the elevator and the doors drew closed.

She said goodbye, but her body shook. Could she make it home? As fast as her rubbery legs would allow, she scooted out through the resort's doors. By the time she reached the stone benches in the little garden on the other side of the circular drive, she collapsed. What if his room was right above her, and he could see her sitting there? She couldn't help it. Her body wouldn't cooperate.

Hanging her head, she tried to pray, but Nason's face intruded, and she could barely breathe. She looked up toward

the western horizon, where the sun would soon end the day
with a few wisps of pink and orange. The wind picked up and
stirred the palm fronds into a frenzy. High emotions and the
evening drop in temperature set Fiona shivering in her thin
top and slacks.

On unsteady legs, she rose slowly, then dragged herself
home.

———

As the elevator went up, Nason's stomach dropped. Fiona's
appearance had rendered him stupid. What a fool. But he
couldn't let her get away without saying *something*. Considering
how that turned out, maybe he would have been better off not
trying.

The ding of the elevator alerted him that he had reached
his own floor. The subdued print of the carpet contributed to
the muted ambience as he shuffled down the corridor. Inside
his body was a totally different matter. His steak dinner
churned in his stomach.

Letting himself into his room, he wished he could go back
and start over with Fiona today. Not just today. Maybe even
back fifteen years ago. Sure, he could have ignored seeing her
today, but how could he have done anything different all those
years ago?

He tossed the room key onto the dresser and succumbed
to the call of the luxury king size bed. Now he kicked off his
leather loafers and allowed his body to drop like his golf ball
sinking into the water trap.

Ping! Uncooperative droopy eyelids failed to open at the
first sound of an incoming text. *Ping!* No. Go away. He forced
himself to roll over to yank the phone out of his pants' pocket.
Longstreet.

LONGSTREET: MEETING MOVED UP TO TUES-
DAY, EIGHT A.M. HOPE YOU'LL BE READY.

He groaned as Longstreet texted again.

LONGSTREET: THEY'RE ANXIOUS.

NASON: CAME IN TODAY. WILL COME IN TOMORROW TOO.

Was there a sigh emoji? Even if there were one, he'd never send an emoji of any kind to a superior. Probably not to any other attorney. It just wasn't done.

LONGSTREET: DON'T FORGET EARLY TUESDAY.

Nason didn't bother to send another text. Checking the time, he figured 9:30 was good enough to call it a night, although he couldn't remember the last time he went to bed before eleven. Irina would be wondering if he were sick. If she were here. Which she wasn't.

He threw the phone on the bedside table and pushed off the bed to get out of his clothes and into lounge pants and a tee-shirt.

As he pulled the shirt over his head, he realized he'd forgotten to ask for toiletries. After he called the front desk, he opened the balcony doors and stepped out to wait and enjoy the cooling evening breeze. He loved living near the Southern California beaches, where the temperature could drop twenty degrees after sunset. Oh, and the murmur of the surf. He didn't believe the poets who said music soothed the savage beast. It was the sweet sound of the surf.

Except for tonight. The waves whispered accusations. He was a schmuck, an idiot, a fool.

Tell me something I don't know.

He'd spent all this money for nothing. Since he'd messed up tonight's encounter and tomorrow was a holiday so a meeting probably wouldn't have worked out anyway. Besides, she said she was busy. And now, he'd promised to work tomorrow.

Well, at least he was cool. At home without air conditioning, he would have sweated, tossing and turning all night. His mind was in such a turmoil, that was still an option.

Someone from guest services arrived with shaving supplies, a toothbrush, and other personal items. He lathered his face and hesitated just as he was about to touch his face with the safety razor. It had been years since he'd used anything but an electric shaver.

Careful you don't cut your throat, buddy.

Scoffing at his ridiculous thoughts, he applied the razor, and, of course, with the first pull, nicked himself. Maybe cutting his throat wasn't so ridiculous after all. He tried again and finished his face with only three nicks. He'd call that a victory.

The tiny toothbrush, encased in plastic, seemed permanently sealed, and he fought to open the package. He threw the toothbrush into the sink and laid both hands on the counter ledge, dipping his chin. Lifting his gaze, he glared at his image. He sighed and attacked the toothbrush package again.

Squeezing the tiny courtesy tube, he dabbed a little toothpaste on the brush and stuck it in his mouth just as his phone pinged from his bedside table. He moved to the table. Longstreet again.

LONGSTREET: LET'S MEET TOMORROW SO YOU CAN FILL ME IN.

A long, deep groan spiraled from him. No. He grabbed the phone with one hand, and with the other, hurled the toothbrush to the table, but it bounced off onto the carpet. *Good one.* He poked at the on-screen keyboard as fast as his shaking fingers allowed. Before he could finish the text, another came in from Longstreet.

LONGSTREET: DID YOU ARRANGE FOR THE DEPOSITIONS?

Nason's body tensed, and his jaw clamped tight. What a jerk. Was Longstreet questioning his ability to do his job? It wasn't like he could snap his fingers and voilá, a deposition just happened. He'd done the hard work all right.

And in record time. They were scheduled for the coming week.

NASON: OF COURSE!!!

He had to get control of himself before there would be no turning back. The little dots bopped up and down revealing Longstreet was formulating a response as he waited.

LONGSTREET: HOPE SO.

Tempted to hurl his phone out through the open sliding door, he instead reined in his anger and tossed the phone to the bed. Safer than trying for the nightstand again.

The trouble was, in the past, Longstreet would have had reason to question Nason's work ethics. But he'd cleaned up his act and tried to redeem himself. He knew his former actions followed him and that he would now have to act carefully to prove himself. Even as a baby Christian, he knew he'd be judged more harshly.

But to have his division head question him was unsettling. He picked up his phone again.

NASON: LET ME REVIEW THE DEPOSITION SCHEDULE AND THE FINANCIAL RECORDS FURTHER TOMORROW.

No little dots dancing.

He waited for a couple minutes and chucked the phone again. The toothbrush lay on the carpet at the end of a trail of toothpaste. He scooped it up and hurried to the bathroom to rinse the brush with hot water, returning with a wet washcloth to scrub away his mess. It could have been worse. He could have hurled the phone out to who knows where.

Sleep was going to be AWOL for a while, so he might as well do something to keep his mind off Longstreet. He opened the mini-fridge and pulled out a Coke.

Gah! One gag-worthy swig that tasted like toothpaste put him off the idea.

Setting the can on the counter, he thought about watching TV, but even at the best of times, it held little enjoyment for him. Sports, of course, were a different story. But at—he checked his watch. Eleven p.m., he doubted there'd be much sports on the limited channels in a hotel. Too bad he didn't have his Bible with him.

Wait. Did hotels still have Bibles in the room? He pulled open the drawer of the bedside table. No Bible. Ah ha! The second nightstand drawer offered a Gideon Bible. He took the Bible, grabbed a bottle of water, and made his way to the balcony.

The nighttime ocean chill on the wrought-iron chair seeped through his lounge pants, but anything cool was welcome. He flipped through the pages, looking for a book and chapter that he remembered about anger. He had a right to be angry, didn't he? His integrity, new as it was, was being threatened. Maybe even his job. What would he do then?

An image of his father floated to the top of his mind. His father grasping his shoulder, encouraging him, telling him he was good with people, with details, analysis, debate. And showing him how to fudge. Just a little. And at that time, he wanted to be just like him in all ways. He'd followed the man's faults for too long. Now he realized he could be like the good parts of his father and toss aside the bad.

Back in the Bible, he continued fingering the tissue-like pages until he came to Ephesians four. Get rid of anger. Well, that was pretty clear. It also said to get rid of bitterness, rage, brawling—thank goodness he'd given up brawling as a teenager—slander, every form of malice.

Nason looked back a few verses. "In your anger, do not sin." What the heck does that mean? He went back to the verse about getting rid of anger. The next verse told him to be kind, compassionate, forgiving one another. *I guess that's my answer.* But how to actually accomplish that?

Closing the borrowed Bible, he stared at the waves. The soft swishing of the sea, mixed with the Word, soothed his soul. If only he knew the Word better. He sighed, remembering his pastor telling him there was an app for that.

He wandered back inside, slid the door closed behind him, and approached the bed. Apparently, he hadn't heard the ping of another message from Longstreet.

LONGSTREET: OKAY.

Now all he needed to do was get some sleep.

Chapter Seven

Fear chased Fiona all the way home. It heckled her into thinking she couldn't make it to the safety of her apartment and convinced her that her head floated above her. Of course, that was ridiculous. *Get a grip.*

Finally, she stumbled through her front door, her body shaking as she collapsed onto the couch.

No. I will not allow a panic attack. Remember what the doctor told me to do.

She closed her eyes and rubbed her hands over the couch's tweed-like fabric, focusing on the roughness of the texture. It meant she was not up there in the clouds. She was here on the couch. Reality.

Soft footfalls on the carpet announced her roommate's entrance.

"What's up, girl?" Lottie whispered as she reached Fiona's side. Perching on the arm of the couch, she stroked her shoulder.

With halting words, Fiona relayed her encounter with Nason. Her trembling lingered beyond the telling, pushing her into the corner of the sofa. She drew her knees up to her chest and wrapped herself with a summer throw, creating a private little cocoon against the ocean air that swept in through the open window.

Lottie handed her a cup of chamomile tea. "Sip this. It's hot, but it'll calm you."

She slipped her arms out from under the throw and accepted the mug. Inhaling the fragrant steam that spiraled up, she focused only on the tea, shutting out the weekend's events.

Lottie, her own mug of tea in hand, lowered herself onto the other end of the couch, jiggling the liquid in Fiona's cup.

"Oh. Sorry. Look, Nason has opened the door for you two to talk. You need to walk through it. You need to get some closure, to forgive him."

"Forgive him?" Fiona's voice was shrill.

"I know you're angry. Hurt. But you've already let it fester for fifteen years. It's eating away at you. You've allowed the bitterness to control you. I think if you talk to the Lord about this, you'll see He's leading you to take care of it." She sipped her tea, watching Fiona over the mug's rim.

"What if he doesn't ask for forgiveness?" She hoped he wouldn't, so she'd have an excuse to keep on being angry at him. Right?

"Doesn't matter. You have to forgive him anyway."

"What?" She shook her head. Had Lottie just annihilated her excuse? "Who says?" She was being obstinate, and she knew it. She also already knew the answer to her question.

Sorry, Lord. "Sorry. I know. I know. I have to. But it's too hard." Tears trickled down her face, and she swiveled to set the cup on the table behind her so she could swipe at the moisture with the blanket. The downy fibers caressed her cheeks, but soon the salty streams soaked the angora.

"You're not alone in this."

"And I appreciate you, Lottie. What would I do without you?" Her clogged nose muffled her words.

Lottie chuckled. "Not me, you silly noodle. Although I will

be here for you, too. I meant the Lord. He's always right by your side. I know it's too hard for you, but it's not too hard for God."

"Oh." Fiona scooted down, pulling herself into a fetal position. "We going to have popcorn and a movie, or what?"

Huffing, Lottie stood, bringing herself up to her full 5'7" to tower over Fiona's curled form. "Look. You have to face this."

"I know. I know. But can I just do a movie and your yummy popcorn for right now? I promise I'll face it tomorrow. Please. This weekend has just been too much."

"You never explained why you were in such a funk when I got home earlier today." She lowered her voice. "What happened yesterday?"

"Nothing."

"Well, it couldn't have been something on Friday. That was a great day for you. A sweet, hunky guy asked you out."

Uninhibited by any sound within the apartment, the swish of the surf echoed loudly.

"Wait? Is that it? Trevor didn't cancel, did he? Or say something stupid?"

Her fear of dating Trevor, or anyone for that matter, rushed back, swamping her. Lottie knew almost everything about Fiona, but did she know how fearful and lonely she really was? She couldn't bare any more of her naked, frozen soul any more tonight.

"Fiona, please tell me."

Sometimes Lottie was like a dog with a bone. She'd never let this go until Fiona confessed. And her best friend would suss out anything less than candid.

"Trevor did nothing wrong." Her voice was soft. "I'm just…I don't want to be let down again." She ended in a whisper.

"Aww, I'm sorry." Lottie knelt beside Fiona and gave her an awkward hug. "That's always a risk when we put ourselves out there. But Trevor's a great guy. And besides, it's only one date."

"Trevor invited you, too. Please come with us. That means it's not really a date, right?" Fiona would feel so much better if it wasn't an official date. And that meant Lottie just had to come.

"Seriously?"

She held back a sigh. "What movie did you pick?"

Lottie sighed loud enough for the two of them. "That new romcom on the streaming service. Okay?"

"Eww. Romance. Tonight. Really?"

"But it's funny. Okay, how about a Disney channel oldie?" Without waiting for a reply, Lottie turned on the TV and scrolled to the Disney channel, clicking on *The Parent Trap*.

Soon the rat-a-tat sound of popping corn and the aroma of melting butter filled the room. Now that was Fiona's language.

How could she convince Lottie to come to Trevor's shoot?

———

He didn't really mind working on a holiday. Irina was still at her sister's, and the office was quiet, devoid of the distracting hubbub. Surprisingly enough, more offices were occupied today than he expected.

Banishing Irina, the situation at home, and Fiona from his mind, he hunkered down in front of the glowing monitor. He still couldn't find anything in the employee pay records that waved a red flag.

Back to the financial records.

He scrolled between files, comparing entries on both sides of the ledger. Another $75,000 deposit payment to the law firm. That would have to mean someone was spending an incredible amount of time on the other case. Or on this case before he came aboard.

Accessing the firm's billing records for the BioTech account, he noted many hours indeed had been billed to the corporation's deposit account.

What was going on?

Could it be fraudulent or double billing? Maybe it was nothing.

Nevertheless, Longstreet would need to get in on this.

But Nason hesitated. What if he was wrong? It could be a simple bookkeeping error.

His traitor brain reminded him that before he joined The MacArthur Group and was on his own, he had double billed. That he'd thought little of it made him cringe now. Worse, after he came to this firm, he quickly found out that it would not be tolerated.

Boy, he'd dodged a bullet on that one. Fortunately for him, the amount was small, and he was given the opportunity to correct his "mistakes." A hand slap by the State Bar, as he'd been required to attend a special ethics class, was all he suffered from that escapade.

On the surface at least. He suffered plenty from the mental kick in the behind he gave himself. If he was to stand for the law, he'd better do what was right. Besides, what would he do if he got disbarred? What kind of job would he be fit for?

Sure, he acted better, but it was an act, a selfish one. He didn't want to get caught. He didn't want to get disbarred. Selfish.

Everything changed when he accepted the Lord.

He'd tried to be a better husband and father. He never even considered until recently that perhaps that should have extended to Fiona, too.

He joined a community service group to serve his neighbors.

Most of all, he wanted to be above board in all his dealings, including billing, to serve the One who died for him even though he was so unworthy.

At least he seemed to succeed in his determination when it came to business. He couldn't say the same for being a husband or father.

Irina could be so demanding that he lost his patience time and again. Rick was a good kid and making something of himself. Nason was proud of him. But now he'd added the pressure of needing more money to pay for the wedding. He understood Rainbow's parents didn't have the dough, and he tried not to be resentful, but when he worked sixty hours a week, it was hard.

Then there was Fiona. But she wasn't his child. He wasn't responsible, was he? Then why did he feel like such a heel? If she just hadn't snubbed him at the hotel, he could forget about her.

And if Irina and Rainbow hadn't chosen the Princessa del Mar Resort for the wedding, he wouldn't be thinking about Fiona at all.

A buzzing from his phone reminded him it was almost time to meet with Longstreet. He printed out a few pages of the pay records and the financials and grabbed them on his way out the door.

How much would he tell Longstreet about his suspicions?

Nason made his way through the ghost town of offices. Even those that had been in this morning had hightailed it out for Labor Day barbecues and picnics.

On the executive floor, it seemed odd sailing through the outer offices devoid of gatekeepers.

He knocked on the jamb of the open door to Longstreet's office, a pain now throbbing in his head.

Longstreet turned from his computer and beckoned Nason in. "Let's sit at the conference table." The man lumbered to the oval table and collapsed into the plush leather chair, setting it to creaking. Although it was fully padded leather, like the division head's desk chair.

Nason's office chair was leather, too, but nothing as rich as this conference table chair.

He settled in and organized the files on the tabletop. He reviewed the details he'd examined and his findings, or lack thereof, that pertained to the client's actual case.

"I really need more time to sift through everything. I feel we're being rushed."

His boss stared at him. "This is an important client. We do whatever it takes to make them happy."

"To the detriment of the case?"

Longstreet's face hardened. "Do your job."

"Sir, with all due respect—"

"You want to debate with me?"

"No, sir." He'd better drop that subject for now.

He'd divert Longstreet's attention to the other concern.

"I think I found something irregular that you should look at."

That got Longstreet's attention. The man raised his eyebrows and looked at him intently. "Go on."

Nason's insides squirmed. This may not be a safer topic. What if he was wrong? He'd asked himself that question for the umpteenth time.

He swallowed. "As I examined BioTech's books, I noticed a second deposit of $75,000. In less than two weeks. Then when I looked at our billing records, they didn't match. I couldn't account for about $10,000."

Longstreet leaned so far back in the chair, Nason thought he'd fall over backward. "What are you saying?" He cocked his head to the side.

"Doesn't it seem suspicious? Or at least something to be investigated? Maybe there's fraudulent or double billing involved."

"Oh, I doubt that." His face was devoid of any emotion.

Wasn't the man concerned about the possibilities? Or was

he just so confident in the staff he knew, or at least thought he didn't have to worry.

Well, Nason wasn't so trusting.

"I can look further into it for you."

The chair clunked as Longstreet sat upright quickly. "No. I'll take care of it. That's my job." He stood. "You concentrate on examining BioTech's case materials and the upcoming depositions. Leave the rest to me."

Nason gathered his files and stood. "Yes, sir."

Why didn't it make him happy that Longstreet had agreed to look into the irregularities? As Nason trudged back to his office, the conversation played through his mind. The man hadn't actually said he'd look into it. Just that he'd take care of it.

He shrugged the dubious thoughts away. Longstreet would do the right thing.

———

Memories plagued Fiona throughout the week, even as anxiety about seeing Trevor on Saturday dogged her. Focusing on the memories, even the bad ones, was better than falling into an anxiety attack. When she could concentrate on the good thoughts of the past, it felt like hot fudge on a sundae, the good feelings oozing over and around her. Somewhere she'd heard eating chocolate made one feel like you were in love. She had loved Nason as a father. He was her father. DNA or no DNA.

Then why did he stop acting like a father? Was she such a horrible person? One he couldn't love? Wasn't a parent's love supposed to be without question, without judgment, without qualification?

Obviously, this didn't apply to Nason's feelings for her. Must be true only if there is a gene match. Even though Maeve's addictions made it difficult for her to show acts of love, she loved Fiona unconditionally. Of that, Fiona was confident.

Yes, it must be due to the real DNA.

But she knew kids whose adoptive parents treated them just as if their biological material matched. Lottie's parents adopted a child from Haiti, and Fiona had never seen an unloving attitude toward the child.

So, what was it? She must not be lovable. But another idea flitted through her mind. Perhaps it was Nason who could not love. And then the idea was gone, not even worthy of contemplating. It had to be her fault.

After all, her high school and college boyfriends had abandoned her. Her college love had broken up with her in a text. At least, the high school guy had said it to her face. Not that it was much help. It still broke her heart.

Trevor. Now those thoughts were back. Did she dare go out with him?

Get real, Fiona. He hasn't asked you to do anything beyond this one time.

Saturday arrived without Fiona solving the puzzle surrounding her parentage or canceling her plans with Trevor, and that was solely because Lottie agreed to go with her on the shoot and changed her plans. She and Lottie fussed in the early morning hours, deciding what to wear.

"Trevor is here." Lottie beckoned from the front door.

"Coming." Fiona tossed on a light sweater and made sure her phone was stashed in its proper purse pocket. As she threw the strap over her shoulder, her phone pinged.

Who would call her at 7 a.m.? She pulled the phone out, and her mother's picture bloomed on the screen. Great.

"Mom. It's 7 a.m. You all right?"

"Dear, I need money to keep my phone from being shut off." Maeve's voice was breathless.

"No, Mom. I paid it last week. Remember?" It was becoming more and more difficult for Fiona to discern whether her mother was getting forgetful, trying to scam her, or both. She leaned toward the latter.

"Well, then. I need money for groceries."

Yes, the latter. Didn't the woman realize her ploys were transparent?

"I can't give you any more money right now. And I'm going out the door, so I will need to talk to you later."

"Going to work?"

"Not today."

Fiona clutched the phone to her ear and ran toward the front door.

"Can you get me some money today?" A whine played out on a long note.

"I'm sorry, but no. I'll call you tomorrow. Now I gotta run." She clicked on the phone's screen, cutting off her mom's complaint.

Cutting off her guilt wasn't so easy.

Trevor's car idled at the curb while he chatted with Lottie. When he looked up at her coming down the stairs, his face transformed into a grin with a flashing dimple.

During the ride up the coast, the ocean view soothed her nerves. At least the ones caused by her mother, but not so much the ones jumping because she sat next to Trevor.

"Where are we going? I thought the shoot was in Temecula." Fiona scrunched up her face in confusion.

"Sorry. I forgot to tell you about the location change. I hope you don't mind missing the wine country. There'll be another chance to go there. But now we're headed to a former Marine Base."

"No problem. We're just along for the ride anyway." What could be as interesting on a Marine Base?

The view of sea and sand, lost when they left the coast and headed across town, gave way to an unusually clear sky with a view of mountains to the north and hills to the east.

Soaring hangars majestically held court on the tarmac of the former Tustin Marine Corps air station.

"How did I not know these were here? They're humongous." Fiona found them as interesting as vineyards.

"These helicopter hangars were large enough to hold six blimps back in the base's heyday." Trevor exited the car and stood, hands on hips, seemingly transfixed by the sight. "Now they're historic landmarks mostly used for photo and movie shoots and events."

"Look. The doors are opening." Lottie pointed as the wooden doors as tall as the seventeen-story hangar slowly moved apart.

Someone across the field summoned Trevor, who saluted the girls and trotted off.

Fiona and Lottie found the visitors' area and settled in.

People scurried about on endless errands leaving Fiona wondering what their jobs were. Trevor and three other male models re-appeared.

They were clad in a style that resembled military attire. Trevor's tall muscular body fit well into the cargo-style pants and tight fatigue tee-shirt. Combat boots completed the look.

On the tarmac in front of one of the hangars, the photographer called out instructions that Fiona didn't understand, but Trevor and the others moved this way and that, achieving a variety of poses as the camera clicked away.

"Fee." Trevor called to her from across the field, the noonday sun beating them unmercifully.

She bristled at his use of such an obnoxious nickname. How could she tell him not to call her that without hurting his feelings? Do those things hurt men's feelings? Fiona scowled.

"Yeah, Trevor. What's up?"

"Move around to this side of the field. You'll have a better view." Trevor pointed to where he wanted them to go. "Near the catering truck."

Lottie put her arm through the crook of Fiona's, and they

hurried to the far side. "I love watching Rex taking photos. I wish he were here doing the photography." Her tone played like a lonely-hearted country tune.

"He'll be home soon."

"How about that Trevor? I seem to remember Rex telling me Trevor was one of his better models."

"Hmmm." Fiona reluctantly found herself admiring Trevor.

The sun slid behind clouds that had suddenly appeared, and there was a collective groan from the group.

"Ok. Let's take a break," the photographer called out. "Maybe the sun will come back out soon."

The technical people melted away from the set. Trevor and the other models chatted for a moment before moving to different parts of the field where the spectators gathered.

Trevor wiped his brow and neck with a towel as he approached Fiona and Lottie. "I wonder who decided September was a good idea to put us in military gear."

Fiona was puzzled. "Aren't you used to this sort of thing?"

"Yes, but these clothes are the worst. Must be the fabric. No way I'd wear them in this weather. And these boots. They're cooking my feet." He grinned and wiped his neck again. "Well, what do ya think?"

How was she supposed to answer that? That she enjoyed watching his lean but muscled body move at the photographer's command? That she was trying to decide whether it was appropriate for grown men to be prancing about?

"I'm sorry it's so hot for you." She was glad the spectators lounged under canopies. "Very interesting. Do you enjoy doing that?" She waved her arm around and hoped she didn't sound judgmental.

"It pays the bills." Someone handed him a bottle of water. He unscrewed the top and took a long pull. "Someday I'd like to get into acting. And modeling is a good steppingstone."

Acting? Oh, my. She was not used to artsy types. When

her mother worked a real job, it was in a variety of retail businesses. Nason was an attorney and Lottie's father and brothers were in business. She hadn't known creative types in college. She supposed Lottie's fiancé was the first one she'd known. And he was a down-to-earth guy, with none of the flightiness she'd always assumed about people in the arts.

Inwardly, the specter of prejudice slapped Fiona, and she recoiled. She'd never thought of herself as prejudiced, but here she was judging by a preconceived notion. Where'd that come from? She vowed to do better.

"I bet it's tough to get into acting. Although I don't know anything about it. What kind of acting?"

"First, TV commercials. My modeling portfolio gives me a natural lead in."

The clouds pulled away from the sun, and the director beckoned the models and crew to hurry.

"Sorry. Gotta run." Trevor followed the others as they scuttled quickly into place.

Lottie must have left Fiona while she was talking to Trevor, but now she sidled up next to her. "What did Trevor have to say?"

"He wants to be an actor."

"Rex says he has great potential."

"Really?"

"Well, you have to admit, he's got the looks." Lottie winked at her.

Fiona's neck heated up and was no doubt turning red. Her pale skin betrayed her every time. "Need more than looks."

Lottie pinched her arm.

"Ow. What was that for?"

"You being lame."

"Am not." Fiona pinched her back.

"Are too."

They fell into a fit of giggles. They were so juvenile sometimes, but it felt really good to laugh. Lottie could always bring her out of whatever hole she fell into. Was she too dependent on Lottie? What would happen when Lottie got married? She needed to learn how to stand on her own.

The clouds had drifted off, and the sun blazed hotter. They found their way to a spot on the grass under a different awning and lowered themselves to the ground. Weeds prickled Fiona's legs through her jeans. She wished she'd worn shorts to combat the heat, but then the grass would really have scratched her bare legs.

The tableau in front of them moved every few moments as she and Lottie watched, whispering their comments.

A director called for a wardrobe change and everyone dispersed.

"It's hotter than blazes out here even under the awning. Let's head over to the catering truck."

"You talked me into it." Fiona giggled.

They stood, wiping grass and debris from their backsides. At the catering truck, they were given tall frosty cans of Coke and plates of chilled cut fruit.

"Hmm." Fiona grinned at the Coke and fruit. "Interesting combo, but it looks cool and delicious."

They found an empty table, sat down, and started in on the chunks of pineapple and watermelon. By the time Trevor sat down, their plates were almost empty.

"Would you like what's left of my mango?" Poor Trevor looked even warmer now in a black bomber-type jacket thrown over a heavy beige turtleneck. "You must be dying in that outfit."

"Outfit?" He grinned. "Thanks, but can't eat when I have my, erm, ensemble, on. If I dribbled, I'd be hung by my thumbs."

"Not even a swig of my Coke?"

A whistle blew. "Gotta get back anyway." He winked again.

Fiona and Lottie stayed in their seats by the catering truck and watched for another hour before the shoot wrapped up.

"I don't know about you, but I feel like I put in a good day's work here." Fiona stood and stretched her back. "And I'm hungry."

"Me, too."

Finally, Trevor showed up in the light tee-shirt and casual slacks he'd arrived in, looking cooler already. "Hey, how about the Kettlebar for Creole food?"

"Sounds awesome." Lottie was always ready for spicy food.

Fiona should not be looking forward to this. It wouldn't end well.

Oh, what the heck. Get over it, Fiona. And enjoy.

Chapter Eight

Waiting for the A/C repair for three weeks had left Nason feeling as if he'd crawled through the desert on his belly. Even taking a swim every night to combat the hundred-degree temps didn't help. But finally, the air conditioning had been set to rights yesterday. Nason planned a relaxing Saturday.

He stretched out on the couch, aimed the remote, and clicked away, searching for a favorite ballgame.

Life was good today. If he could forget about the case, Longstreet, Fiona, and Maeve.

"Nason, when are you going to fix that leaky faucet in the master bathroom?" Irina's demanding voice cut into his head.

He'd have to add Irina to that list of people he wanted to forget today.

"Ah, Irina. Just let me relax today and enjoy the two thousand dollars' worth of cold air." He kept his gaze on the ever-flipping channels. The bill, on top of the wedding costs, was ill-timed, but what could he do? He needed the temperature controls so he could sleep.

"What was your excuse for the last month?" Irina set her coffee mug on an end table and flopped onto the matching club chair next to him.

"Any of that left?" He lifted his chin toward her coffee.

She huffed and lumbered out of the chair, returning a few moments later with another mug that she thrust toward him.

"You didn't answer my question."

He concentrated on the scrolling TV screen.

"Nason. Really. Answer me. Please."

"What was the question?" He kept his face turned toward the TV. Maybe she'd tire of her game and stop talking.

"You know very well what I said."

So much for her tiring of talking about the faucet.

"Just call the plumber." He winced inwardly. Another costly bill was ill-advised, but he needed some downtime.

"And you were complaining about the HVAC bill." Irina whirled out of the room.

"You're right. You're right," he called out to her retreating back. And she was right. He needed to cut back on expenses. "I'll take a look after I rest a little."

After bouncing through the channels for another five minutes, Nason slammed the remote to the coffee table. Saturday, no football, and the US Open hadn't looked appealing. Tennis was okay if you were on the court, but he wasn't a fan of watching it on TV.

Might as well fix the faucet. As he stood and stretched, his phone chirped. Maeve's name flashed across the screen. He groaned. This would not be good, but he snatched up the phone. If Irina flew back into the room, he didn't want her to see who called. He thumbed the icon to answer and walked out onto the patio, sliding the glass door closed behind him.

The air, hot and heavy, collided against his body. Going outside had not been a good move.

"Maeve. What do you want now?"

"No, how are you?" Her voice contained a permanent whine. "By the way, I'm terrible. Thanks for not asking."

"I'm in no mood for games. What do you want?"

"If you're going to play it that way." She huffed and then

stayed silent for two musical beats. "Nason, darling, I just need a little cash to tide me over until payday."

He drew in a slow, steady breath. "First," he said, his jaw clenched, "don't call me darling. Second, how many times do I have to tell you, I'm not giving you any money?"

Two more beats of silence. "Nason." In those short seconds, her voice morphed from childlike to steel. "You owe me."

"How do you figure that?"

"You deserted us. Leaving me to support Fiona all alone."

"You haven't supported Fiona for years. By the looks of things, I'd say Fiona's supporting you."

"What do you mean, 'by the looks of things'? You been snooping?"

Ouch. She'd caught on to the slip of his tongue.

Suddenly, Maeve let out a banshee-like wail so loud he had to move his phone away from his ear. He couldn't make out the words. Her screams were those of a wounded animal.

"It's all your fault. Your fault. If you hadn't left us, we'd be a family now." Maeve now spoke between sobs. "If you hadn't married that home wrecker."

"No, Maeve. Never a family. Not when you lied to me about being her father."

"Stop saying that. You *are* her father."

"We've been through this a dozen times. DNA tests, get that, tests, plural, don't lie." Now he was screaming. He lowered his voice or Irina would be out here joining the fracas. "Why are you lying?"

"I promise you. You're her father."

The same old story. They'd been over it. And over it. For years now. He'd known she was a great liar, but maybe she was delusional too.

"Not gonna discuss this with you again."

"Might as well end it then. I'm just a burden." Her voice

became a whisper. "You won't have to put up with me anymore."

"Oh, now. Cut it out. You wouldn't do something like that. You want to break Fiona's heart?"

"But you wouldn't care, would you?"

How did he answer that? Of course, he didn't want her to harm herself. Certainly not anything like suicide. But truthfully, he didn't want her around either. But not that way. He had to bite his tongue to keep from vocalizing his thoughts. How callous. Horrible. In God's eyes, with his next response, he might hand her a weapon to use against herself. But she wasn't serious. Couldn't be.

"Maeve. Be sensible. Don't go do anything stupid."

"That'd make you too happy."

Did he hear a cackle just as the phone disconnected?

He dropped his hand and cellphone to his side and looked off toward an unusually brilliant blue expanse. With this heat, the sky should have been hazy, obliterating the view, but instead he had an unobstructed view of the mountains.

If only his thoughts about Maeve and Fiona could be as clear.

Did he owe Maeve something? Fiona?

His chest tightened. He didn't like the answer that kept pushing its way up from his gut. The truth was, he had been her father for the first twelve years of her life. A DNA test didn't wipe that out. Or shouldn't have. But he'd been so angry at Maeve's deception and manipulation. And Irina had demanded he distance himself from both of them. She'd made it a condition of their continued happy marriage.

What could he have done differently?

Stand up like a man. It wasn't the child's fault.

Nason could swear someone said the words out loud. His neck prickled. Of course, no one was there. Was that his conscience speaking? The Holy Spirit? He would be kidding himself to think the Holy Spirit was talking to him. Right? He didn't know enough about his faith to believe that.

He had to make this right. Somehow. But how could he do that? He couldn't go back fifteen years and start over.

At least he could start with a conversation. Would Fiona agree?

———

Fiona perched on a bistro chair staring out the cafe's window, knowing cars whizzed by on the busy street, but not really seeing them. The whooshing sound of the cappuccino machine and the clink of glassware faded into the background.

A week since she'd seen or heard from Trevor. But that was okay. Today she had to focus on a different man.

But who was this man? She stopped calling him Daddy when she was five or six. He was Dad even after the DNA tests showed he wasn't her father. Fiona knew he couldn't be her biological father, but after twelve years of being his daughter, shuttling back and forth between his house and her mother's, he was Dad. He had cared for her, fed her, bought her clothes and treats, told her he loved her, and even took her side against her mother occasionally. Then he up and disappeared from her life without a word. Somewhere in her head, he had still been Dad.

Until she was sixteen anyway. That day Lottie was falling apart because she was worried about the debate that would qualify her for the elite debate team. Her father cancelled his business trip, a critical one from what Fiona understood, and stayed home simply to be with Lottie and give her moral support. That, she realized, was a picture of a real dad. And Nason wasn't.

Ever since, to her, he was Nason. Just Nason.

She tried to put him as far out of her mind as he had put

her out of his life, but he was like a phantom, always returning to disturb her equilibrium, haunting her at her high school graduation, her college graduation, and every other important day of her young life.

Why had she agreed to meet him now? Didn't she have enough to stress her out? Her boss was on her back to "upgrade" her clients' contracts, Lottie was leaving her to be married, and her mother was on her latest downward drug spiral. Her mother. She couldn't even tell her mother about Nason's sudden reappearance. It would rocket her mother downward toward the abyss, and there might be no turning back.

She wanted to blame Nason for that too. But the truth was, Maeve had been messed up before Nason left. Her mother would not talk about her past, her years before becoming Fiona's mother. What was it? Fiona knew her grandparents were distant. Had they always been that way? Or just when Maeve became pregnant without being married? No joy had entered her grandparents' picture when she had introduced Nason as Fiona's father.

The sound of throat clearing brought Fiona back to the present and her head up to the man standing next to her. Nason. He was perfectly groomed, with his sandy-blond hair looking as if it had been cut and styled in a high-end salon and his meticulous wrinkle-free polo shirt and slacks.

"Hello, Fiona." Nason's voice was smooth and rich, sort of like that salesman who tried to sell her a fancy car she couldn't afford. "May I sit?"

Meticulous manners, too. She nodded, lips glued in place with no possibility of a smile.

She held his gaze for a few moments, then looked away.

"Thank you for seeing me." His cappuccino cup clanked as he set it on the marble table. "Order you another coffee?"

At the shake of her head, he stilled for a few moments. "What a surprise seeing you at the resort."

"A ghost of your past. An unwanted ghost."

"No. I've thought a lot about you recently."

"Just recently? No thoughts about me the other fifteen years?"

Fiona saw him visibly wince. Maybe that was a good sign.

"It hasn't been easy for me, Fiona—"

"Of course, it has been a piece of cake for me. No worries. Who needs a father?" A bitterness much more potent than she knew existed inched its way up from her gut, hitting her chest so hard she wanted to double over in pain.

"I said that wrong. I mean…There are circumstances you can't understand."

"Your wife. Your male child. My drug-addicted mother. Oh, I understand." She sipped her coffee and grimaced. Cold.

"I wasn't a free agent." He licked his lips, his expression looking as if he were eager for her to understand.

But she didn't. The image of Irina's cold gray eyes bored into her mind, and she shuddered. Thoughts of the eight-year-old mop-headed boy she'd loved and thought was her brother added to her pain. Not only had she lost a father, she'd lost a brother. A semblance of a normal family when she was at Nason and Irina's. Homelife with Maeve had no similarities to a happy family. Her mother skated just this side of the line between an adequate home and child services.

Until she shot to the dark side and child protective services removed her. Fiona was temporarily given to Nason while her mom went into rehab and ordered to earn the right to have her back. Given as if she were some prized cow at the county fair. At least that's how she thought about it now. Back then, she was ecstatic. She hadn't known it would be the beginning of the end.

Her breathing became shallow, and dread washed over her. She couldn't have a panic attack here. Fiona shot up from her chair. "I can't do this right now." She grabbed her purse, poised to flee.

"Wait. Fiona." Nason put out his hand as if to grasp her arm.

She shrunk away from him and stumbled from the cafe. *Outta here. Outta here. Gotta get outta here.* The words were like an ear worm she couldn't shake from her head.

Tears clouded her vision as she searched for her car in the lot. Where had she parked? It seemed like hours ago. Her little car beckoned from its spot at the end like a homing beacon. She rushed forward.

"Fiona."

Nason's voice sounded faint, but she had the feeling he was right behind her. She jabbed at the key fob. As soon as the car door lock clicked, she yanked it open. The leather-like vinyl burned when she threw herself into the seat, but she couldn't let that stop her. She turned the key and threw the car into reverse.

Outta here. Outta here. Gotta get outta here.

He stood on the sidewalk near the cafe's front door.

Tires squealed as the car lurched forward out of the parking lot and onto the busy street.

———

Nason mentally slapped himself as he watched Fiona speed away in her little red Mini Cooper. What a fool he was. He'd handled everything all wrong. Said all the wrong things.

But if she wouldn't listen to him, how could he prove to her he'd had no choice?

Irina had given him an ultimatum. No. Several ultimatums. Take the DNA test. Prove she was or wasn't really his. Break all ties with the child who wasn't his, or she'd take Rick and walk out.

He couldn't lose his wife and son for a child who wasn't really his, could he? He couldn't deal with a drug-crazed woman who asked for money every time he picked up or dropped off Fiona, could he?

Too much. It was all just too much. Had God really told him to make amends with Fiona? It had to be a mistake. Surely, He wouldn't expect him to fight his wife on this.

No, he needed to concentrate on his job, his cases, and the problems at hand. How else would he pay for Rick's wedding? Keep Irina happy?

BioTech's CEO had taken to contacting him directly instead of Longstreet. Which was odd. Longstreet seemed to be in his office less and less frequently, causing Nason to wonder about both BioTech cases. He knew nothing about the case that Longstreet was handling alone. And the case he was handling was getting complicated. To say nothing of the still unresolved billing contradictions.

This distraction with Fiona was not helping.

Distraction.

Was that all she was to him? She was a person. One he'd loved and cared for. Didn't she deserve more than being thought of as a distraction?

But with work and the wedding, he had more than he could handle. And Maeve's constant interference ate at him.

Did Fiona tell Maeve they'd seen each other? And what about today? Did she know they were meeting to talk?

Look how well that turned out.

The September sun seared his head and shoulders. He'd had enough of that too. Once in his Mercedes, he turned the air conditioning up full blast and headed home. Irina thought he was at a meeting. And so he had been. Just not the sort of meeting he'd led Irina to believe. Shoving down any more guilt over that little white lie and Fiona, he tried to focus on his cases, including a new one added to his case load yesterday.

And Longstreet was ghosting him. Nason hadn't seen him since their meeting nearly three weeks ago. Now the man wouldn't answer his calls. It smelled. Like his old fishing boat. Were the rumors more than gossip?

Fiona. Longstreet. Wedding. Irina. His troubles did a bongo beat in his head. If he was going to make it through the day, he'd have to chuck that drum out now.

Nason rolled his neck and shoulders, trying to relieve the spasms that complicated his drive. He tuned his radio to the news, then thought better of it, changing to a Christian music station. Until last year, he would rather have scratched finger-nails on a blackboard than listen to religious music. But now he immersed himself in lyrics and melodies that soothed his soul.

And, boy, did he need that right now.

One musical note was very much like every other one, so he winced when he heard himself singing along. *Better just listen, dude.*

———

His house came into view. How had he made it home? He had no memory of the freeways and streets he'd used to get there. Talk about distracted driving.

He pulled his silver Mercedes coupe into the driveway next to Irina's black Cadillac Escalade just as she slid out of the vehicle. How did she stay upright in those stiletto heels? She gathered several shopping bags and hung them from every finger.

"Hey, babe. Need help?" He moved around to her side and held out his hands.

"Yeah, sure." She untangled the straps and slid three bags from her fingers to his. "Thanks. Your meeting's done already? I expected it to last hours."

He grunted, then added, "Looks like a good shopping day."

Once inside the house, Nason and Irina dropped the paper shopping totes onto their bed.

"I finally found my mother-of-the-groom dress." She extracted a lot of fluffy fabric from one of the bags, shook it, and held it in front of her. "Like it?"

"Beautiful. What's for dinner?" Not waiting for an answer, he ambled out of the room.

Just as he made it to the kitchen, Irina's growling voice slapped the back of his head. "You really ought to curb your enthusiasm. You know you're involved in this wedding, too. When are you and Rick going for a tux fitting?"

"Don't know. Waiting for Rick to tell me." He opened the refrigerator door and peered inside. "What did you say was for dinner?"

"I didn't say. By the way, you didn't answer my question about your meeting." She pushed him aside with her hip and extracted a casserole dish covered in foil.

"Yeah, it was fine." He reached around her and grabbed a Dr. Pepper. It would be prudent for him to get out of the kitchen. He moved to the other end of the great room and poked at the remote, turning on the TV. Ah, a baseball game. He settled onto the couch and proceeded to shut everything out of his mind except the game in front of him and the cold can in his hand.

"Nason. Darling."

His head snapped up. He must have dozed. Fortunately, the soda can was sitting on the coffee table. How'd that get there?

"Nason?" Irina cozied up next to him on the couch.

Her form fit perfectly next to him, but he'd appreciate it more if he didn't know by her tone that something was coming. Of its own volition, his arm found its way to her shoulders. Traitor arm.

"Yeah?"

"I saw this great deal today on a Mediterranean cruise

that leaves two days after the kids' wedding. Seven days. The really low price includes air fare and all expenses." She sounded like a sales brochure. "We're really going to need to get away by that time to relax. What do you think?"

A cruise? Was she serious? "And just where do you think I'm going to get the money for that after paying for the wedding?" His voice took on an edge. He brought his arm off her shoulders, dropping his hand onto his lap.

"I thought we could use the money you got from selling your fishing boat."

"That's supposed to go toward a new boat." There was no comparison between having his own fishing boat and going on a cruise. At the end of the day, he'd still have a boat. What would they have after the vacation? *Memories, dude. Yeah. Yeah. Make his wife happy?* Well, that trumped them all. If he loved his wife, and he did, he'd want to make her happy. "Irina. I dunno."

"Well, how about we sell a few stocks? Or I could let the outside wedding planner go and do the job myself. That would go a long way to pay for it."

Maybe now she was talking. She could definitely do the work. And probably better than anyone else. Irina could have been a professional event planner. She'd organized a few events for family and friends. But she'd always said making a job out of it was too much like a job. He hadn't cared whether she worked or not, so he left it up to her.

"Do you want to do that? I mean, take over the wedding planning?"

"I want to go on that cruise." Her jaw clenched. "Besides, you owe it to me."

Ahh. Now here it came. Her usual ace in the hole. Every time she wanted something she played the "You were a bad boy and hurt me" card. Which of course, was true, but for how long could she count on successfully winning with that card trick?

"If you're willing to take on the wedding planner job, I'll think about it."

"*Think* about it?"

He supposed there was no getting out of this. Anyway, they hadn't been on a vacation together in a few years. By the time the wedding was over, they'd need to relax, just as Irina said. Have some fun.

"Yes. Think about it. At least give me a couple of days to get used to the idea."

———

Fiona loved living in a beach town, but the rent was outrageous. What would she do when Lottie got married? To stay in the apartment, she'd need a roommate, and she was out of best friends, except maybe for Teagan, but she'd never leave her grandmother. Breaking in someone new would be a nightmare.

She pulled into their underground parking garage, shut off the engine, and stared at the padlocked storage cabinet on the wall in front of her. Padlocked, just like her emotions. Her history. If Nason wasn't her biological father, who was? Maeve was no help. Despite the irrefutable DNA test, not once, but twice, her mother insisted Nason was her father. Maybe she didn't know who her father was. But then why not just say so? Apparently, her mother was in denial. Big time.

The heat in the closed car took away her breath. The fringes of a panic attack loomed. Better get inside. She threw open the car door, stumbled out, and plodded toward the staircase. It looked like Mount Everest. Feet heavy, she dragged herself upstairs.

"Fiona. There you are. You're back early. How'd it go?" Lottie sat at the kitchen table, her hands poised over her laptop's keyboard. "From the look on your face, I'm guessing, not so good."

"You could say that." She stood in the center of the room, a little disoriented. Must be the heat, the threat of anxiety. Rest. She needed rest.

"Nason didn't apologize?"

"He was—is—*not a free agent.*" She added air quotes.

"What does that even mean?" Lottie's tone and expression became indignant.

"Yeah, I dunno." Fiona dropped onto the couch and curled up into a fetal position. "I just want to take a nap."

"Okay. But how about going out to dinner after?"

"Let me sleep for a while." She closed her eyes again, willing herself to nod off.

Slumber seemed a lost cause as her mind chased thoughts up and down dark alleys, the specter of unforgiveness lurching out from dark corners. She couldn't forgive him. Could she? Well, he hadn't asked for it or even said he was sorry. What was it the Bible said about forgiveness?

How many times must I forgive?... Seventy times seven.

Were there any exceptions? She tried to remember the passages in ...

She sighed, got up, and retrieved her iPad. Opening her Bible app, she tried to remember which book talked about that seventy times seven.

"Lottie, which book says you have to forgive seventy times seven?"

"Probably Matthew eighteen."

Poking her iPad screen, she found the chapter in Matthew and read through until she finished verse twenty-two. "I guess seventy times seven means a lot of times. Isn't there anything that says I don't have to forgive if they don't ask to be forgiven?"

Chuckling from Lottie made Fiona look up. "What?"

"No loopholes. Did you read the whole chapter?"

Fiona continued to the end of chapter eighteen, then

looked up at Lottie. "What does this mean? I get that the servant was pretty nasty."

"Regardless of whether someone asks you to forgive them, you are that servant in the parable if you don't forgive 'em. And you'd be offending the God who forgave you for all of your sins. Remember?"

"I don't know if I can. Or where to start."

"Read verses fifteen to twenty again."

"Okay."

"Go back to Nason and tell him he's wronged you."

Fiona blew out a long breath. "But I did that already. Oh, let's just forget this right now and go out to dinner." She clapped her iPad case shut and tossed it to the couch.

If only her life could be more like Lottie's, calm and peaceful. Except for the chaos she subjected her poor friend to. Her own life was always in such an uproar. Where could she find that same peace in the midst of that?

Wait. Blinded by a new thought, she sat up. She'd been looking on outward events. *Lottie's peace comes from within.* From being a Christian. Not from lack of bad stuff happening to her. Her mother had cancer a few years ago, and Rex had broken off their engagement once. Thank goodness they reconciled, and their relationship seemed stronger than ever now. Despite how the army had sent him on a temporary duty to Washington, D.C., and he wouldn't be back until the wedding.

But I'm a Christian, too. Why don't I have that peace?

She cringed inwardly, a sneaking suspicion that forgiveness was somehow at the bottom of it all. *But, Lord, don't you know how much it hurts?* Silly question. Of course, He knew.

"Hey. I thought you were hungry. Shall we go?" Lottie stood by the front door, purse and keys in hand.

Fiona jerked out of her thoughts and hurried after her friend.

Their favorite sushi place was crowded, so they sipped tea while waiting to be seated.

"Fiona."

She saw it in Lottie's expression. "Don't go there. Please. I need to chew on this by myself for a while. Please."

Her friend patted her arm. "Whatever you need."

As they stood among the other waiting diners, she forced herself to relax. Head, neck, shoulders.

"Can we talk about Trevor?"

And, just like that, everything tightened up again. "Must we?" She concentrated on relaxing.

"But Rex said he really likes you and plans to ask you out again."

"Is that good news or bad news? You know I don't want to get involved. Can't." How did she feel about Trevor asking her out again? He seemed to be down to earth and fun. Could they go out just for fun? No romantic junk?

"No need to get serious. Just have some fun. I don't think Trevor is looking for anything serious anyway." Lottie was mind reading now.

The hostess called their name and seated them in a little booth up against the little "river" situated shoulder high on a raised counter. The flowing waterway meandered around the restaurant. Little "boats," artfully piled with colorful fish and rice concoctions, floated by waiting to be scooped up and savored by the diner.

Chopsticks poised, the girls grinned at each other, and at an unheard command, clinked their bamboo utensils together in a toast. "Mazel tov!"

If she could eat with two little sticks, she could surely manage a just-for-fun friendship with a nice man. Right? Besides, it would take her mind off Nason and the status of his fatherhood. Or the lack thereof.

Yeah. Right.

Chapter Nine

A Monday morning at the resort gave Fiona little time to entertain personal thoughts. Sunday she'd banished Saturday's anxiety by going for a long overdue run along the beach. Better than any medication.

But today she reviewed contracts and audiovisual orders, calculated costs, and fielded client phone calls.

As she finished her tenth call of the morning, her desk phone beeped, signaling a voicemail. She entered her code, and Nason's voice was in her ear.

"Fiona, can we try again? I'd really like to help you understand. My schedule is slammed until Thursday, so how about Thursday evening? Dinner? Coffee? Call me."

Her chest tightened, short, fast breaths escaping in puffs, and a hollowness bore into the pit of her stomach.

I don't want to deal with this. Not today. Not ever. Even if she did, what good would it do? He wouldn't ask for forgiveness, but she'd be obliged to grant it anyway. And she didn't need to see or talk to him to begin that process. She knew it needed to start in her heart.

No, she wasn't ready.

The mail clerk dropped a stack of envelopes in Fiona's in-tray, drawing her from self-absorption. Ready for the distraction, she nodded her thanks and grabbed the bunch. Dealing with four envelopes didn't take much time. One was an invitation to her client's big gala.

Her mind still went back to where she started. Wouldn't she ever get Nason out of the forefront of her mind?

Get back to work, Fiona. She clicked her mouse on the icon representing the waiting project, putting every mental molecule into the effort.

When she next glanced at the time in the corner of her computer, she was surprised to see she'd made it to four o'clock somehow. Closing out the documents she'd been working on, she prepared to check her email, always the last task of her day, but with just enough time to deal with any minor issues.

She clicked on the email icon, and her in-box rolled with a dozen or so new entries. What was Rex's photo studio doing emailing her? The email looked like it contained attachments. Photos?

"Hi, Fiona. I'm from Rex's photo studio. He thought you might like to see these photos from the recent shoot."

Photos of Trevor popped open on her computer screen. Mingled with the seriously posed shots were a few of Trevor mugging for the camera. There were even a few photos of the visitor's gallery, including her and Lottie. Someone had taken a photo of the three of them.

Fiona peered at herself. Shock registered when she saw a smile on her own face instead of the frown she normally adopted when being photographed. And she could swear there was a gleam in her eyes. Trevor had his arm across her shoulders, his own face aglow. Did men's faces glow?

Had Lottie seen these? She looked up hoping to see her at her desk, but she wasn't there.

Fiona grabbed her mobile phone off her desk and found the number she wanted, poking at the screen in earnest.

"Trevor speaking." His voice was rich and business-like.

What was she doing? Calling Trevor? Was she insane? Her mouth was dry, her voice in hibernation.

"Hello? Anyone there? Hello?"

"Uh, hi, Trevor. It's Fiona. Sorry, you caught me off guard answering so quickly." She rubbed her sweaty palm on her linen-clad thigh.

"Oh, hey, Fiona. Nice to hear from you. How are you?" The business tone was gone, replaced by what sounded to Fiona like genuine pleasure.

"Good. Good. I just received an email from Rex with photos from the shoot. I had to tell you how great you look, er, how great the photos turned out." Had she really said how great he looked?

"Did you see the one of the three of us draped over the catering truck? Priceless. You're a great sport."

She was a good sport? Not sure anyone had called her that before.

But it had been fun.

"Trevor. I was wondering if you'd like to accompany me to an event sponsored by one of my clients. I'm sort of obligated to go, and having a friendly face would help."

Left field. That's where the idea must have come from. It had jumped out of her mouth with no forethought. He'd probably decline and then she'd be embarrassed.

"Sure. I'd like that."

What?

"When and where?"

"Thursday night?" How could he be available that soon? That was sure to upend the arrangement.

"Sounds great."

What? Quick. Before he changes his mind.

"Can you pick me up at my place by five? We have to drive to Coto de Caza. It's dressy. Hope you don't mind."

"Don't mind at all. How dressy? Tux?"

"No, I don't think that's necessary."

"Dinner?"

"Dinner? Oh, they'll be feeding us. I wouldn't be surprised if it's steak and lobster. Maybe even caviar and champagne." Fiona chuckled.

Trevor laughed, too. "I'd be delighted, Fiona. See you at five Thursday night."

She clicked off her phone and set it on her desk with a shaky hand. Not only had she broken her own dating mantra, she'd made the first move. Well, maybe the second move, but still.

"What are you grinning about?" Lottie stood at her cubicle opening, arms crossed, eyebrows shooting toward her hairline.

"Oh, uh, what? I'm not grinning." She patted her face. Was she?

"Your grin is so big it's gonna break your face."

Fiona picked up the gala invitation and waved it at her. "Just asked Trevor to be my escort for the Brodermans' big charity thank you bash."

"Why you little dickens. Scoring such a big invite AND Trevor as an escort. Whatever got into you?" Now Lottie was grinning.

"I know. Right? I didn't even think about it. I just picked up the phone and called him. It must've had something to do with a message from Nason and photos from Rex's studio."

"Explain." Lottie's grin turned to confusion.

Fiona told her about Nason's voice message and showed her the photos.

"Proud of you, girl. Let's pack it up and go home."

She was proud of herself, too.

Now she had to pull off the actual date. And somehow deal with Nason's message.

———

Monday. A new week. A fresh start. Five days ahead to accomplish his goals. So much potential. What was wrong with people that they didn't get this about Mondays? Nason often overheard others grumbling as they arrived, reluctant to face the week. If they'd only prepare themselves over the weekend, they'd be so much further ahead.

Of course, he didn't always succeed in that respect. Fiona had thrown him off kilter on Saturday with the meeting disaster. If she'd only stayed and talked. Irina hadn't helped with the Mediterranean cruise suggestion.

Mediterranean cruise. Ha. The idea produced a growl in the back of his throat. He wasn't made of money. Great. He was saying that phrase more and more. He was becoming his father.

Why on earth he felt the need to start the day, the week, with trying to call Fiona again, he couldn't guess. The call had gone to voicemail, and he was caught off guard without having a plan. He always liked to have a plan. So, what did he do? Left a lame message for her to call.

Dude, you are losing your touch.

He sat with his hand on top of the desk phone's handset for several moments after he hung up. As if he'd lost the connection with Fiona and was trying to recapture it. If it were only that easy. If she'd listen and understand.

Could he be going about this all wrong? He wasn't one to share himself with others, and no one outside his family knew about what happened with Fiona. It helped that his current circle of buddies had been acquired after the blowup over her DNA. But maybe he should talk to someone. But who?

Pastor Luke. Nason's pastor had been discipling him. Well, at least as much as Nason was willing to make the time for attending their Bible study.

Baring his soul was not high on his list of desirable activities. High? It wasn't even on the list.

Do it, buddy. How difficult could it be? He cringed. Did he dare find out?

Just as he'd made up his mind to call the church, his computer pinged with a new email.

An email from a legal assistant at The MacArthur Group's head office in Chicago. He clicked on the email. As it opened, he suppressed the growl that was crouching at the back of his throat.

Was he Longstreet's keeper? Where was that blasted man?

"These two cases and your job depend on you finding him."

"My job? What about Longstreet's?" He muttered at his computer. Besides, what authority did this legal assistant have? He wasn't even the senior partner's assistant.

He had a vague recollection that he was about to do something, make a call, but it scattered. Instead, he tried to keep his mind stayed on the Longstreet problem.

Gazing out his window toward the 405 freeway from his fifth story office, he peered at the parched, brown hills in the distance. With the dry air and Santa Ana winds kicking up, all that was needed was a spark, and those hills would be aflame. Fire season.

He dragged his mind back to Longstreet. Where was he? Where to start? It was time to put a little pressure on his secretary. He jumped up and headed to Selena's office.

"Selena, can you go see Longstreet's secretary and put a little pressure on her? Find out where he is? Tell her our jobs, including hers, depend on it." So what if they were vague threats from a random assistant?

She stared for a moment and scooted out of the room.

He paced his office, peered out the window, and finally sat down in front of the threatening email. Would she tell Selena what they needed to know? What would he tell that pesky person at the main branch?

His elbows on his desk, he dropped his head into his hands.

The outer door to Selena's office opened and clicked shut.

This better be good news.

"Boss? She finally admitted Longstreet's been out of town."

"Where, for Pete's sake?"

Looking like she might be sick, she whispered, "Palm Springs."

"Not on business, I assume?"

"No. Unauthorized vacation. He swore her to secrecy. So she's taken a big risk by telling me. She's worried Longstreet will fire her."

"No risk from Longstreet. He'll be lucky to keep his own job." He jumped up and resumed pacing. "Unauthorized? What's the matter with him? He's getting himself all jammed up. And taking us with him. What hotel?"

She scrawled something on a notepad, tore off the sheet, and handed it to Nason, withdrawing her fingers as if they'd been burned.

"Thank you, Selena."

What was his next move? Longstreet might ignore him if he just called. But to drive all the way out to Palm Springs? Nearly a hundred miles in traffic and off-the-charts desert heat?

He shoved his laptop into his computer bag. Grabbed his keys and sunglasses. As he zoomed past Selena's desk, he threw an explanation over his shoulder. "Heading to Palm Springs to find Longstreet. Won't be back today."

The elevator doors slid closed as his mobile phone beeped. Irina.

"Hey. Can't talk now, but I'm glad you called. Gotta run out to Palm Springs."

"Today? I wanted to talk about the cruise. The tour company says we should book now or lose the cabin."

"I really can't talk about that right now. I have to find Longstreet, and he's supposedly in Palm Springs. I have to go. My job may depend on it. Then there would be no cruise."

"So, there will be a cruise? I can book it?"

His wife was nothing if not persistent.

"Irina, I'll be home very late tonight. We'll talk about it tomorrow." He clicked off the call, not waiting for her reply.

The building's glass doors slid open. The heat blasted him, nearly propelling him backwards. The wind had picked up and was now frantically shaking the palm fronds.

Not good weather to be driving through the desert for a couple of hours. He let the growl loose.

Hovering over his mind was a vague thought that he'd left something undone. But he shook it off and focused on the long drive ahead.

———

Jim Longstreet's face paled under his sunburn. "Nason, whadda ya doin' here?" He bolted upright from where he had been sprawled on a poolside deck chair.

Nason planted his feet wide with arms crossed over his chest. "What are *you* doing here? For Pete's sake, we're in the middle of two huge cases and you're on vacation? An unauthorized one at that." His voice rose, and no doubt so did his blood pressure.

"Hey, don't take that tone with me, man." He pulled himself out of the lounge chair and matched Nason's stance. "Remember, I'm the division head. Your boss."

And Nason was only a junior partner. A fact he needed to remember.

"Bah. You can't be here and be getting the job done."

"As a matter of fact, I can. My clerks are meeting all the benchmarks."

"Yeah? Well, the main office disagrees. Our jobs are on the line. And that includes yours."

Longstreet sputtered, then seemed to recover. "I'll call and straighten them out. It won't be a problem."

"Better not."

"You come all the way out here just to tell me that?" He added a smirk.

A muscle in Nason's jaw jumped. "If you'd answer your phone."

"Hey, you've had a long drive. Let's go in out of the sun and have a cold drink." He shouted to his wife and children who were splashing in the pool, pointed to him, and then to the building. His wife gave him the okay sign.

Longstreet took Nason's elbow and steered him toward the hotel restaurant.

As they sat sipping a mix of iced tea and lemonade, Longstreet ignored the issues and relayed funny stories about their stay in Palm Springs.

What was this guy thinking? Didn't he understand the severity of his desertion? And the risk to the cases? And what about those billing irregularities? The man wasn't stupid or new to the job. What was Longstreet not telling him? Something was up.

Desertion. The word burned into his mind. He hadn't deserted Fiona and Maeve. Well, not Maeve anyway. She was nothing to him. Fiona was…what? What was Fiona to him? She wasn't his blood. Sure. He spent twelve years acting like her father. When he thought he was her father. But he wasn't. He had to honor his vows to Irina first. And to Ricky. Right?

"So, you see. Nothing to worry about."

What? He'd missed whatever explanation Longstreet had offered. He couldn't admit he'd been distracted.

"And that means you'll be back in the office when?" Hopefully, that wouldn't give away his lack of attention.

"Like I said, Wednesday."

So much for that strategy.

"What do I tell the main office?"

"I told you. I'll call them personally. Now how about some dinner with me and my family? Are you staying here tonight? You're not driving all the way back to Orange County, are you?"

"No thanks. Heading back. I have a full day tomorrow." As Longstreet knew full well. He hesitated for a moment, but he'd driven a long way to not bring up the other issue. "Longstreet, what about the odd billing I mentioned?"

Sweat broke out on Longstreet's upper lip. Or maybe it was moisture from that last swig of his drink. No. Beads appeared on his forehead too.

The man lumbered to a standing position. "Don't know anything about that. See you Wednesday."

"Wait. We're not—"

Longstreet turned hurriedly to the nearest exit.

"—done here." He fought the desire to track the man down and belt him one. That would not be a good Christian witness. Besides, Longstreet outweighed him by at least twenty-five pounds. Maybe more.

What now?

He picked up his cell phone and dialed Selena. "Hey, it's me. Do I have meetings set up with those five witnesses on the BioTech list I highlighted?"

"Let me check."

Nason drummed his fingers on his knee.

"Boss? The system indicates someone has already met with them. How's that possible?"

"It's not. Unless Longstreet met with them. But why would he do that? They're part of my case. Can you tell who signed off on them?"

"Initialed by NBW. You. Or is there someone else with those initials?"

"Not that I know of." This was getting more and more bizarre. "Call each person and set up a meeting with me."

"Do you think someone else actually met with them? Should I ask them?"

"Ask them who they met with."

"Your meeting schedule is already crammed this week. Should I set them for next week?"

"Yes, as soon as possible."

"If they actually met with one of our attorneys, won't they get irritated if we book a second meeting?"

"Can't be helped. Thanks. I'll see you tomorrow."

"Wait. Did you see Longstreet?"

"In a manner of speaking."

"What does that mean?"

"Sorry. I'll tell you tomorrow. Got a long drive ahead of me."

And yet, he remained where he was, the murmur of voices in the restaurant playing in the background.

Someone was falsifying records. At least it appeared that way. But why? Were they targeting him specifically? Or was something larger going on? And who was it?

He'd take bets it was Longstreet.

Chapter Ten

The last thing Fiona wanted to do that night was attend a fancy event with a man she hardly knew. Sure, he was really nice and fun to be with, but doubts about starting something with him nagged her.

Remember, you're the one who called him.

Yeah, yeah. I remember.

Maybe it was the train wreck she'd had this week. Monday morning had started off with that message from Nason pleading for another chance to meet—well, maybe not pleading. Pipe and drape for an incoming show failed to be delivered today. The client threatened to sue. On top of that, she'd forgotten to file the audiovisual proposal for her newest client. That hadn't made a great impression. And she couldn't exactly tell the new client another client had distracted her by threatening a lawsuit. Talk about a rotten impression.

Maeve had called again, alternately whining and, through slurred unintelligible words, threatening mayhem if Fiona didn't give her some money. Against her better judgment, she'd delivered another fifty dollars to her late last night.

Now, although Trevor would pick her up in an hour, she loitered in her bedroom totally unprepared. She still had to take a shower and dress. Days like this she was glad her hair was short and only needed to be tousled with mousse.

Every time she tried to put Nason's call out of her mind, it came back demanding attention. It hadn't helped that Lottie had been badgering her to call him back and agree to a meeting. No wonder she couldn't put it out of her mind. In her heart, she knew Lottie was right, and she knew she was being stubborn. But that same heart was sore and just the thought of poking at it caused her pain.

Her mind whipped back to Trevor. Relationships never worked out for her. Why start something that would just end badly? Maybe they could just be friends. Friends.

And how's that worked out for you in the past?

She shuddered as a knock on her bedroom door brought her back to the present, and Lottie's head peered at her around the edge of the opened door.

"Hey, you haven't even started getting ready. It's almost 5:30. Get a move on."

"Aww, Lottie. Okay. Okay." She grabbed her robe and slipped past Lottie to get her shower.

It was a good thing she wasn't one to fuss about her looks because she was able to shower, dress, add make up, minimal though it was, and finger comb her hair by one minute to six.

She stood in front of her full-length mirror, turning this way and that, checking she hadn't missed something in her whirlwind attempt to get ready. She loved the deep sapphire color of her new dress, and the twirly fabric that skimmed her knees, adding a feminine touch that she sometimes felt was lacking in her wardrobe.

Her mom had tried to dress her in frilly dresses whenever she was going to spend the weekend with Nason, but at home Fiona was lucky just to get clean clothes. Maeve had never been one to worry about laundry and dishes, much less providing her with jeans and tee-shirts without holes. After Nason married, he and Irina provided an up-to-date wardrobe that stayed at their house, but Irina's taste in clothes ran to tailored classics.

No wonder her closet was mostly devoid of dresses. Lottie had talked her into this one. In her mirrored reflection, she saw an all too infrequent smile play at her full, pink lips.

"Trevor's here." Lottie called from the living room.

Fiona's gut knotted. Why was she putting herself through this? Career-wise, she needed to attend. But she could have gone alone. Adding Trevor to the mix was asking for trouble.

Fidgeting with her dress, she assessed her image once more, the smile gone. She wouldn't win any beauty contests. She threw her shoulders back and stepped out into the living room.

"Wow. You look great."

Was that admiration in his eyes? Or was he just saying it to be nice?

"You look great, too." Fiona gulped as she appraised his fit body encased in a tux that looked tailored just for him. And being a model, it probably had been.

"I know you said I didn't have to wear this." He waved his hands over the deep black of his tux jacket. "But it's new, and I wanted to take it for a spin."

"At least I won't be the center of attention." Oh great. How egotistical did that sound? As if she would be anyway.

———

They eased into companionable chatter as Trevor drove through the hills toward the upscale area of Coto de Caza, home to celebrities and Orange County moneymakers. This included her clients, the Brodermans, banking superstars who held a posh fundraiser at the resort each Christmas. A party that was a small thank you to those behind the scenes.

Lush vegetation flanked the guarded gate of the Los Ranchos estates, an elite section within the already exclusive properties. Fiona flashed her invitation at the guard who insisted on examining it more carefully than Fiona thought necessary. He must have thought they didn't belong. Finally satisfied, the guard pushed a button and the gate swung open, allowing them to pass.

"Well, what was his problem?" Trevor's tone was light. "Maybe he thought we were gate crashers."

"Just protecting their multi-million-dollar residences, I guess." She couldn't keep the note of irritation out of her voice. *It was nothing personal.* At least that's what she kept telling herself as they wound their way toward the Brodermans' mansion.

The late afternoon sun kissed the golden walls of the European-style mansion, accentuating the glow of lights shining from every window of the two-story manse. Peaked, slate-gray roofs elevated above multiple wings of the home gave the structure a massive appearance.

Trevor's Mustang purred around the circular drive that flowed between a large pool with a fountain and a group of red-vested valets in front of the house. Her door opened and a white-gloved hand reached out to assist her. She emerged in front of a peaked archway set over soaring front doors constructed of glass and wrought iron.

"Toto, I don't think we're in Kansas anymore." Trevor's head was thrown back as he stared.

Corny. But somehow endearing. She chuckled.

They stepped onto the white and black marble of an entryway four or five times larger than her entire apartment.

"Fiona." Mrs. Broderman floated toward them in a champagne-colored floor-length gown. "I'm so pleased you could make it." She took Fiona's hand in both of hers and pressed gently. "And who is this handsome young man you've brought with you?"

"This is my friend Trevor Thomas." She realized she was enjoying Trevor's attractive good impression. *This isn't who I am, is it?* Looks, money, and impressing people had never been part of who she was. At least that's what she thought.

Mrs. Broderman gave them a quick tour of the party layout. "Please help yourself. We'll be making some boring speeches in about an hour, but there may be a not-so-boring something special for you, Fiona." She winked and walked away.

What in the world? She didn't know if she was intrigued or scared. Definitely scared.

Silver trays of the predicted champagne circulated about the rooms on the gloved hands of black-tux-clad servers. Trays with every imaginable hors d'oeuvre followed. Except caviar. She watched for it, but it never appeared. *Maybe it was out of season. Or maybe it was a myth that all rich people served caviar.*

Fiona and Trevor nibbled off every tray offered to them and extolled the virtues of all as they chatted and moved about. A few people recognized and greeted Fiona.

Roaming the grounds, she admired the towering bronze fountains, manicured lawns, and formal rose gardens.

Over-stuffed with the fancy fare and her high heels pinching, she was ready to make their excuses and head home. Their exit was cut off by Mrs. Broderman at her elbow and Mr. Broderman at the microphone as he called everyone to attention.

An elegantly appointed terrace displayed a simple platform where their host stood.

"Friends, Marlena and I can't thank you all enough for the generous support during our fund-raising events that brought in $500,000 for cancer."

Mr. Broderman continued explaining about their charities, then began individually thanking those who had assisted at various events.

"And we couldn't have done it without the first-class assistance of the Princessa del Mar Resort. Thank you to J.R.

Evans, VP of sales, and Miss Fiona Hanlon, sales manager extraordinaire. J.R and Fiona, won't you please step up here?"

Effusive clapping roared in her ears as she shrank back, trying to hide behind Trevor. But the traitor moved behind her and, hand at her back, scooted her forward. She had no choice but to follow Mr. Evans up onto a small dais.

After more embarrassing accolades, Mr. Broderman handed Mr. Evans and Fiona each a white envelope with his best wishes. She mumbled her thanks and practically raced from the platform.

Fiona thanked Mrs. Broderman for the gift and for the evening with what she hoped sounded like the genuine gratitude she felt. Unfortunately, it was overshadowed by the embarrassment of being singled out. Mortification forced her to stuff the unopened envelope into her handbag. She grabbed Trevor's hand and pulled him through the house to the front doors.

Breathe, just breathe. She would not allow a panic attack to overtake her in front of the valets and, a more horrific possibility, in front of Trevor. He kept her hand snugly in his as they waited for his car. The car arrived and she rather ungracefully plopped onto her seat despite Trevor's gentle help.

Neither of them spoke until they passed through the Coto de Caza gates.

"Fiona, you okay?" His voice was low and tender.

She swallowed and modulated her speech. "I'm okay. Now."

"How about some chai tea in a little coffeehouse I know? It's quiet, and you can relax a bit before I take you home."

Coffeehouse? She really just wanted to go home, but it would be rude to say so, right?

———

The coffee house was softly lit and something she recognized only as a classical music piece played quietly in the background.

Her chai tea, with a hint of heady spices, felt like silk as it glided down her throat. *Thank you, Trevor, for suggesting it.*

He took a sip of his tea and set the cup down. Leaving his hands cradled around the warm mug, he leaned toward her. "I gather you don't like to be the focus of attention."

"It was that obvious?" She cast her gaze to her drink's shimmering beige liquid.

Trevor chuckled. "Maybe. But I get it. I didn't used to like any kind of attention either."

"What? But you're a model."

"That's why I said 'used to.' My mom enrolled me in ballroom dance classes when I was in junior high. Talk about embarrassing, but eventually, I came to really like the classes. And I became a pretty good dancer, so I started competing."

"Wait. You're also a competitive ballroom dancer?"

"I quit when I graduated from high school. Didn't have time while I was in college."

"What did you study?"

"I have a bachelor's and master's in history from Stanford."

The formerly silky chai tea now felt like a rock going down. Who was this guy? "Wow. And how did you get from history to modeling?"

"That's a long story for another day, but the short version is my birth mom suggested it."

"You're adopted?" Duh. Stupid question.

He grinned at her. "Yep. It was mostly a positive in my life."

"Mostly?"

"My adoptive parents loved me and gave me great opportunities, like Stanford. When I expressed an interest in finding my birth parents, they encouraged me. It was hard connecting with my mother at first, but we worked it out, and we have a great relationship. My birth father, not so much."

"I'm sorry." Should she mention her own father issues? No, this was the time for his story. Maybe she'd share her story some other time. But she'd only shared it with Lottie so far. So maybe not.

"It took me a long time to forgive him for abandoning my mother when she was pregnant with me."

He forgave his father?

"How's your relationship now?" She should have been asking how in the world he managed to forgive his father. Had his father asked for forgiveness?

"He's no longer in the picture, so I had to forgive him for my own spiritual health."

Before she knew it, she threw all her resolutions out the window into the dark night and told Trevor about Nason. He listened without commenting, and at the end of her marathon story, she was breathing as if she'd run those twenty-six miles.

Trevor clasped her hand in his. "I'm so sorry, Fiona. That's tough."

She didn't see the expected pity in his eyes, only compassion. "How were you able to forgive your father? Did he ever ask for forgiveness?" Her voice trembled.

He squeezed her hands and put his own around his mug again.

"No. It wasn't—isn't—easy. It takes a courage I don't have naturally. I have to pray about it daily, asking Him to increase my faith so I can continue to forgive him."

Unreal. Had God put Trevor in her path? She mumbled some sort of response, but it didn't even make sense to her. She swallowed and tried again.

"I can't do that."

"Can't? Or won't?" His tone was gentle. "Sorry, don't mean to be harsh, but forgiveness is a command, not a suggestion."

A gut punch. Was he judging her? How dare he. She sat up straight, ready to let him have it.

"I'm sorry." Trevor held his hand up, palm out. "You didn't ask my opinion."

But you gave it to me anyway, didn't you?

As she sank back in her chair, her breath whooshed out. He was right, wasn't he?

"S'alright. It's nothing Lottie hasn't already told me. But really. I just don't know if I can."

"If I can do it, so can you." He sipped his tea and made a face. "Cold. Shall we head out?"

At her nod, they gathered their belongings and made their way to the car.

Trevor was quiet on the way home, which left her to her own thoughts. The similarities in their hurts astounded her. It couldn't be a coincidence that their paths had crossed. The timing was too perfect.

Yet Trevor's situation was not really similar to hers. He never knew his birth father. Well, neither did she, but the man who had acted like a father toward her had abandoned her. Wasn't it better that Trevor never knew his birth father rather than be hurt later?

Hurt was hurt, right? Lottie had once told her not to compare miseries. One person's discomfort was just a blip on the weather radar to some, but that same circumstance could be a Cat 5 hurricane to another. It was all painful. She couldn't dismiss Trevor's pain.

How had Trevor reached a place of forgiveness? Or even wanted to forgive? And what had he meant by for his own spiritual health?

It seemed the only way to begin the forgiveness process was to call Nason and arrange another meeting. That alone would take more courage than she possessed. Could she really pray for more faith like Trevor had? Would He answer? Of course, He would.

Could she handle His answer?

———

His answer had been swift and unequivocal.

Call Nason.

But she hadn't been as swift. Before she knew it, two weeks had drifted by.

Today, she arrived at work just before nine with every intention of calling Nason right away. But first she stowed her purse and lunch in her desk drawer, being careful to nestle both items in the bottom just so. The temperature in the office was warm for a change—or was it just her? She took off her sweater and straightened it neatly on a padded hanger, only then depositing it on the cubicle's hook. She smoothed the soft fibers. Re-straightening every item on her desk took another half hour.

The office was abuzz with chatter, and she listened to each conversation within earshot. At least Teagan was silently tapping away at her keyboard.

Fiona. Enough, just call him already.

Taking a deep breath, she reached for her phone handset. The buzzing beneath her hand startled her, and she withdrew her hand as if it were a rattlesnake shaking its tail.

Silly girl.

She picked up the phone and dealt with a client request. The morning got away from her as her boss, co-workers, and other client calls demanded her attention, one after another.

Lottie was out on calls, and Fiona longed to talk it over with her. That's what she got for keeping her plan a secret this morning before Lottie left for the day. Not exactly keeping it a secret, but she had been afraid if she shared with Lottie, then chickened out, she'd catch her best friend's wrath.

And she didn't share such things with Teagan.

Now she was on her own.

Lunch first. She nibbled at a turkey and cheese sandwich on brioche and swigged a Dr. Pepper.

Her computer clock showed she had about five minutes left of her lunchtime. It was now or never.

She took a deep breath and dialed Nason's office number. Her leg jiggled, and her breath backed up in her lungs. No time for an anxiety attack. She forced her breath in and out.

Voicemail.

"Hey, Nason. It's me. Fiona. Maybe we could try meeting again? Call me." She set the handset back in its cradle as her heart banged out a lively Christian rock beat.

Relief she hadn't had to speak to him fed her guilt. She'd done what the Lord asked. She'd called Nason. It wasn't her fault he didn't answer. But now she had to wait.

Would he call her back? Maybe he was over trying to talk to her. Ignoring her would be a fitting punishment.

"Get back to work, Fiona."

Teagan glanced at her and mouthed, "What?" Fiona shook her head. She'd been caught talking to herself. Although that was nothing new.

Estimates for three new clients called for her attention. She dove in. Details and dollars and cents took over her brain, pushing away thoughts of anything else.

"Fiona."

She jumped and realized Heather looked over the top of the cubicle at her.

"You startled me."

"At least you were hard at work this time."

This time? When wasn't she hard at work? What did Heather mean? Was that a dig because she received the promotion over Fiona? "What?"

"Never mind. The Skinner-Williams wedding."

Just when Fiona thought she'd gotten Nason out of her mind.

"Mrs. Williams wants a quote on greenery, trellises, and

latticework. Don't know why she called me." Heather thrust a page of notes at her. "Can you get to this right away?"

"Sure." She took the pages and glanced over them. "Pretty straightforward."

Heather nodded and walked away.

Thankfully, her diligence this afternoon meant she had completed the estimates she'd started on after lunch.

Fiona's mind wandered as she culled through Irina's requests. What was Ricky like as an adult? What did he do for a living? Had he gone to college? She sure could have used Nason's financial help for her own college. Her mother certainly hadn't helped. She'd worked hard at several jobs, received grants and scholarships. Fiona was proud of herself, for a change.

What did Nason think of Ricky's fiancée? His wedding plans? Probably didn't think of it at all. Although he was footing the bills. Wonder why Rainbow's parents weren't paying for the wedding?

She reined in her thoughts and got to work pricing out the decorations for Ricky and Rainbow's wedding.

Nason would have to wait.

Irina's estimates complete, she pushed herself away from her desk and made a trip to the ladies' room. She took the long way there and back to add some steps to her day. She'd been sitting at that stupid desk for hours. Maybe she'd go for a run right after work.

Returning to her desk, with her mind on her upcoming run, she glanced at her phone's blinking message light, and absently punched in her code. The computer voice announced two messages.

Trevor had phoned apologizing for taking so long to call her. He thanked her for taking him to the party and for confiding in him afterward. Would she like to have dinner next week after he returned from another out-of-town shoot?

Warmth spread throughout her chest, and she smiled. *Yes.*

How had she gone from being afraid to date Trevor to being excited about the prospect? In one date? Two dates, really, she supposed.

Whatever. *Call and accept the invitation before he changes his mind.*

"Trevor, I would love to have dinner."

"That's great." The smile in his voice reached through the phone. "I'm heading out tomorrow for Mexico. I'll be back on the twenty-sixth. So, pick you up Saturday the twenty-seventh about seven?"

She readily agreed. After they said their goodbyes, Fiona checked for her second message. A few clicks and whirs later, Nason's voice greeted her.

"Hey, yeah, glad you called. Let's meet again. How about Saturday the twenty-seventh? Sorry, can't meet before then. Family obligations. Same place and time? I'll wait for your call."

Family obligations? Oh, yeah. She was not family. But she had been. How does one get excommunicated from a family?

DNA.

She huffed. Her breathing became rapid. Family. Family. Family. The word reverberated in her head.

Stop. Breathe in and out. Count.

The anxiety attack averted, she picked up the phone and dialed Nason again. Voicemail. Just as well. She left him another message.

Same place and time. Hopefully, it wouldn't be the same results.

She'd focus on her date with Trevor. Which, she realized was the same day as she was to meet Nason. She prayed meeting him wouldn't ruin her date with Trevor.

Chapter Eleven

Weeks had tiptoed by now and Longstreet still hadn't returned. No phone call. He'd trusted Longstreet to follow through on his promise to contact the main office and return to the office. Maybe he did since that legal assistant hadn't emailed again demanding his response.

At least he was confident everything progressed for the BioTech employee case. To get there, he'd racked up some startling billing hours.

Longstreet needn't have brought Nason in on the case at all. So why did he?

He guessed there was no need for Longstreet as long as the main office wasn't bugging him.

BioTech would only receive his best legal work. Nason was done with fudging.

"Boss?"

Selena stood in front of his desk with an expression he couldn't quite identify.

"Selena."

She fidgeted, the papers in her hand fluttering. "I think you need to see these." She thrust them into his hands.

"What are they?" He skimmed the first page. Then the next. Faster and faster with each additional page. "Where did you get these?"

"Can't say. Confidential."

His heart beat rapidly. "Must be a mistake."

"No. I've confirmed the figures and the documents."

Confusion wrapped around him like cotton batting.

"But—"

"Nason, this is no mistake."

Selena was the most trustworthy and loyal legal assistant he'd ever had. *Listen to her.*

Rage built in his chest.

Longstreet was claiming all, one hundred percent, of the billable hours that would come out of the BioTech case. That meant Nason was getting no credit for his efforts. In fact, despite working so many extra hours on this case, he was going to fall below his monthly required number of hours he was supposed to bill. He was being shafted.

He jumped from his chair and paced, slapping the pages he'd rolled up against his palm. From the beginning, he'd thought there was something weird about the BioTech case. He hadn't been able to put his finger on it.

"Have you set up meetings with those other five?"

Pink blotched Selena's tanned cheeks, and Nason was pretty sure it wasn't from makeup.

"I have not been able to reach any of them. Left three or four messages for each without one response. I'm sorry."

"It's not your fault, Selena. But why wouldn't they respond if they wanted to win against their employer?" A white bolt flashed through his mind. "Are these even real, legitimate people?"

"It seems so."

This was nonsense, and he was going to fall short on billable hours for this?

"Where's the senior partner?" His voice was low and menacing. She cringed. Poor Selena. She didn't deserve that.

"In Detroit. Won't be back in Chicago until Monday."

"Sorry. I'm not angry with you. Of course, I'm not. You may have just saved my bacon. What about Longstreet? Any news?"

"Rumor has it he's also gone to Detroit." She moved back a step.

"What?" He rubbed his hand down his face, from hairline to chin. "He and the senior partner are colluding?"

"I didn't find evidence of that. Nor did my source. I don't believe any of the senior partners are involved. Or that they would ever be involved. I think he's gone to Detroit to convince the senior partner he wasn't responsible for any double billing problems."

"You know this how?"

"I don't *know* it. But apparently MacArthur hasn't received these reports yet. The senior partner's secretary said she delivered them after he went out of town."

He plopped back into his leather desk chair. "Either I fly to Detroit or sit here on my hands until Monday."

"His secretary told me the meetings were over today, and he was spending the weekend with his son and daughter-in-law on some lake island. By the time you could get there, he'd be gone."

"No telling where Longstreet's gotten to then."

"Rumor mill is still crankin'. They say he's coming back to OC tonight. Won't be in until Monday."

Nason swallowed a sigh. "Hey, thanks. Selena."

"I was afraid you were gonna shoot the messenger."

"You know better than that."

"Just messing with ya, boss." A grin tipped the corners of her mouth, but her eyes still seemed worried.

He tried to return the grin, but only succeeded in twisting

his mouth into something half-hearted. "You'll keep an eye on your sources and the rumor mill, won't you?"

"Of course."

"You're the best. Thanks again."

"One more thing. Longstreet's secretary let it slip that he went to Palm Springs to rest because he's sick."

"What kind of sick? He didn't look sick to me."

"No idea. Couldn't get any more out of her. She probably knew she'd already said too much."

What on earth did that mean?

Before she could get out the door, his phone rang. More bad news? He yanked the phone off the base and jammed it to his ear. *Careful, dude. Don't give yourself a concussion.* "Williams."

"Nason? It's Fiona." She sounded breathless.

He tensed.

"Hello, Fiona. Sorry, we've been playing phone tag."

"Yeah. No problem. But...Just confirming. Same time and place next Saturday are fine with me. If it's still good for you."

"Perfect. I'll see you then."

Nason could have sworn he heard her grinding her teeth.

He was more careful with the phone as he settled it back in its home. Was this going to be another fight? Of course it was. Fiona was angry. And she had every right to be. If only she understood.

How could he explain it to her?

Forgiveness.

Again, with the voice in his head. Was that God, the Holy Spirit? What did it mean? Monday's decision to call Pastor Luke finally resurfaced.

His phone call to the pastor was unsuccessful. Another voicemail.

As soon as he hung up, the phone rang again. He couldn't handle any more bad news. Fortunately, it was Rick confirming tomorrow's golf game. At last. Something to look forward to. He would get to spend time with his son while Irina spent time with Rainbow and her mother. Guilt that he was glad Rainbow's father didn't play golf nipped at him. The foursome would be rounded out by one of his buddies and his son.

While he'd been making arrangements, Selena dropped off another batch of deposition transcripts. He had his work cut out for him this afternoon. A good distraction.

But was he going to get paid for this? What about those five witnesses? It could not be a coincidence that none of them had returned Selena's calls. No way.

The big question was what he was going to do about it all. Digging into all the complex paperwork would take a couple months at least.

———

"Good shot, Ricky." Nason pounded his son on the back. The last shot of the game put Nason in first and Ricky third. Not bad for a beginner.

A silly grin on Rick's face was his only response.

Congratulations and handshakes all around preceded the goodbyes to Nason's buddy and son.

His arm slung over Rick's shoulder, they headed toward the clubhouse. "Let's get something cold to drink before we head home. If we get home too soon your mother might put me to work."

They shared a chuckle before Rick replied. "So, I guess that's how it's going to be for me. Rainbow giving me all those honey-do things, huh?"

Wide red brick steps led up to the Mediterranean-style clubhouse. Inside, the Grill walls were blond oak and matched the oval bar in the center. A white stone fireplace on one end broke up the endless beige. Even the club chairs were beige.

Nason liked a little more color in a room, but as long as

the lemonade was sweet and tart and the food cooked right, he'd put up with it.

Settling into chairs overlooking the course and the ocean beyond, they sighed in unison.

"Hey, I'm the one getting old. You're too young and fit to be tired after only one round." Nason couldn't help teasing his son.

"It's been a hectic week at work, and Rainbow's got me going crazy with wedding stuff."

"Sounds like Rainbow's already got you into the honey-do this and that."

"Oh, yeah. I guess so." Another silly grin split Rick's lean face.

A waitress took their orders for lemonade and artichoke dip, winking at Rick just before she turned away.

"You need to start looking hen-pecked so the girls will leave you alone."

"Dad." Rick's neck turned pink.

"So. You said work's been busy. It's going good?"

Rick described the bridge project he was working on until their drinks arrived.

"How's work going for you, Dad?" Rick gulped half of his lemonade in one long swig.

Nason flapped his hand. "So-so. Some good and some bad." He related some of his work-related woes but left out mentioning Longstreet and the mystery situation. He didn't know how to explain it.

The same waitress returned with their artichoke dip and French bread, smiling broadly at Rick whose neck colored again.

"I'd say you have an admirer."

"Wow. She's pretty out there with her flirting. How do you tell a woman you're not interested? Without hurting their feelings, of course." He grabbed a chunk of bread and scooped up a large mouthful of the chunky dip.

"When you figure that out, let me know. Sometimes you just can't do it with subtlety." Nason copied his son, digging into the dip.

"You talking about Maeve?" Rick said around another mouthful.

Nason wanted to bite his tongue. Instead, he grunted. She was not a subject he'd intended to bring up. In fact, he'd avoid it and her at all costs.

"Dad, you've never explained Maeve."

"There's no way to explain that woman."

"Stop. You know what I mean."

Yes, he knew what Rick meant, but he could not have this conversation with his son. "There are some things a father cannot talk about with his children." He stuffed another bite into his mouth.

"But you've always told me I could talk to you about anything. That's not a two-way street?" Rick's gaze bored into Nason's, challenging him.

He looked away from his son, his gut tightening. "No," he whispered. *Leave it alone, Ricky.*

"C'mon, Dad. I'm a big boy now. I can handle it."

Yeah, but I can't.

He turned back to his son. "Look. I was just young and foolish. And she was...she was really not much more than a one-night stand. Well, more than one night, but you know what I mean. I'm not proud of it, and I tried to make up for it by supporting Fiona." Now he did bite his tongue. *Ouch.*

Rick stared at him for a moment. "But she wasn't your child. Maeve lied to you, and they've been interfering in our family ever since." A bitterness laced his words.

"It's not Fiona's fault, you know. She's an innocent party, catching all the flack."

And Nason needed to set things right with her. How could he do that? What could he do? *Ask for forgiveness.* But it wasn't his fault.

"You don't think Fiona has some ulterior motive for coming back into our lives?" Rick's tone made it clear what his answer to that was.

"Remember, she didn't come to us. At least not at first."

"What do you mean 'at first'? Has she been in contact with you?"

"Hm. Once or twice. In fact, we're having coffee next week." Now why on earth had he told Rick that?

"What? No."

"What's your problem with this, Rick? She's not going to inherit your fortune. There isn't one anyway. She's not going to replace you in my heart. What's the problem?" Anger mounted in Nason's chest. How had he raised such a selfish child?

Look who's being selfish. Humble yourself and ask Fiona for forgiveness.

"It's not fair to Mom. Maeve and Fiona are not our family. We've got Rainbow to consider now."

"You don't think I can be a good father-in-law to Rainbow and have a relationship with Fiona?"

A relationship with Fiona? Where'd that come from? He hadn't even considered that he or she would want that. But somehow it seemed right that he should have one with Fiona.

"So, you're planning to have some sort of daddy daughter thing?" Sarcasm and bitterness added fire to Rick's words.

The flirty waitress sidled up to them again. "Ready for a refill?" She spoke directly to Rick, her tone honeyed.

"No. No. Thank you." Rick looked away after only the briefest of glances at the young woman.

"Just the check, please."

"Of course." She flounced away.

Father and son looked everywhere but at each other until the waitress brought the check, and Nason signed it.

"Rick. This isn't Fiona's fault."

"You gonna tell Mom?"

"Let's just get out of here."

No way was he going to tell Irina. At least not yet. But he didn't want to admit that to his son.

Would Rick tell his mother first?

Chapter Twelve

Saturdays, when she didn't have to go into the office, allowed her time to take longer runs, runs that really made a difference. And she had never been so glad it was Saturday. Already warm at six-thirty a.m., the temperatures would surely soar before noon. But now the ocean breeze evaporated the sweat on her drenched body, cooling her after a five-mile run.

She savored the activated endorphins and the resultant euphoria. Before she became a runner, she stupidly rejected the message that exercise could be an analgesic.

With feet planted wide and hands on hips, she breathed in and out, savoring the high that running gave her. She considered running to be one of God's blessings. Grateful for any and all gifts from the Lord, she turned and jogged home.

The apartment was stifling despite the open windows and the puffs of gentle breezes off the ocean. She punched the household fan's max button, swiped a cold bottle of water from the fridge, gulped down half, then slowed to sipping.

Time for a cold shower to ease her aching muscles.

Her phone rang, and an unknown phone number glowed. Unknown numbers were not welcome. She'd wait for a voicemail. Usually there was no voicemail, which meant she'd avoided a sales or scam call.

As she grabbed her robe and clean clothes, an incoming voicemail pinged. Who could that be then? She clicked on the voicemail icon, then the unknown number. Her gaze latched onto Ricky's name in the voicemail transcription. He wanted to talk. What could he want to talk about?

Maybe he was excited about finding his sister. They had acted like brother and sister once. But it had been weeks since they first saw each other. He couldn't be all that excited. Of course, he had a wedding coming up, and presumably a job or college. Who knew what else? Had he delayed because he didn't know what to say?

Wait. Where'd he get her cell phone number?

Curiosity nudged her to push the call back icon.

A voice totally unlike his eight-year-old soprano answered on the first ring. She'd heard his voice at the site visit, but she hadn't exactly listened well in her distracted state.

"Ricky?"

"Hello, Fiona. Thanks for calling me back."

She waited for more, but the silent vacuum urged her to fill it.

"I'm so glad to hear from you, Ricky. By the way, how'd you get my cell phone number? Not that I mind you calling, of course."

"Oh. I...uh. Got it from my dad."

Hmm. That sounded fishy, but she'd let it go. "How are you? How are the wedding plans going?"

"I leave that up to my mom and Rainbow. Fiona, what are your intentions?"

What was he talking about? "Excuse me?"

"What do you want from my father?" His voice had gone from cool to cold as a winter snowstorm.

Want? *His* father? His choice of words had been no accident. Did he think she wanted to steal him away? Have Nason cut Rick out of the will in her favor? Was there a large bequeathment involved?

She mentally shook her head. Didn't matter. She didn't expect anything or want anything. At least not monetarily.

But maybe an apology. A request for forgiveness. An explanation.

"Very little." She kept her voice warm to take the high road.

"But you want something? Why have you made contact after all these years?"

"You're kidding, right?" *Me* make contact?

"You obviously want something."

This kid was nuts. It was going to be difficult holding onto any civility, much less a warm, fuzzy tone. "May I remind you that your mother came to our hotel. My boss assigned me to your event. I instigated NO contact." She cleared her throat, and before she knew it, more words spewed. "Actually. I do want something…"

"Ah ha."

"I want an explanation why all of sudden I was no longer welcome to any kind of relationship with Nason." *Bite back that tremble.* No need for Rick to catch on to that.

"Obvious. Your mom lied. You aren't a member of our family."

He'd stuck the stiletto between her ribs. "Stay out of our lives."

"Hard to do when I'm working on your wedding."

"I can have my mom request you be taken off our event."

And twisted it.

What excuse would they give? Would that get her fired? At the least, it would mar her reputation with her boss.

"Look, Ricky. Really. I don't want anything from you guys. Just let me do my job."

Lord, don't let me sound desperate.

"Then keep it professional."

Like she hadn't been keeping it professional?

Her phone suddenly seemed quiet, empty. She pulled it away from her ear and checked the screen. He had ended the call.

The exhilaration from her run dried up like her body sweat as she stood in front of the rotating fan. Her muscles quivered, and she couldn't tell whether it was from the exertion of her run or the anger that was building up in her body.

How dare Rick accuse her of somehow seeking, what, retribution? A slice of some inheritance pie? Why was the thought of returning her to a place at the family table such a threat?

And where was Nason in all of this? Did he, too, think she was finagling for something? Did he know Rick was calling her?

What would she say to Nason later today? Oh, she had so much to say.

———

Nason chose a small bistro table in the back corner of the cafe to wait for Fiona. He tested the double espresso macchiato and, finding it satisfactory, took a larger taste. The caffeine fortification would help him through whatever happened in the next hour.

Determined to get his explanation across this time, he fidgeted in the too-small cast iron chair. The chatter and clanking of stoneware added to the edginess that set his leg twitching.

Why should he be so nervous? He was a mature adult male. Strong. Decisive. A leader. A boss. Yet, he was keenly aware he would be addressing a hurt child in an adult body.

One who had fifteen years to build up her anger. That outrage had been pretty clear the last time they'd talked. Or at least tried to talk. She'd bolted before he had a chance to really explain himself.

As he took another sip of the creamy brew, he saw Fiona standing in the open doorway. He raised his hand to get her attention. Her blonde pixie cut made her appear younger than her twenty-seven years. Or maybe he just wanted to think of her as the young, sweet child he remembered, rather than an angry adult.

From the fire blazing in her amber eyes, he surmised he would be dealing with that adult today.

Nason stood and gestured toward the nearby chair. "Fiona, I'm glad we could meet again."

Sparks continued to flash in her gaze, although she remained silent.

"Can I get you a coffee? Latte? Espresso?"

"A sugar-free vanilla latte, please." Her voice was hard. Her body rigid.

"Of course." He headed to the counter. Glad of the few minutes it would take to get her latte, he tried to make sense of her attitude. He'd expected her to be skeptical, but not so evidently enraged. Her phone message had seemed almost friendly. What had changed? How would he break through to get a listening ear?

He set the cup and saucer on the table, the stoneware clanking against the wrought iron.

"Thank you." She averted his gaze, staring out the door she had entered only minutes ago.

Was she already planning another escape?

"Fiona, I'd really like to explain how things were—"

"Did you know Ricky called me this morning?" She finally looked at him, her eyes as hard as her voice. "Did you know he practically threatened me to leave you alone?"

"What? No." Rick had called her? He knew he shouldn't have let it slip that he was seeing Fiona. "I'm sorry. I had no idea."

"He even threatened to have me removed from his wedding account. Which could get me fired."

"No. He wouldn't do that."

Would he?

"Ricky seems to think I'm angling to get, I don't know, maybe an inheritance or something. Look. I didn't seek you out, and I don't want anything."

He almost missed her whispered, "Maybe just an apology."

An apology? Could he give her one? Could he at least give her that? But it wasn't his fault. Really, it was Maeve's and Irina's fault. Between the two of them pulling him in opposite directions, he'd been between the proverbial rock and a hard place.

"Fiona, I'm sorry you felt that it was unfair. Your mother and my wife made it impossible for me to keep up our relationship."

"You're sorry I felt it was unfair?" Her voice was shrill and loud.

Patrons in nearby tables turned to stare.

He'd finally said he was sorry. What was wrong with that?

———

Adrenaline surged through Fiona, and she clutched the edge of the table to keep herself in her chair. The barista's constant calling out names roared in her ears. The hiss of the cappuccino machine sounded like an old-fashioned steam engine barreling toward her.

Nason's eyes were vacant, his jaw slack.

Obviously, he didn't get it.

What was the matter with this man? Was he obtuse? Or so self-absorbed he couldn't pick up on anyone else's emotions?

She relaxed her grip on the metal and slumped against the back of her chair. Her emotions alternated between pity and disgust. If he thought she was going to let him off the hook with that pathetic "sorry," he was more delusional than she imagined.

"Unfair? It wasn't unfair. It was selfish and cruel."

How could she explain her feelings about him cutting them off? After her mother told Fiona she wouldn't see him anymore? She couldn't find the words to tell him she felt abandoned and lost.

It wasn't just the lack of vocabulary. It was the fear of tearing open her soul to reveal her innermost pain. To ask him why he couldn't love her, and to admit she was unlovable.

A loneliness so intense it became an ache that suffocated her spirit.

But you are not alone.

Sure, she had her mother, but she was emotionally distant and grasping. There was Lottie, but she was getting married and would have to concentrate on her new husband. Trevor. She didn't know what that was yet, and, by her past record, would probably amount to nothing.

Deep inside that suffocating spirit, a whisper tried to get her attention. Whatever it was, she couldn't take a large enough breath to acknowledge it.

Rick. He'd been the proverbial last straw this morning.

"And Rick. Threatening me? Was he just being unfair? No. He must have learned selfishness and cruelty from you."

"Believe me, I had no idea Rick would call you. And, honestly, it's unlike him. Usually, he's kind and considerate. Maybe his wedding is getting to him. Making him testy."

Seriously? He's got to be kidding. "That's no excuse to be cruel."

"No. You're right, but maybe he misunderstood something you said."

"I said nothing." She narrowed her eyes at him. "What have you been telling him? Maybe you think I'm out to get something from you. After all, you're a big, hot shot attorney. Right?"

"Hardly. I'm just a junior partner in a large firm. And, no, I haven't said anything like that. Nor have I thought it."

"Considering we met by accident, I certainly hope not. But let's get back to why you left."

"You know why. I've told you. Irina gave me an ultimatum. Would you expect me to sacrifice my wife and son to...to…"

"To what? To have a relationship with a child who wasn't your daughter, even though we thought so for twelve years of her life? She didn't matter. Did she?"

"Fiona, please understand. I did what I had to."

He did what he had to? A little doubt creeped in. Maybe he really did. Was she in the wrong? But even so. Was she supposed to just move on? Didn't he at least owe her an apology? And what about Rick?

She jumped from her chair. "Until, and unless, you and your family can apologize, really apologize, I can't, won't speak to you. Except in my professional role concerning the wedding."

Nason put his hand up to stop her. "Wait."

"And Rick better not have me removed from that. Because if I get fired, I will want something from you. And if I have to take you to court, I will."

She turned her back and, once again, fled from Nason and the cafe, her chest heaving. Shouldn't she feel good about standing up to Nason? Instead, regret already added to her inability to breathe.

Take him to court? What on earth possessed her to say

that? To an attorney, for Pete's sake. One thing she was sure of, she wouldn't speak to any of them until they apologized.

———

"So, you've spoken to Nason?"

Fiona's heels thudded against wooden planks as she strolled beside Trevor on the boardwalk away from the seaside restaurant where they'd had dinner.

Twilight had given way to night, and the waning crescent moon did little to illuminate the darkness. Instead, lights spilled from the windows of neighboring establishments creating golden pools on the promenade.

She tried to appreciate the night, the dinner, and the walk with Trevor, but in the six hours since she'd left Nason open-mouthed in the cafe, her heart had been closed off.

"Yes," she finally said.

"It didn't go well, did it?" His tenor voice was gentle.

"Pretty obvious, huh?"

"You've been quiet tonight. I'm sorry. Do you want to tell me about it?"

"It was horrible. Nason was horrible. I was horrible."

"So. I guess it was horrible." Trevor took her arm and squeezed it gently as he wrapped it in the crook of his elbow.

"I don't think you really want to hear about it."

"I do. That is, if you want to."

She'd already made a fool of herself in front of Nason, even if he was, what had she called him—oh yes, selfish. And cruel. She couldn't forget cruel.

Did she want to tell Trevor how stupid she'd been? It would be sure to turn him off and prove she wasn't worth even dating.

Get a grip. Trevor's been nothing but encouraging.

Fiona gathered her pluck and plunged ahead, describing her short and volatile meeting with Nason.

"I don't know what possessed me to threaten a lawsuit. I could never do that. Not to mention he's a lawyer." She let out a long, shuddering breath, glad the telling was out.

"We often say a lot of things we don't mean in the heat of the moment. You were rightly vexed."

Rightly vexed? She had indeed been vexed. Rightly? She wasn't sure of that.

"You think I was right to be angry?"

"He actually said he was sorry if you felt it was unfair? Unfair?"

"His exact words."

"That was certainly no apology. Much less a request for forgiveness."

"Humph."

"Although he's hurt you—again—you realize you still have to forgive him. Right?"

She yanked her arm from his and turned toward him, fisting her hips. "So you and Lottie keep telling me. But how? The hurts just keep coming."

"Even the most unlovable need grace and mercy."

Unlovable. He'd used that word, the word that struck her with such terror.

"What about me?" Her voice squeaked on the sentence.

"God gave you grace and mercy when He died on the cross for you. He did it because He loves you. He forgave you for everything. Now it's your turn."

Intellectually, she knew that was true. In her heart? She was having trouble feeling it right now.

The image of herself the day she accepted Christ as her Savior rose in her mind. Kneeling on the steps by the pastor's lectern, Lottie by her side for support. She tried to capture the feeling she'd had when the weight of her sins lifted from her when she'd prayed that day, sensing God's love. But it eluded her grasp.

"You know, it's not just a feeling. It's faith. Taking God's Word as absolutely true."

Had Trevor read her mind? How had he known she was trying to feel—to feel loved, worthy of God's love?

Fiona blew out a long breath. Trevor took her arm again and moved them forward, continuing their walk.

"Pray about it, Fiona. Open your heart and pray."

Open her heart?

That seemed to be the crux of the problem. Her heart was wrapped in chains. Padlocked. She merely had to find the key.

Chapter Thirteen

What ever happened to relaxing weekends? Nason's weekend had been punctuated with a lingering rage at Longstreet's continued absence and his seeming deceit. Confusion over how Fiona had reacted in the cafe last week added to his anxiety.

He told her he was sorry. How had he been selfish and cruel? He had no choice when he'd distanced himself from Fiona and Maeve. Over and over, he reminded himself that he'd never been married to Maeve. Besides, DNA proved Fiona was not his child. His wife had a right to demand he not be involved in their lives.

Irina, still asleep at his side, snored softly. He gave up lying in bed. So what if it was only five in the morning? He'd get his shower and life-giving caffeine, then head into the office early.

He slid out of bed and, in another fluid movement, drew the satiny cover into place on his side. With bare feet, he padded from the carpeted bedroom to the bathroom.

Oh, molly! The cold marble on his feet jolted him. A disadvantage they hadn't considered when choosing marble for the bathroom flooring. *Just wear your slippers, man.*

If he hadn't been awake before, there was no doubt that he was now fully conscious.

Bustling through his shower, shave, and getting dressed, he filed the meeting with Fiona into the recesses of his mind.

When he pulled his car out of the garage, the night sky greeted him. The time change. No wonder he couldn't sleep. If he hurried, he could beat the early morning commuters on the canyon road and make it to the office by six-fifteen.

Yes. He beat his best time. Six-thirteen. At least he could appreciate the little things.

He let himself into the building where only the night security guard hunkered behind the receptionist's desk.

"How's it going, Sarge?" The man was probably not a sergeant, but the guy seemed to get a boost out of the promotion. Besides, he didn't know the guy's real name. Probably on his name tag, but that would mean Nason would have to stop, look, and chat. Not today.

"Mr. Williams. You're the first one in today." His voice was gravelly.

Nason offered a two-finger salute and kept walking.

After plopping down at this desk, he skimmed the perfect piles. Each was neatly marked with post-it notes telling him what kind of attention they needed. Thank God for Selena. Each was even marked with a priority number.

Which he immediately ignored.

He pulled each stack toward him, evaluated the priority, and re-marked it before returning it to a spot on his desk.

Starting with his number one priority, he got to work before rattling noises in his outer office announced Selena's arrival. Seven forty-five already?

"Selena?"

"Good morning. You're in early."

"It was better than tossing and turning. Any word from Longstreet? It's been weeks."

"Not even scuttlebutt. However, I heard the senior partner is on a month-long vacation."

Without him, the problem was not likely to get solved any time soon. He'd just bide his time. Surely, Longstreet would show up soon.

"Let's forget that and get back to business. My first appointment is at ten. Right?"

Several hours of appointments and copious follow-up notes later, it was too late to call the main office in Chicago, and the senior partner wouldn't be there anyway.

And what about Fiona? What was his next step with her? Was there a next step? Perhaps he should leave it up to her.

He didn't have time for all this drama. After all, he had a living to earn. A wedding to pay for.

Yep, he'd leave the next move to Fiona.

———

For weeks Fiona had carried the weight of anger and loneliness, and she was sick of it. She'd doubled down on her Bible reading for the past couple days, and the words were slowly seeping into her heart.

The Lord—how else could it have been so perfect?—had presented her with passages that spoke of perseverance and doing good. She certainly hadn't been doing anyone good, not even herself.

Lottie had mentioned that lately her face resembled someone sucking on a sour pickle. Leave it to her best friend, who never pulled any punches, to draw an image Fiona would find deplorable.

When she'd mentioned to Trevor she'd been reading about doing good, he told her a great way to help a person look outwardly was to do good for someone else.

Yes, she needed to stop being so self-centered and to think of someone else for a change. Her mother came to mind first.

Fiona had been short with her on the phone lately or ignored her calls altogether. What kind of a daughter did that?

Thinking about talking to or spending too much time with her mother caused the hairs on the back of her neck to lift and vibrate. Her mother was toxic, and their relationship followed suit. But Maeve was *her* mother, given to her by the Lord. He must expect Fiona to honor her by doing things for her. And probably giving her some quality time.

She didn't know where the courage came from, but she broke through her icy shell enough to call her mom and suggest a shopping trip.

Now she wasn't so sure this do-good thing had been such a great idea.

Fiona and Maeve ambled through the South Coast Plaza, Orange County's largest shopping center, getting jostled by the throngs. It didn't help that this very high-end mall carried merchandise costing way beyond her salary, much less her mother's meager income.

Added to that, Maeve complained every five minutes about the crowds, prices, and clerks who, in her opinion, were snubbing her.

"Mom, the saleswoman didn't mean to be rude. She probably works on commission, and when you said you were just looking, she needed to move on to someone who was actually buying. Besides, it didn't help when you said the clothing looked cheap." Fiona gently moved her mother away from the offending store.

"Well, those dresses did look cheap." Maeve huffed as she tugged her arm out of her daughter's grasp. "We have better in the thrift store."

Fiona caught herself rolling her eyes and decided on a new tactic. "How about some lunch? We could go to that little bakery. They have great clam chowder that comes in a sourdough bread bowl."

"Oh, it's much too hot for clam chowder."

"C'mon. There are plenty of other choices. Sandwiches and salads. And delicious cookies for dessert."

Maeve grumbled but allowed Fiona to lead her toward the escalator.

They wound their way through the crowds, following the pathway's twists and turns, finally reaching the bakery. Yeasty and sugary scents greeted them at the door.

"Ooh, look. Jumbo chocolate chip cookies." Maeve's attention had finally been captured. "I want one of those."

Fiona bought salads and cookies that were quickly devoured as they sat at a courtyard table. Her mother looked happy after the meal, and that made Fiona happy. If you didn't count her momentary horror when her mother licked the melting chocolate off her fingers. Maeve was only forty-seven, yet sometimes she acted like an old lady in her dotage. It must have been the drugs.

"What now, Mom? Some more window shopping here? Or maybe that nursery down the street?" Occasionally, when her thinking was clear, Maeve liked to create miniature succulent gardens in pretty earthenware pots that were abundantly available at the thrift store where she worked.

"I want to go buy that lovely blouse we saw."

Fiona almost choked on her iced tea. "What blouse?" Although she knew very well what her mother was talking about.

"The lovely teal blouse in that last store." Her voice held a tone that said, "How could you forget?"

"But, Mom—" Fiona sputtered, not sure how to say her mother was out of her mind for even considering it. "That was the blouse you said was too expensive and cheap looking. You must mean a different blouse, a different shop."

"I never said that. I know what I'm talking about." Maeve's jaw was tight.

"Even so, you can't afford it. It was two hundred dollars."

"Surely, you can afford that. You're a big wig at the resort. Right?"

What was this woman thinking?

"No. You know I can't afford that much money. I am no big wig." Where had she gotten that idea?

"Maybe you can get it from your father then." Her mother looked at her straight-faced.

Fiona felt as if the blood had drained from her head to her toes. Her mother was serious. "Wh...what are you talking about? I...I can't get anything from Nason."

"Sure you can. You two've been pretty chummy lately."

Did she know she'd met with Nason? Even so, they definitely had not been chummy.

"Mom, whatever you think you know, you're dead wrong."

"Am I?"

Her mother's icy tone and stony glare pinned her to the chair. The silence that followed made her squirm as if she were guilty of something.

"I do not have a relationship of any kind with Nason."

"But you've been meeting with him."

"I'm part of the resort team working on his son's wedding."

"Really? I didn't know that." She wasn't being sarcastic, but she continued to glare at her daughter.

Then what was she talking about? She couldn't possibly know she met with Nason at the cafe. Could she?

"Mom, I—"

"I saw you drive up to the cafe where he was waiting."

Her mother had been following Nason.

"What have you done? Have you been sneaking after him?" Fiona knew her mother had stalked him before.

"That's none of your business. But you don't deny it, do you?"

"It is my business. What if he files for a restraining order? Or worse, files a police report for stalking? You could go to jail." The last sentence was punctuated by a tone so sharp it could have severed her vocal cords. It didn't stop her toe from briskly tapping the tile.

"I want to go home now." Maeve stood, knocking her chair over. Without a look back, she marched away.

"Mom. Wait." Where did she think she was going without her?

———

Fiona's foray into doing her mother good had failed. It didn't just fail, it failed spectacularly. She'd caught up with her mother at the mall and got her home, but they still weren't speaking to one another.

As she shut off the engine, Fiona opened her mouth, but Maeve jumped out and slammed the door, shaking the car. She flounced off toward her apartment, her back stiff.

"Mom." It was a feeble whimper.

Dropping her forehead to the steering wheel, she allowed the tears to fall. How could she have allowed that conversation to get so far out of hand? Was her mother really stalking Nason again? She couldn't even guess what that meant for any reconciliation for her and Nason.

Stupid. There was no reconciliation anyway.

She had to forget Nason and figure out how to move forward with her mother. But how in the world would she do that?

Reaching into her purse for a tissue, the ringing of the phone startled her, and she yanked her hand away as if it were a rattlesnake. She moved her hand to her racing heart.

The phone continued to ring, then quieted.

Rather than attempt putting her hand in her purse again, she allowed her nose to drip.

Yuck.

When she could stand it no more, she grabbed a tissue,

wiped, and fished for her phone. A voicemail notification from Trevor appeared. *Drat*. She should have answered.

"Hey, Fiona. It's me. Trevor. Just checking to see how your day is going with your mom. Praying it is going well. Call me later and tell me all about it. If you're up to it. See you."

Oh, Trevor, if you only knew how botched up it was. She was too much of a mess to talk to him now. It would have to wait.

People walking along the street gave her the evil eye. Probably wondering why she was taking up one of their parking spaces too long. Better move along.

She started the engine, then shut it off again.

This was no good. She needed to make it right.

Fiona, her belly queasy, but her shoulders back, ran up to her mother's apartment.

"Mom." She knocked twice, then again. "Mom. It's me. Fiona. Let me in please. I want to apologize."

Rustling noises inside meant Maeve should have heard her knocking.

"Mom? Please let me in. I'm sorry."

The rustling stopped, then everything went quiet.

Fiona knocked again. Still no answer. She tried the door. Locked.

A key. She remembered she had a key to her mom's door. Digging deep into her purse, she finally pulled it out. Her fingers trembled. The screen door squeaked as she held it farther aside. She missed the keyhole but made it on the second try.

"Mom, I'm coming in." She nudged the scarred wooden door open. "Mom?"

Maeve sprawled on the couch. Her eyes closed.

Adrenaline pushed Fiona to the still form and shook it. "Mom. Mom." She fumbled for a pulse. Thank God she was alive.

Her mother yanked her arm from Fiona's grasp.

"Whatta ya doing? Leave me alone." Maeve threw one

arm over the other, protecting the one that Fiona had held, as if she'd been hurt.

Fiona sagged to the floor. "Oh, Mom. You scared me."

"Well, that's what you get for barging in here. Whatta ya want anyway?" The scowl on her face enhanced the age lines that were like a road map of her mother's hard life.

A lot of it was of her own choosing, but she'd been beaten back more than Fiona figured was her fair share. The thought softened her heart.

"I'm really sorry. I had wanted our day to be fun."

The scowl lines eased. "Aww, I'm sorry too, pet." Maeve struggled to sit up, but she waved Fiona away. "Ican'tdoit." The words slurred together.

Had she taken something in the few minutes Fiona had sat outside feeling sorry for herself?

"Let's have some coffee, shall we? You do have coffee. Right?" She stood up and picked her way from the tiny living area to the minuscule kitchen just around the separating wall.

Her mother said something unintelligible.

Fiona found a grimy drip coffee maker, but no ground coffee. She spotted a jar of instant coffee. That would have to do. *Who in the world drinks instant these days?* Maybe she'd buy her mom a one-cup coffee machine. No, the individual pods would end up being too expensive.

An equally grimy tea kettle sat on the stove. She washed it thoroughly, inside and out, filled it with clean water, and set it back on the stove. They'd have hot water in no time. Next, she scrubbed two coffee mugs.

"Almost ready." Fiona stepped around the wall to see her mother. "Mom?"

Maeve had resumed her sprawled condition and added snoring.

Fiona shut the stove off. She didn't really want instant coffee.

She cleared a spot on the once over-stuffed chair opposite

her mother. Her phone would be a companion while her mom slept.

Fiona texted Lottie so she wouldn't get worried. Then she texted Trevor.

FIONA: CAN'T TALK RIGHT NOW. @ MOM'S AND SHE'S SLEEPING. BUT TODAY WAS ANOTHER DISASTER.

Trevor must have been hovering by his phone, because his text came back immediately.

TREVOR: I'M SORRY. WHAT HAPPENED?

FIONA: IT'S TOO MUCH TO TEXT. BUT I THINK SHE'S BEEN STALKING NASON. WE ARGUED OVER IT.

TREVOR: THAT DOESN'T SOUND GOOD. I MEAN THE STALKING PART.

FIONA: RIGHT?

TREVOR: BUT THINGS CAN'T BE ALL BAD IF YOU'RE STILL WITH HER.

FIONA: I TOLD HER I WAS SORRY. BUT SHE FELL ASLEEP. BEFORE WE COULD TALK.

TREVOR: SO WHEN SHE WAKES UP.

FIONA: YEAH, IF SHE DOESN'T SLEEP TOO LONG.

TREVOR: DO YOU WANT SOME COMPANY?

What? No. A chill swept over her. She did not need Trevor coming to her mom's place. Did she even want him to meet her?

Her fingers flew over her phone, a text to Lottie.

FIONA: Want to catch a movie tonight?

Fiona's leg jiggled. *C'mon, Lottie. Answer.*

LOTTIE: Sure. What time?

FIONA: Soon. I'll text when I'm on my way.

Close call. She didn't want to lie. Back to Trevor.

FIONA: That's sweet of you. But I promised Lottie we'd go to a movie tonight.

TREVOR: How about lunch tomorrow after church?

Now that was a plan she could get behind.

FIONA: Yes. I'd love that.

A few more texts and her fingers stilled.

Six p.m. Her mother had fallen on top of a bunch of clothing and some other indistinguishable fabric piled onto the couch. The woman looked like she was out for the night. Fiona recognized a dingy throw and pulled it out from under her mother's dead weight. She draped it over the thin body.

Should she wait? She plopped down again. A translucent brown bottle with a white cap lay under the coffee table. Fiona's breathing hitched as she scooped it up. Sleeping pills.

Frantically, her gaze ran over every inch of the room, looking for a clean horizontal surface. She swept her arm across the coffee table, pushing everything to the floor.

Digging into her purse, she found the little package of tissues. With two fingers, she yanked one free, then spread it out onto the newly empty tabletop. She uncapped the bottle and carefully spilled the contents onto the tissue. The label said thirty were in the prescription. Filled yesterday.

Two, four, eight, sixteen, twenty-four, twenty-eight.

She sat back, calming her racing heart. Only two missing. She couldn't overdose on two. But just in case, she refilled the bottle and stuck it into her purse. Fiona would go home and let her mother sleep.

The door clicked shut softly behind her, but the screen door screeched, pulling Fiona's shoulders up to her ears. She waited a moment while the dark sky and cool night air whispered their reassurance that her mom was all right.

An okay ending to a not okay day.

Next time would be better. It had to be.

Chapter Fourteen

Nason felt like one of those animals at the zoo, pacing to and fro in a cage. Roaring at anyone who dared spy on him. He'd yelled at Irina and turned down a chance to play golf with Rick.

What was he thinking? That would have at least taken his mind off work. Instead, he was boxed in at home with Irina expecting him to be Sunday sociable.

How could he be?

Weeks without a word from Longstreet. What was that all about?

In the meantime, he tried to keep up with the BioTech meetings and depositions. The case progressed well. Except for the missing employees he needed to meet with. Not getting in touch with all involved would be a terrible reflection on him, the case, and The MacArthur Group.

Selena had not been able to make contact with the five employees Longstreet—at least he thought it was Longstreet—had added to the witness list. The five that suspiciously hadn't responded.

Nason had to forget about the MIA five. He didn't believe they existed anyway.

Perhaps he would have to fly to the MacArthur Group's main branch in Chicago to confront—who? The senior partner was nowhere to be found. Supposedly on extended vacation. But they had staff he could talk to. But was that a good idea?

Yes, tomorrow he'd have Selena book him a flight.

That thought seemed to settle something in his mind, and Fiona took up the newly empty real estate there.

It had been weeks since he'd seen or heard from Fiona, too.

Why did this pile of nonsense have to drag out?

The more he thought about his last encounter with Fiona, the angrier he got. What right did she have to be upset with him? He'd tried to reach out to her. She just didn't want to understand his predicament.

He changed into swim trunks and vowed to swim as many laps as he could to cut off those thinking patterns.

Although the day was in the eighties—the weather for a California November was always a surprise—the water was just on the edge of warm yet cool enough to be refreshing. He was grateful for a pool heater. Back and forth. Back and forth. Long strokes. Powerful kicks. Back and forth. Back and forth.

As he swam, his mind cleared, allowing him to pray. There were no words, just a yearning toward God.

He swam to the side and grabbed the edge to pull himself up. Twisting his body, he plunked with a splat onto the ledge. He shook his head, flinging pool water from his hair. Nason ran his fingers through the wet mass, combing it back.

No towel. He'd raced so fast into the pool, he hadn't brought one out with him. Just as the thought formed, Irina stood on the other side of the rectangular shaped pool, a stack of towels in hand.

"Looking for one of these?" Irina's tone was smooth, and one corner of her mouth tilted up.

She continued toward him, and when she made it to his side, held the stack out to him.

"Thank you. Just what I needed." He took a towel and wiped his face and the top of his head. The swim must have washed away some of his anxiety, because a calm settled over him. It helped that Irina was in a good mood.

She thrust the towels onto the outdoor rack and moved to his side again. She lowered herself to sit and dangled her legs, swishing the water. "I've got some steaks marinating. Wanna barbecue them outside?"

"Sure."

They sat side-by-side in a comfortable silence.

How long had it been since they'd been comfortable in each other's company? Suspicion worked its way into his mind. Why now? No, he wouldn't spoil the moment. Instead, he'd take whatever this was at face value and enjoy it.

"I better go finish the potato salad. You can start the barbecue anytime." She brought her legs out of the water and curled them to the side to stand.

Nason watched her walk away, leaving wet footprints in her wake, her golden ponytail swishing with each step. She was a striking woman. All too often her shrewish temperament made him forget.

They consumed their steak, Caesar salad, and potato salad dinner on the patio, the hickory smoke pungent in the air. The good mood prevailed, allowing an unruffled conversation about nothing important. Even their phones cooperated and remained silent.

Irina cleared the table and Nason basked in surprising contentment. Where had the tranquility come from? Was it from praying? Had God heard him? He couldn't remember praying for anything specific, but it seemed as if his spirit had called out for peace.

They spent the evening sitting on the couch, hips touching, watching the latest television shows. Walking to their bedroom arm in arm, Nason tried to remember the last time they had such a peaceful afternoon and evening. None came to mind.

No, he wouldn't head to the main office yet. Matters were bound to sort themselves out.

As sleep crept over him, the word forgiveness played on a non-stop loop through his brain matter. Was he supposed to forgive someone? It made little sense. He let the thoughts slide away as he succumbed to slumber.

———

Nason picked up his favorite insulated travel mug from his desktop, threw his head back, and tipped the mug to his mouth. Empty. *Oh, molly!* He craved a coffee refill, but he'd already had two this morning. And it wasn't a small mug. His doctor would have his head.

He swiveled and plunked the ebony black mug on the credenza out of the way, out of sight. Out of sight, out of mind, right? He doubted it would work, but he had to try.

Leaning back in his chair, he cradled the back of his head in his interlocked fingers. Yesterday with Irina had been a balm to his soul. They hadn't had such an enjoyable evening in a long time. In the beginning, they'd fit so well together. Shared nearly everything.

But then Maeve worked her black magic on their lives, interfering, stalking him. While sharing Fiona, he couldn't avoid her mother. Although he tried. But parents had to communicate over their kid.

When Irina began sharing her suspicions about Fiona's parentage, he dismissed it as just his wife's jealousy. The more bizarre Maeve got, the harder Irina pushed, demanding a DNA test. Fighting that idea for two years, he finally gave in when social services had put Fiona in their home. He couldn't put up with Maeve demanding he divorce Irina, the "home wrecker," and make the three of them a family. She didn't listen when he told her they'd never been and never would be a family. She still wasn't listening.

He couldn't blame Irina when finally, she gave him an ultimatum. It was a DNA test, or she and Ricky were gone. What could he do? The DNA test proved he wasn't Fiona's father. Just thinking of Maeve's response to the test set his belly aquiver. He had no choice but to stop seeing Fiona. But it never really took her mother out of the picture.

Poor Fiona was the loser. Admittedly, he missed Fiona at first. The relief at not dealing with Maeve quickly overshadowed the loss. Now his conscious pricked him about Fiona. Three times he'd tried to explain, but she wouldn't listen. What could he do?

Maybe he should ask her for forgiveness. But why? He hadn't done anything wrong.

His heart felt like it had been pricked with a pin. Two or three times. Was he guilty?

A brief knock at his door, then Selena entered. Nason dropped his hands from his head and brought his chair down with a clunk.

His trusty legal assistant looked sick.

"What's up?"

"The senior partner is on the phone for you. Line two." She grimaced.

"I thought he was on vacation."

Selena shrugged and ducked out.

Finally. Maybe now they'd get to the bottom of this. Why was Selena scowling?

"Hello, sir. How are you today?"

"Williams, I have instructed your legal assistant to book a flight to Chicago for you. I'm sorry, but I need you here as soon as possible. Make sure your case files are in order."

"Yes, sir. I understand you want me to be in Chicago right away, but I don't know why."

"Let's discuss that in person."

"Does this have to do with Longstreet?"

"Don't worry about him. Let's focus on your situation."

"What situation, sir?" The inside of his head sounded like he was standing in the bell tower of his college. Right next to the bell clapper as it struck.

"Again, we'll discuss that when you get here. I'm sorry if this is personally inconvenient for you. But it's quite important. Have your legal assistant send my secretary your itinerary. Goodbye, Williams."

After he hung up, the only part of him that moved was his tongue as it raked his lips. His mind swirled at warp speed. What in the world was going on? Was Longstreet involved? It certainly didn't sound like anyone was pointing a finger at his boss. So, what then?

He planted his palms on his desk and eased up from his chair.

What did Selena know?

Striding to the door, he pulled it open and came to stand next to Selena at her desk.

"What's going on?"

She was a petite woman, but she seemed to make herself even smaller as she huddled down in her chair. "I don't know, Boss. Really, I don't. I only know Mr. MacArthur told me to book you a flight to Chicago as soon as you have your case files in order. Except. Except he also told me to hand your case files over to Mr. Smith to handle."

"What? Smith? Why would I do that?"

His legal assistant's eyes grew wider as she stared at him.

"Maybe he expects me to be in Chicago for an extended period. But I could just bring my files with me."

"No, Nason. He said to book your flight to Chicago on Wednesday night's red-eye and your return for Friday's first flight."

Now it was his turn to stare.

———

Red-eye flight fatigue added to Nason's weariness from three days of gathering and organizing all his case files so he could catch the flight to Chicago. To say nothing of the suspense. It weighed on him like he carried his boat's anchor.

Now he hitched his carry-on bag up higher on his shoulder and transferred his briefcase to his left hand. He used his right to haul open the heavy glass door that led him into The MacArthur Group's corporate offices.

He made his way to the black marble reception desk and to the goateed young man sitting behind it. Nason flashed his badge.

"Nason Williams to see Mr. MacArthur."

"Let me check on that for you." The receptionist spoke quietly and scrolled through the computer.

Speaking of his old fishing boat, this guy was slower than his boat at anchor. Well, maybe the system was slow, not the man. No, it couldn't be that slow.

"Ah, yes. Here you are. Please have a seat. I'll let his secretary know you are here."

Despite the cool weather, sweat pooled on his lower back and under his arms as he waited. Great. His dress shirt would be ruined. His suit coat would have to stay put.

Mentally, he reviewed the case files he'd handed over to Selena for Mr. Smith. For the umpteenth time.

"Mr. Williams, you can go up now. Suite 500. Fifth floor. Mr. MacArthur's secretary will be waiting for you."

Suite five hundred. Fifth floor. *Got it.* Sarcasm had taken control of his mind. Heaven help him.

The elevator doors whispered closed.

Nason rode the silent elevator, exited, and headed down a plushly carpeted hallway. As he passed a glassed-in law library, he coveted the impressive collection of law books neatly organized on shelves that spanned the room. The California office had a nice library, but nothing like this.

He tugged open one half of the double entry doors.

A gray-haired woman stood behind a desk and held out her hand. "Nason Williams? Please sit down." She gestured toward a plush barrel chair on the far wall. "Mr. MacArthur will be with you momentarily."

If he was going to get anywhere, he'd better adjust his attitude.

He eased into the chair, reclined slightly, thought better of it, and sat up straight. He didn't want to look uneasy, but he couldn't appear nonchalant either.

A box on the secretary's desk buzzed. "You may go in now." The crow's feet around the woman's eyes didn't move when she smiled. Or at least attempted to smile.

Another set of heavy double doors. Like Fort Knox here. He entered a rectangular office that sprawled to the left and right of him. To the left was a seating area made up of two modern white sofas and two sets of white side chairs. Beyond was a floor to ceiling bank of sleek windows devoid of any coverings.

In the center stood a black marble-slabbed conference table for eight. A desk that matched the conference table commanded the center of the right-hand side. Two white leather box chairs facing the enormous desk contrasted starkly against the enormous black furniture.

"Ah, Williams. Let's sit at the conference table."

The founding senior partner, grayed at the temples, was probably close to sixty-five. Nason wouldn't be fooled by age. The man was at the top of his legal game.

Nason eased himself onto the edge of the chair.

Mr. MacArthur's bushy gray eyebrows formed a deep vee. "Williams, do you know how much trouble you're in?" His voice was gruff but not unkind.

"Me?" His voice squeaked. "What do you mean?"

"We've received a complaint that you have been not only double billing, but billing for hours spent on non-existent witness meetings. This is a serious charge."

"Sir, I'm not guilty of either of those charges. There's been something off on this BioTech case from the beginning. There are five witnesses that I can't locate, much less bill hours for meeting with them." A pain worked its way up through Nason's tightening neck muscles toward his head. "Where's Jim Longstreet? You should ask him about this."

"I've already met with Longstreet. I want to hear your side of the story."

MacArthur walked back to his desk and grabbed a file. He returned to the conference table and pulled a few pages from the file and handed them to Nason. "Are those your initials?"

Nason rubbed the back of his neck. They were the same papers Selena had shown him weeks ago. "Sir, those are my initials, but that is not my handwriting. And these are the same five witnesses I haven't been able to locate. I've seen these pages and am baffled. I have no idea why my initials are on these documents, so I've started looking into the issue."

An elbow on the table with his knuckle supporting his chin, MacArthur seemed to be absorbing Nason's words. "What have you been looking into? Have you come to any conclusions?"

"Sir, I'm not quite sure yet. I have seen some inconsistencies and errors with time sheets and account records. The one thing I am sure of is I haven't met with these witnesses and the documents are not mine."

"Mmm. I see. Have you any evidence of these errors or inconsistencies?"

"Well, the most glaring evidence is that those documents aren't mine. However, I printed some spreadsheets showing hours billed, as well as our client's account with us and marked items that don't match up. I still need to compare those items with the rest of the file before I can be certain. But you know how complex the paperwork is. It's taken me two months to get this far."

Nodding, MacArthur said, "I think at this point, we'll take over this matter. Do you have the spreadsheet printouts with you?"

"No, sir. But I can have my legal assistant email them to you right away."

"Fine. I have a lunch appointment in a few minutes. Have your legal assistant email those to me, and we'll meet again at two o'clock." He stood and extended his hand. "Until then, get a little rest."

Standing outside the building, he looked up and down the sidewalk, his breathing ragged. What hotel was he booked into? Chicago wasn't called the windy city for nothing. His coat flapped while he pawed through his briefcase. What had he done with his reservation info?

This could not be happening to him. Maybe it was a dream. No, a nightmare, and he'd wake up. He shivered, and not just from the fifty-degree temperature. No, he was too cold to be asleep.

A small token of relief eased his breathing as he found what he was looking for. The Hyatt. It was only a few blocks from where he stood in the business district of Chicago's Loop.

Taxi or walk? A taxi would probably be smarter in the chill wind. But who'd accused him of being smart lately? He checked the map to get his bearings. Turning on his heel, he headed right.

Sleep or rest? Out of the question. Despite the excellent mattresses at the Hyatt, his usual hotel of choice. Even if he'd been at the high-priced Trump International, he wouldn't rest today.

He paced his hotel room, stopping occasionally to stare out the windows. All he saw were the granite walls of the neighboring towers anyway.

MacArthur appeared to be a reasonable man, and he hadn't founded and maintained a successful law firm by jumping to conclusions or allowing himself to be blindsided. Nason just hoped the man's standing as an excellent attorney extended to his case.

Stomach grumbling, he headed to one of the hotel's restaurants. If nothing else, it would be a diversion from brooding about the afternoon's inquiry.

Yeah, right, dude.

———

Nason felt as if he were a piece of meat fresh from the barbecue. He'd been totally grilled. Still, while MacArthur had been thorough, the man had listened and followed up with thoughtful questions. He had no doubt now the senior partner's talent had rightly earned him his reputation as a top attorney. He was grateful the man was also kind and understanding.

"You will take some vacation time until I finish my investigation. And, of course, if wrongdoing is found, the California State Bar will have to be notified and conduct its own investigation." MacArthur straightened the file folders in front of him.

Vacation. Ha. Some vacation that will be. After enduring three hours of questioning, he needed a real vacation. But what if they didn't believe him? Of course, it wasn't a matter of MacArthur being persuaded by his side of the story. What if they couldn't find enough evidence to exonerate him? Was it still innocent until proven guilty?

Particularly since he'd been guilty of double billing in the past. Way in the past.

"Head home to California. But remember, since you are on vacation until further notice, you are required to stay away from your office." Those distinctive eyebrows couldn't hide the compassion in the man's eyes.

"You're kidding, right?" Why did he say that? He knew the rules.

"You know I'm serious. In the meantime, your cases will be handled by Smith. You understand we have to take every precaution, but I'm confident we'll get to the bottom of this soon."

MacArthur walked him to the door and put one hand on Nason's shoulder as they shook hands.

Despite MacArthur's reassurances, Nason wasn't convinced they'd get to the same bottom. Would they find the truth and exonerate him? He was grateful he was being put on vacation and would eventually receive his salary. Or else how would he pay for Rick's wedding? That assumed he'd be back to work and getting paid soon. And not thrown out on his ear.

Irina was going to have a fit. The night before he left for Chicago, she'd raged at him. Blaming him for getting himself in such a fix. He tried to explain he hadn't gotten himself into anything. It was all Longstreet. She'd just have to get over it. Would she come to his side and support him?

And where was Longstreet? He was getting sick of asking himself that question. How dare that man accuse him? And Nason knew it was Longstreet who'd pointed the finger. MacArthur never said it directly, but the inference was there.

Even if he were found innocent, Nason didn't think he could forgive Longstreet for putting him through this. And he surely wouldn't forgive him if, for some reason, he was falsely charged and had to appear before the State Bar.

If MacArthur couldn't find the evidence to clear him, not only would he lose his job and face disciplinary action from the State Bar, but the senior partner could even file a report with the police. His legs threatened to drop him right there in the building's lobby.

Get a grip. You didn't do it. They'll have to figure that out. Eventually.

This time, he didn't have enough strength to walk to the hotel. He took a taxi with every intention of sleeping until his return flight at dawn.

But somehow, he doubted he'd sleep.

Chapter Fifteen

Every muscle ached. Had he just gone ten rounds with Mohammed Ali? Every nerve quivered. The six-and-a-half-hour flight from Chicago was a blur. Had he slept through it? He didn't think so.

He shook his head to clear away the cotton that seemed to be wrapped around his head as he tried to remember where he'd parked his car. Was it yesterday? Or the day before? He didn't know anymore. Next time he'd use valet parking. Why hadn't he taken a photo of his location?

Twenty minutes of wandering while hefting his carry-on bag and briefcase left him even more exhausted. He stopped and leaned against a square cement post. Why was he sweating? It was cool in the underground structure. Nevertheless, he wiped his brow with his coat sleeve. As he dropped his hand, his gaze landed on a familiar silver Mercedes.

Nason wanted to slap his forehead but was just too relieved to find his car.

The new-car leather smell greeted him when he threw open the door. There was nothing like that aroma. What if this mess didn't get straightened out, and he lost his job? His prize Mercedes would have to go.

He'd have more to worry about than a car, even if it was a prized possession. Plenty of his possessions might have to go if he no longer had a job. He might not even have a profession. Then what would he do?

Abolishing the negative thoughts, he threw his bags into the back seat and slid into the comfort of the luxury leather. He laid his head back on the headrest. What was next? He should formulate a plan. Irina. He needed to call her first. No. He'd call Selena first.

He glanced at his phone. 10:30 a.m. She'd be in the office. Punching in her number, he suppressed a groan.

"Selena speaking."

"Hey, it's me. Nason. I just got back to the Orange County Airport."

"Boss...you...uh, how are you? Everything okay?" Selena's tone was hesitant, reluctant.

"I'm heading straight to the office."

"Then everything's okay?" Her tone brightened.

"Not by a long shot." He gave her a short rundown of yesterday's events.

"Boss, I'm so sorry. We can fight this, right?"

"I hope so. See you in a few."

"Wait. Forgive the insubordination, but if you've been put on vacation, surely you were told not to set foot in the office?"

Selena knew her job well. Maybe she should have been a lawyer.

He allowed his lips to flap as he expelled a long breath.

"I'll take that as yes. Then you mustn't come in. You'll just make it worse for yourself."

And for her, because she'd be forced to notify security. She wouldn't want to, but she would be duty bound.

"Of course. But would you let me know if you hear anything? Especially about Longstreet?"

"You know I won't be able to tell you any details of the inquiry. But if it's just scuttlebutt..."

"I understand. Thank you, Selena." He clicked off the phone and didn't move.

Selena's voice had held pity. He didn't like that one bit.

Better let Irina at least know he was back in Orange County.

NASON: BACK FROM CHICAGO. ON MY WAY HOME.

Just as he was about to hit send, he added *Love you, babe.*

Winding his way out of the airport, he wasn't sure he was ready to go home. He slammed his hand to the steering wheel. This whole episode was a stupid nuisance.

More than a nuisance, dude. Better start praying.

Some Christian he was. He hadn't even thought about praying. Pastor Luke. He'd never met with his pastor either. If there was ever a time he needed some words of wisdom, it was now. And maybe Pastor Luke would pray for him. No maybe about it.

He spoke into his dashboard system. "Call Pastor Luke."

Little noises that indicated the call was being dialed and ringing filled the car.

"Pastor Luke. How may I help you?" His sermon rich voice boomed through the speakers.

"Hello, Pastor. It's Nason Williams. Wondering if I could make an appointment to see you."

"Of course. When would you like to come in?"

Now? No, he needed sleep first.

"Sometime next week?"

"Of course. How about Wednesday? If you're okay the day before Thanksgiving. Or do you need to see me sooner?"

How fortunate he didn't attend a megachurch. None of those pastors would suggest an appointment that soon. He knew from experience. That's why he attended Pastor Luke's church. Bonus was it wasn't far from his home.

"Next Wednesday would be fine. Thank you."

"Eleven okay?"

He agreed to the time and hung up.

———

Classical music played softly in the background of the bridal salon. Saleswomen spoke in muted tones. A shriek of joy from a bride-to-be who had found the perfect dress occasionally punctuated the air.

Fiona sat in a private area created especially for the lucky bride. Secluded from the rest of the patrons, it was furnished with velvet club chairs in a rosy pink, a plush pink rug underfoot, and a small white platform nestled in the center of a three-way mirror. A crystal vase of white roses adorned the small pink table between the chairs.

Lottie had her final fitting and was now inside the dressing room, trying on her special gown. Fiona leaned back in the plush chair and closed her eyes. Just what she needed, a day off after three frantic fifteen-hour days running a show. Besides, she wouldn't have missed sharing this day with Lottie for anything.

At least she had called her mother every day since their Saturday debacle, and they'd had pleasant conversations. She was proud of herself.

Of course, the sleeping pills weighed heavily on her mind. Would she get another prescription? The alcohol and so-called recreational drugs were bad enough. Fiona needed to get her mother into a rehab facility before she took too many sleeping pills or stepped up to something like heroin. Was she sure Maeve hadn't already?

Memories wormed their way into her mind. Memories of her six or seven-year-old self fixing a peanut butter and jelly sandwich for dinner while her mother lolled on the couch, wasted from booze and drugs. That was a good day. Sometimes there was no peanut butter or bread. So she ate spoonfuls of jelly. When there was no jelly, she went without dinner, thankful she'd had lunch at school.

But there seldom was a lack of liquor, cigarettes, or those little orange pills that her mother said kept her from getting fat.

A shudder coursed through Fiona's body and soul.

Lord, please keep my mom out of those hard drugs. Convince her she needs rehab. Please.

Soft footfalls and a rustle of fabric coaxed Fiona to sit up. Lottie's simple sheath dress of satin began with a modest scoop neckline, flowed gracefully over her curves, and ended just above where her toes peeked out. As she turned, a Watteau train hung in gentle folds from her shoulders down her back.

Her eyes twinkled above a grin that said it all.

"Oh, Lottie." Fiona wasn't sure why she whispered. It just seemed fitting. "You look gorgeous."

"Do I? Is it all right?"

"All right? It's fantastic. It looks like it was designed especially for you. Simple, but elegant."

The bride-to-be clasped her hands at her waist as if she were holding flowers. "What do you think about violets for my bouquet?"

"You sure you want violets? I mean, I love violets. But do you?"

"Ever since you introduced them to me."

"Well, then, go for it."

Violets were Fiona's choice for her some-day wedding. But that was okay. She could share with her best friend.

"I want the trim at the top of the train to be visible, so I've decided not to wear a veil. Just a simple crown of white roses and a few violets for accent. What do you think?"

"You will be the most beautiful bride ever. And in only five weeks."

"That's so soon. I'm not ready."

Fiona made soothing noises, but she was the one who wasn't ready. Not seeing and confiding in her best friend whenever she wanted. Technically, after the honeymoon, she would see her every day at work. But it wouldn't be the same.

The swish of satin followed Lottie back to the dressing room, leaving sadness in its wake. Fiona shook herself. She would not be depressed. After all, she was really happy for her friend. Her groom-to-be was a wonderful man who loved her.

Maybe someday she would find a great guy who loved her. She'd had little luck so far. Her mind swung to Trevor. No. A half a dozen dates was too soon to go there. And it wouldn't be luck. She would hold out for God's choice. That is, if He had a choice for her. What if He wanted her to remain single all her life? What if there was no one to love her?

If her so-called father didn't love her—

"Have you tried on your maid-of-honor dress yet?"

"Got it right here." Fiona lifted up a garment bag with her emerald-green dress safely tucked inside.

"Well, then. Ready for a celebration lunch?" Lottie practically floated toward her. With one arm laden with her own garment bag in white, she thrust her free arm around Fiona's and propelled her out of the bridal salon.

They splurged on antipasto and lasagna at Maggiano's and headed home.

"Why'd you make me eat all those carbs?" Fiona rubbed her aching midsection. "I need a run. A long run. If I can stay awake, that is."

Lottie giggled and kept her gaze on the freeway in front of her. "Better hope I don't fall asleep. So, are you and Trevor coming to the wedding together?"

"Together? Since he's a groomsman and I'm the maid of honor, we'll both be there. There's no need to come together. Besides, we haven't even talked about it."

"Oh, well." Lottie flapped her hand. "You'll be together plenty. Too bad he's not Rex's best man. He's married."

"Who?"

"The best man. Anyway, you and Trevor will be seated at the head table. And…you'll be together plenty."

"So you said. What do you have up your sleeve?"

She flapped her hand again. "Say, how are things going for Nason's son's wedding?"

A knot grew in the pit of Fiona's stomach. She really didn't want to think about Nason or Ricky. "Everything's fine."

"Really. When's their wedding?"

"A month after yours. January 5."

Only two more months of putting up with the Williamses. After Ricky's wedding, she could wipe all of them out of her mind.

And how's that worked out for you so far?

————

He pulled into the parking lot of the former elementary school that now housed his church. The office door was propped open, so he let himself in.

"Pastor Luke?"

"Back here."

Nason followed the pastor's voice down the hall and found the man half obscured behind stacks of books.

"Come in, Nason. I apologize for the mess. Diving deep into some research today. Let's sit over here."

Pastor Luke guided him to a group of chairs in the corner. What a contrast between MacArthur's office and this humble pastor's.

"You might need a larger office, Pastor." Nason lowered himself into a simple but comfortable chair that looked to have been rescued from someone's living room.

"Well, I'd surely have my pick if I wanted a large class-room, wouldn't I?" He chuckled. "I know the school is more space than the church needs right now, but I dream of someday filling all the empty classrooms with Sunday School attendees. Maybe a church-sponsored Christian school, too. Now, how can I help you?"

Nason poured out his story. Well, two stories. Fiona and Maeve. And his legal morass. His spiritual mentor nodded, asked a few questions, but mostly listened until Nason was spent.

"Sounds like you are carrying some heavy issues. But they're not too heavy for the Lord."

"But what should *I* do?"

"Have you prayed and asked for guidance?"

Nason figured his neck was red. "Not as much as I should...to be honest, I've prayed very little. I know that makes me a horrible Christian."

"Well, not horrible. But let's rectify that." Without waiting for his guest, he moved his hand to Nason's shoulder and bowed his head.

The prayer was detailed and earnest. *Man, he needed to learn how to pray like that.*

"Amen. Now, Nason, what do you think? Did the Holy Spirit reveal anything to you while we prayed?"

How to tell this godly man that he'd heard nothing?

"I see."

Pastor Luke must have figured from Nason's silence, nothing was getting through to him.

"Nason, both dilemmas seem to be all about forgiveness. You already know that you have to ask Fiona to forgive you, and you will have to grant this other man forgiveness. Despite the outcome of your inquiry."

Forgive Longstreet? His gut burned with bitterness. The man needed to beg him for forgiveness first.

"I can't even locate the man to talk to him. How am I going to forgive him if I can't find him?"

"You know that forgiveness doesn't rely on you seeing him

or him being present. Forgiveness is really between you and God. Think of how much the Lord has forgiven you."

Oh. Jesus had forgiven him so much. Because there had been so much to forgive. *And I just keep making the same mistakes. More to be forgiven of. Daily.*

As he pondered these thoughts, thoughts of how much Jesus had forgiven him, shame swamped him, threatening to drown him. But even that was part of the Lord's forgiveness. No matter how many times he forgot.

"Just go back to the Lord daily. Hourly if you need to. Ask him to help you forgive others as He has forgiven you. And when you forget about His mercy, ask him to forgive your forgetfulness."

"I'll try, Pastor. But, frankly, the threat of losing my job over these false charges is overshadowing everything else."

"Don't you have any evidence you can present to prove your innocence?"

"I'm banned from the office, so even if there were evidence, I can't go looking for it. Although…"

What about those papers Selena found last month? Surely, there were files. If she could find them, she could follow up and uncover some evidence. Why hadn't he thought of this before?

"Pastor, you have given me an idea. Thank you. And thank you for your counsel." Nason shook his pastor's hand. "I will pray more earnestly for the Lord to remind me of all he's done for me."

"And forgive this man? Whether you see him or not?"

Nason nodded. It would be hard, but he'd try.

For the first time since this whole mess started, he had hope. Excitement propelled him to his car. He slid into the front seat. Before the dashboard system was fully functional, he started speaking into it. No response. *Calm down, man.* He turned the key off and on again, giving it time to engage.

"Call Selena's office phone number."

"Calling Selena office phone number," his onboard assistant repeated in her computer voice.

"Selena Garcia. How may I help you?"

"Hey, it's Nason."

"Hi, boss, how are you doing?"

"Okay. Okay. Listen, do you remember the records you found in which Longstreet was claiming all the billable hours? Well, could you use those to trace back the origins? And could you get to Longstreet's withdrawal records to show he was not only double billing, but falsifying billable hours to non-existent witnesses? There may be more records, as well."

"I'm not sure I'd have access to some of the banking info, but perhaps I could persuade Longstreet's secretary to help. She's been temporarily assigned to another attorney."

"Really? Then what's the rumor about Longstreet?"

"She won't say much, but there's still talk he's ill. Maybe in the hospital. For some long-term medical problem."

"Can you try to confirm that, too? You know I'd do all of this myself if I could."

"Sure, boss. I'll do what I can."

"What are you doing without me?"

"Assisting Smith on your cases. But he's either doing most of the clerking himself or he isn't working too hard on your cases, because he doesn't give me much to do."

Nason didn't like the sound of that. Smith better not mess up his cases. He planned to return and win those.

"Perhaps that's a Godsend. It'll give you more time to follow-up for me. Thanks, Selena. You're the best."

"Sure, boss. We gotta get you back. I prefer working for you over Smith any day."

What a gal. He chuckled and hung up.

Maybe. Just maybe, he could lick this thing. His confidence soared.

Nason looked at the time on his dashboard, but it wasn't the time that caught his eye. The date. It was the day before

Thanksgiving. Neither Selena nor the main office would be getting much accomplished over the next four days.

What a Thanksgiving he was going to have. Worrying about the inquiry. About forgiving Longstreet. About Fiona.

He was already forgetting what the pastor said. Already forgetting the Lord's mercy. Forgetting prayer.

Lowering his forehead to the steering wheel, he prayed.

Chapter Sixteen

Thanksgiving Day was almost over, and Fiona still struggled to get in the spirit.

If she'd only accepted Lottie's invitation for her and Maeve to have dinner at the Butlers' house. But she'd remembered the last time Maeve spent time with Lottie's family. Embarrassing. Her pride wouldn't let that happen again.

What was that about pride going before a fall? Maybe it wasn't a fall exactly, but she'd had better days.

Fiona let herself into her dark and silent apartment. No aromas of leftover turkey or pumpkin pie greeted her. She bet Lottie's house smelled heavenly.

Her mom had complained throughout dinner, and Fiona couldn't blame her. How could a restaurant serving Thanksgiving dinner not smell like Thanksgiving? Because she'd had better turkey and mashed potatoes from the grocery store's frozen food aisle.

She hurled her purse to the sofa and plunked herself down next to it. So she'd chosen a terrible restaurant, so what? There was always next year. If she got an invitation to Lottie's parents', she'd definitely go. She'd even take her mom.

A memory of her last Thanksgiving at Nason and

Irina's surfaced with all the good smells and feels. Nason had cooked most of the gourmet meal and, even as an eleven-year-old, she savored every bite. Ricky was a little annoying in a seven-year-old little brother way. With Nason and Irina's parents present, it was the big family experience she coveted. That day, even Irina treated her as if she belonged.

She snorted. One of the very few times. Had Irina known in just a few months Fiona would be exiled from the family? Was that why she'd been nice?

Why was it so dark? *Silly*. Only the light over the stove was on. Enough wallowing. She jumped up and turned on all the lights. Comfy clothes were her next order of business, a Thanksgiving routine she really didn't need this time. Only the turkey got stuffed today.

Clad in her raggedy sweats, she opened the refrigerator door, searching for something to fill her empty stomach. Old leftover mac and cheese. She hurled that toward the trash can. An almost empty yogurt container. Who left that in here? Another toss. Milk. Lots of condiments with nothing to put them on. Someone hadn't done the grocery shopping.

She slammed the door and tried the cupboard they laughingly called their pantry. Boxes of mac and cheese she didn't have the energy to prepare. Pork and beans. Not without hot dogs. Popcorn. Cereal. That would have to do.

Just enough fruity loops for a small bowl. She dumped what was left into a bowl and splashed some milk on the top. Tea would complete her meal. She filled the teakettle with fresh water and lit the stove. Tea and cold cereal. What a Thanksgiving treat.

A murder mystery on TV was just the right ending to the day. She settled in front of the glowing screen, the tea within reach, and the bowl of cereal cradled in her lap.

Two or three murder mysteries later, the handsome detective had all the suspects assembled and was just about to reveal who dunnit. The suspense was interrupted by the ringing of her cell. She huffed and pushed pause.

Blocked phone number. She usually ignored calls from unknown callers, especially when it was ten o'clock at night, but she clicked on the screen to answer anyway.

"Fiona Hanlon?" The voice was not unfriendly, but brusque.

She sat up straight. "Yes."

"Your mother is Maeve Hanlon?"

Her grip tightened on her cell phone. "Yes."

"We need you to come to Fountain Valley Regional Hospital as soon as possible. Your mother is ill."

She shoved her feet into her running shoes. Where were her keys? Grabbing her purse, she rummaged inside. Not there. Her gaze roamed the room. There they were. On the table by the towel rack. She snatched her keys and coat and bolted out the door.

"Fiona, where are you going?" Lottie stood at the bottom of the stairs, one foot poised on the first step.

"Mom's in the hospital. Gotta go."

"What's wrong?"

"Don't know. They just said she was ill." Now at the step just above Lottie, her roommate grabbed her by the arm and spun around.

"I'll go with you. I'll drive." Lottie steered her toward the parking garage.

The Kia's interior was still warm as they sped off.

Lottie tried to make small talk. At least, that's what Fiona thought she was doing. It sounded like when the adults talked in the Charlie Brown cartoon. Wah, wah, wah.

Her friend must have given up talking. Only the swoosh of traffic echoed inside the car during the rest of the thirty-minute drive.

They raced into a parking space and flew to the emergency room doors. A line formed in front of the only open check-in window. Fiona crossed her arms over her chest and tapped her foot.

At last, a nurse emerged from the back and called a patient.

"Excuse me, please." She called out and everyone's heads turned to her. "Excuse me. The hospital called. My mother was brought in. Maeve Hanlon."

"Yes. One moment. I'll tell the doctor you're here." He turned and ushered his patient into the inner sanctum.

More foot tapping.

Hours of waiting, but only five minutes on the clock. That can't be right.

Finally, the nurse returned, and Fiona let a breath out.

"For Hanlon? Come this way."

"May my friend come with me, please?" She clutched Lottie's arm, and she wasn't going to let go.

He nodded and led them through the door. On each side of the blue-curtained aisle, occupied beds caught her gaze. She tried not to look at the patients who must have been in various levels of discomfort. Murmuring from a few cubicles added to the beep of machinery.

They stopped at an intersection in the aisles.

"Doctor, this is the daughter. Ma'am, the doctor will help you." The nurse turned on his rubber clogs and squeaked off.

A tall man in a white lab coat looked up from his clipboard. "Ms. Hanlon? Hello, I'm Dr. Werner. Your mother had a rough time for a while, but she's doing better now, and should make a full recovery."

A weight Fiona didn't know she had been carrying lifted from her shoulders. "But what happened?"

"A neighbor found her unconscious outside her residence. She had ingested a lot of alcohol and too many sleeping pills. Your mother is very lucky the neighbor came by when he did and called 911. It probably saved her life."

Sleeping pills. Obviously, she refilled the prescription Fiona had confiscated a few weeks ago.

"You can go in now." Dr. Werner pulled back a curtain. "Mrs. Hanlon, someone is here to see you."

Maeve, who was not and never had been a missus, lay with eyes closed, her face devoid of any color. She didn't stir.

"She may sleep for a little while. We're going to keep her overnight for observation. You can wait here with her until we move her to a room."

Fiona nodded. "Thank you, Doctor."

One chair stood beside Maeve's bed. "You take this, Lottie. I'll go find another one."

Her friend raised a hand. "No. You stay here. I'll find a chair."

Legs shaky, she didn't argue. She sank onto the chair and took her mother's slim hand.

Oh, Mom. What did you do? She forgot to ask the doctor if he thought she'd done it deliberately. Her mom wouldn't do that, would she?

A chair scraped as Lottie pushed it into the room. "Sorry about that."

Fiona's heart felt a little scraped, too.

———

Black Friday and everyone was out shopping, buying things they didn't need with money they didn't have. At least Fiona dodged that bad habit.

Instead, after a struggle mounting the stairs, she and her roommate escorted Maeve into their shared apartment.

"I could go to my own place, you know." Maeve's voice was still shaky from her ordeal.

"Mom, we talked about this. You aren't strong enough yet to be on your own."

Girls flanking her, Maeve shuffled to Fiona's bedroom.

"You take my bed, Mom. I'll sleep on the couch."

"No. Now, I don't want to be too much trouble. I can sleep on the couch."

It never bothered her to be too much trouble before. Perhaps a near-death experience would do that to you. Fiona ignored her mother's protests and helped her to the bed.

"Lie down for a while and then you can change if you want. I picked up some clean clothes, your toothbrush, hairbrush, you know. That kind of thing. I'm taking a few days off work to see that you rest."

Lottie followed them into the bedroom and dropped Maeve's overnight bag onto the armless chintz chair. "Here you are, Maeve. Whenever you want it. I'll go look over the takeout menus and find something good for dinner."

Someone would have to go shopping soon. Maybe Lottie would go so Fiona could stay with her mom.

"Okay. You need anything?" She draped a furry throw over her mother. "Mom?"

Maeve shook her head and settled back against the pillows, closing her eyes. Fiona drew the drapes against the late afternoon sun. She padded out of the room, shutting the door behind her.

Her roommate looked up from the table where she'd fanned out a dozen menus. "What do you think your mom would like? Pizza? Chinese? That Mediterranean place is delivering now. And there's that new delivery service."

"It's not new, actually. Been around for a few years. We just never heard of it until now."

"Oh, really? Well, whatever. What should we order?"

"Hey, didn't you bring home any leftovers from your mom and dad's house?" Her salivary glands were perking up just thinking about homemade turkey and gravy.

"Left them in the car overnight. I don't think we should chance eating them. We don't need to get sick, too."

Fiona's hopes deflated. They decided on a hardy meal

from the local diner.

After dinner, Lottie trotted off to the grocery store while Fiona and her mother rested on the couch.

Dr. Werner had told Fiona it was hard to tell whether Maeve had intentionally taken too many pills on top of the alcohol. And, so far, her mother hadn't offered any answers. Time to try again.

Fiona sat sideways on the couch so she could face her mother. "So, will you tell me what happened now?" She kept her voice soft and her tone non-accusatory.

"It was nothing, pet. I just had a few too many drinks after you left. Then I needed something to help me sleep. It was nothing."

"It wasn't 'nothing.' You could have died. You cannot continue to drink and take drugs."

"It was just an accident." Maeve sprinkled her words with her usual whine.

"Maybe so, but if you continue to drink, you'll continue to have accidents. Mom, listen to me. You need to consider a rehab program. What if your neighbor hadn't come by in time?"

Her mother turned to her, eyes wide. "Do you mean I could've died?"

Fiona held back an exasperated sigh. "You almost did die." When was she going to get it? Fiona had been praying since she'd learned her mom had overdosed, and now she sent up some more quick prayers. *Please, Lord. Help me make her understand.*

"I need you around for a long time." Despite all her complaints about her mother, Fiona meant every word. "Please consider a rehab program. As soon as you feel better, I'll look into it for you. Please."

Maeve's deep brown eyes shimmered as they regarded her daughter. "I–I'm sorry, *Iníon.* I know I've been a terrible mother to ya."

Iníon? Daughter. Her mother hadn't used Irish for years. It was usually just *pet.* What did it mean? Maybe it meant nothing. A slip of the tongue. Or maybe she was falling back into the Irish ways of her parents.

"No, *Mamaí*, you did the best you could." Fiona wanted to believe that was true. But why the lies about Nason? Nevertheless, she had to hold out some sort of carrot to get her mother into rehab. And if that meant calling her mommy in Irish or telling her she did the best she could, she'd do it.

And maybe it would be true.

Now tears tracked across Maeve's wrinkles, down her chin, and splashed onto her lap.

Fiona grabbed a box of tissues and handed one to her.

Her mother bowed her head and dutifully wiped her face and nose. "Okay. I'll go." Her black curls bobbed as she snapped her head up. "But. How will we pay for it?"

"I don't know yet. But I'll figure it out, and as soon as you get your strength back, I'll take you."

Had her mother really agreed to rehab? Fiona's heart lightened, nearly floating out of her chest.

The only thing better than this would be if her mother had accepted Jesus. That would be next. Right?

What if Maeve had said yes just to get Fiona off her back? When the time came, would she actually go?

———

Fiona guided Maeve through the holiday weekend without too much strife, confirmed about her time off with her boss, and set about locating a rehab facility and figuring out how to pay for it.

Lottie emerged from her bedroom as she shrugged on her leather jacket. "I'll see you later. I have some wedding errands to run."

Looking up from her laptop, she swallowed hard.

Wedding? How could she have forgotten about Lottie's wedding?

"I'm a lousy maid of honor, aren't I? I should be helping you."

"Everything's on track. I'm off until after the honeymoon, and my mom's back from her mission trip so she'll help me. You just take care of your mom."

"But it's in five days." She punctuated her words with a wail.

Her roommate stopped next to Fiona's chair at the table and patted her shoulder. "Read my lips: It's all under control."

If only everything else was under control. How could she get her mom into rehab and support her best friend as she got married?

"In your spare time, could you figure out how to pay for rehab?"

"Maeve has MediCal, doesn't she?"

"I was just kidding." Somewhere the proverbial light bulb went off in Fiona's head. "But I think you've solved my problem."

Her fingers flew over the keyboard as she logged in to her mother's MediCal account. Lottie looked over Fiona's shoulder as her cursor flew over the page, clicking here and there.

"I'll leave you to it. Praying for good results." Lottie waved and headed out the door.

Two hours later, she'd contacted a rehab counselor, and with his help, filled out the paperwork and application for the recommended facility in Santa Ana. It seemed too easy. Was she missing something? She chose to trust that the Lord had pulled it all together for her.

A faint cry came from her bedroom. She shot out of her chair.

"Mom? What's wrong?"

"*Iníon,* I thought you'd left me alone." Maeve took Fiona's hand. "It was so quiet."

"I wouldn't leave you alone, *Mamaí.*" She eased onto the bed next to her mother. "Good news. I found you a nice place to go for rehab and found out your insurance will pay for it. Isn't that great?"

Maeve's eyes filled with terror. "You...you're going to make me leave here?"

"Mom, we talked about this." And talked and talked. "You agreed to go to rehab. It looks like a really nice place."

"But I'll be all alone."

"I'll come visit as often as they let me. You'll have the best people helping you get well. And I'm counting on you to get well."

Her mother turned away, toward the window, sage green drapes blocking her view.

"*Mamaí?*" Fiona dragged her palms down her sweats-clad pant legs. She knew this had been too easy.

Where's your trust now? The enemy's annoying voice in her head taunted her. No. She would not give up yet.

"*Mamaí,* we'll talk about this later. Now, it's time you got up. Let's get some lunch and go for a walk." She leaped off the bed and threw the covers back. "Here. Let me help you."

Fiona eased her mother out of bed. She came reluctantly, but she didn't resist. Together they managed to get her face washed, her clothes on, and her hair combed.

It only took half an hour. At this rate, it would be time to get her back to bed.

After consuming grilled cheese sandwiches, apple slices, and milk, they were ready for their walk. Despite the Southern California warm November sun, they bundled up against the cold drafts off the ocean.

They stood, arm in arm, on the sidewalk outside of Fiona's building.

"Would you like to walk over to the resort? We could stroll

along the beach. If it isn't too cold."

"That would be nice. I haven't visited your hotel in a long time." Maeve's voice was stronger than earlier in the day.

Must be a good sign.

Usually, she made it to the resort in ten minutes. Today, she clocked their trek at twenty minutes. Maeve couldn't help it if she wasn't up to a power walk. A far cry from it.

"I forgot how beautiful your hotel was."

Fiona and Maeve had stopped halfway up the resort's driveway to admire the Mediterranean architecture of the building and the lush growth surrounding it.

"One nice thing about living in a Southern California beach town is the colorful flowers and plants, even in November." She drew in a deep and satisfying breath. "Isn't God wonderful? He's blessed us with so much beauty."

"Mmm. If you say so."

They needed to have that talk about her mother's need for Jesus. This seemed like the perfect segue. Except her mom had pitched a fit over similar conversations in the past, and Fiona didn't want to be part of that right in front of where she worked. It could wait until they got home.

"Do you want to go through the lobby? Or straight to the beach?" She patted her pocket to make sure she'd brought her employee pass. Otherwise, they wouldn't be allowed through the private gate. Yes, there it was.

As she waited for her mother's answer, she glanced toward the main doors. She was sure her heart stopped.

Nason, Irina, Rick, and Rainbow clustered in front of the valet stand.

What were they doing here?

Fiona tightened her arm against her mother's and steered her quickly toward the side entrance and the beach gate. "The beach it is." She forced a brightness she most certainly didn't feel into her voice.

Her pulse resumed to normal when her mother didn't

protest, and they reached the gate. She swiped her card, and the gate clicked open.

"Fiona? Maeve?"

Mother and daughter swung around at the sound of Nason's voice.

Fiona swallowed hard. "What are you doing here?" She could feel Maeve stiffen through their clutched arms.

"We had an appointment. You stood us up." His tone was matter of fact, not angry.

"I'm taking a few days off."

Nason glanced between the two women.

"My best friend's getting married Saturday." The truth, even if it wasn't the real reason she wasn't at work. She wouldn't give Nason the satisfaction of finding out about Maeve's overdose.

"I see." He moved his gaze to Maeve's and held it. "Maeve. How are you?" His tone had gone tight.

"Perfectly fine. And you?"

Two cheers for her mom.

"Never better."

But Fiona detected hard lines around his eyes and mouth that hadn't been there a few weeks ago. She was sure of it. And now the hardness overpowered his gaze as well.

What was his problem? He didn't have to come talk to them. He had deliberately left his family to trek over to where the beach gate was.

"Nason." Irina's distinct shriek came from their car where the valet held open the passenger door for her.

"Maeve. Fiona." He spun on his heel and strode toward his Mercedes.

Anger flamed up inside of her. What right did he have to approach them? Just to give them dirty looks and walk away. Hit and run.

Requiring her to forgive him was growing into a tsunami that she didn't think she could survive. *How, Lord? How?*

Chapter Seventeen

Nason stalked toward his Mercedes where Irina waited, her face one angry storm cloud.

Once inside the car, he got his jab in first. "Don't say a word. Not one word." He clamped his jaw so tight he thought he'd break a tooth.

What was he thinking approaching Maeve and Fiona? It didn't make sense. He had no purpose in talking to them. Had he thought about it, he would have realized it could only end badly. Well, that was the problem, wasn't it? He didn't think. Some cosmic hand had just propelled him toward the women. It couldn't have been the Lord, could it?

It would have been bad enough if it had been Fiona alone. But Maeve, too? And right in front of Irina and the kids? What happened to Rick and Rainbow? They must have been so disgusted they didn't want to wait around to hear Irina lay into him. Not to mention not wanting to witness his lame excuse.

Because he had no excuse. No reason.

"Nason." Irina's voice was surprisingly calm. "You want to tell me what's going on?"

No. "Nothing's going on. I just wanted to see why Fiona hadn't been at our meeting."

Irina snorted. A very unladylike snort, too. "And what did she say?"

"She was taking a few days off for...for her friend's wedding."

"Really? And why was Maeve with her? By the way, she didn't look too well. Maeve, I mean."

If Nason didn't know better, it sounded like Irina cared.

"I don't know, and I don't care."

His conscience ripped that glib statement to shreds. Maybe he didn't have any of his former feelings toward Maeve, and maybe she'd been a pain in his backside, but—

Shame burned in his chest. But what could he do about it? He had more important things to worry about. Selena was still working to find the evidence he needed. Would he get exonerated? Was his career in shreds? If only he could prove himself innocent. This forced vacation was anything but relaxing time off.

Thanksgiving had been better than he expected. He remembered to be grateful to the Lord for all He'd done for him. Irina, Rainbow, and Rainbow's mother had laid out a grand feast. And Rainbow's father hadn't irritated him much. Much.

Once the guests were gone, the leftovers stowed, Thanksgiving Day was just a memory, Irina was on his back. Fix this or that. Do some wedding chore. The woman just didn't have enough to do, so she spent her time finding things for him to do. To be fair, there were plenty of fix-it projects to be done, and he should be taking this time to do them. Once he got back to work—if he went back to work—he would need to spend all his time racking up billable hours.

"Look, babe, I'll start working on your honey-do list when we get home, okay?" He wasn't just trying to smooth over her current snit. He needed to adjust his attitude toward his wife—again.

Forgive me, Lord.

Nason, Maeve and Fiona are my children, hurting children. You must care.

But, Lord—

No buts, Nason.

What can I do?

For now, pray.

I'll try.

Don't try. Do it.

Yes, Lord.

"Nason? Did you hear me?" Irina used her you're-going-to-pay-for-this voice.

"I'm sorry. What?" He hoped he sounded conciliatory.

"You missed the freeway transition."

Oh, molly.

———

Would she ever get off this emotional rollercoaster?

Running into Nason on Monday had thrown her into a pit of bewilderment and anger. He'd made a deliberate detour of a hundred or so feet from the valet stand to the gate where Fiona and Maeve had been about to enter the beach area. For heaven's sake, they were going in opposite directions.

Yet, he'd chosen to go out of his way and then was— what? What was he? He was curt. No, rude. Cold. He was all those things without saying more than a dozen words. What had been his purpose?

He'd asked why Fiona hadn't been at the wedding meeting, but surely Heather had explained. And what if she hadn't? Did it really matter?

Afterward, Maeve shut herself in Fiona's room and wouldn't come out for dinner. Even when she finally came out for breakfast the next morning, she wouldn't talk about the encounter.

Fear that her mother wouldn't follow through with entering rehab plagued her for the last two days. Where getting into rehab normally took two to three weeks, miraculously, everything had been approved yesterday. Maeve allowed herself to be taken to the facility. She'd been surprisingly docile.

What joy that her mom was finally getting help, but guilt that she'd forced her into it. In the week Maeve had been at Fiona's apartment, her mother had wild rages while asking for sleeping pills.

As she drove away from the facility after admitting her mom, all Fiona could think about was how much she wanted uninterrupted sleep.

But Lottie and Rex's wedding demanded attention.

More sadness mixed with joy. Joy for Lottie. Sadness for herself over losing her best friend and roommate. An ache of loneliness added to her wild, emotional ride.

Now, Fiona sat in a church pew next to Trevor the evening before the wedding, while the pastor spoke quietly to Lottie and Rex about what to expect for the ceremony.

"Looks like this is really happening." Trevor's million-watt smile rivaled the glow of the chandelier.

Fiona let out a long sigh. "Yes, I'm afraid so."

"You don't want them to get married?"

"Oh, no. I do. It's just that I'm going to miss Lottie so much. She's been my best friend for a long time. Roommates for three years."

"It's not like she's moving to Siberia or something. She'll be around."

"I know. I know. But it won't be the same." Didn't men have the same kind of friendships? "Do you have a best friend?"

Trevor gave her a puzzled look. "I have a couple best

buddies. Rex is fast becoming another one. But—I don't think I'd get—uh, well—upset if they moved away or something."

"I'm not upset." She fisted her hip. "Just sad."

"Okay, if you say so."

"What's that supposed to mean—"

The pastor raised his voice to get everyone's attention. "Thank you. Okay. Ladies and gentlemen. Let's do a quick walk-through."

Nursing her indignation, she shot from her seat and followed the pastor's directions. They went through their paces twice, and he sent them away with a "See you all tomorrow for the big day."

"Fiona, I'm sorry." Trevor touched her arm and peered down at her. "I didn't mean to offend you."

She nursed her irritation for a few seconds but let it out. Like a balloon someone had pricked with a pin. "I know. I'm just being silly."

"Ride with me to the rehearsal dinner?" He tucked her arm in his. "You didn't drive here, did you?"

"No, I came with Lottie and Rex. And, yes, I'd love to ride with you. Thank you."

By dinner's end, the laughter and joking around lifted her mood, and she actually looked forward to the wedding. Trevor had been attentive and kind, contributing to her sense of peace. Maybe she should keep him around.

She stole glances at his profile as he drove her home. He acted like he wanted to continue seeing her. Why would he have asked her to ride with him to the dinner if he had no intention of sticking around? But she'd been in this situation before. And those men had run away faster than Olympic sprinters.

Trevor parallel parked his little red Mustang near her building and shut off the engine. His face was somber as he turned toward her.

Uh oh. She didn't like the look on his face.

He took her hand and stroked it. "Fiona, maybe I could keep you cheered up. You know, so you don't miss Lottie so much."

Didn't seem like he was dumping her.

"What did you have in mind?" She held her breath as her gaze wandered around his classically handsome face.

"We could spend more time together. Like a standing date every Friday and Saturday night. Maybe Sunday afternoons." His face broke into a grin. "What do you say?"

A standing date? Wasn't that what she wanted? Then why did she mentally back away? If there were no promises, there'd be no desertion.

"Oh, Trevor." How could she say this without putting him off altogether? "I would love to spend time with you. But—"

"I don't like the sound of that."

"I like you very much. And I would like to spend time with you." Her voice trembled. "I'm pretty sure I'll say yes when you ask, but no standing dates. I'm not ready for any commitments." She watched his face, looking for signs of disgust.

Why couldn't she be ready? Maybe it was because his request surprised her. Would he tell her he was out of here if she wouldn't even commit to a standing date?

"I understand. I'm glad you want us to see each other." His words and tone were still the epitome of kindness. "So. How about next Saturday? I found a great new restaurant."

Fiona's heart resumed its natural rhythm.

"It's a date." She rewarded him with the biggest smile she could manage.

"And do you need a ride tomorrow morning?"

"No. The girls are all riding to the wedding in the limo with Lottie." She wanted him to know she meant it when she said she wanted to spend time with him. "But I think I could use a ride home."

"Ok. It's a date."

They chuckled in unison.

Had she missed her chance to have something with Trevor? Something more permanent? She wasn't thinking as far as marriage, but what if she could have said yes to standing dates? Maybe after a few weeks or months, she would be ready to say yes to standing dates. But he may not ever ask again.

————

Nason grunted as he knelt over a hole in the sod that housed a broken sprinkler head. He'd made good on his promise to his wife. For a week, he had been checking items off her never-ending honey-do list while Irina worked day in and day out on wedding tasks.

Today, it was the sprinkler system. With a drought in play, if he wanted a green lawn and healthy shrubs, he had to revitalize the system.

Mud-caked gloves hampered his dexterity and fitting the new head onto the pipe. With one last grunt, he succeeded. He replaced the sod and eased to a standing position. Ouch. Creaking knees told him he was getting old.

Since when was fifty-four old? He was middle-aged, not old. Then why did it hurt to walk a few yards to the sprinkler system controls?

He flipped a few switches, and voilà, let there be water. Immense pride expanded his chest. Yes, indeed, he could do more than the law. Not that he wanted to become anything other than the attorney he was—and hopefully he would win the right to continue to be one. He especially didn't want to be a gardener. Not that he had anything against gardeners. He just didn't have the knees.

This week's energy was thanks to Selena. Despite being barred from the office, he had worked with Selena over the phone, directing her where to look, what details to watch out for.

They'd found the documentary evidence of Longstreet's

malfeasance. Plural. He had indeed falsified billing records, double-billed, and withdrew money from his client's trust accounts.

Selena, bless her heart, had forwarded everything to MacArthur. Now if the man would review it all, he'd find Nason was not guilty. It had been several days already. What was taking so long?

Vibrations from his pants pocket buzzed against his hip. He tugged his gloves off and laid them on the brickwork before yanking the phone out.

Blocked phone number. He didn't like answering his cell phone when the number was blocked. So often it was a sales call. But these days, it might be important.

"Nason Williams."

"Williams? MacArthur. "

It was as if he'd conjured MacArthur up. But, of course, he didn't believe in such things. Was it the Lord's prompting?

MacArthur continued. "I'm pleased to report the documentation your legal assistant sent has proven valuable and exonerates you from the charges."

If his knees didn't still hurt, he'd do a happy dance. As it was, he could barely talk through the grin splitting his face. "Thank you, sir. I appreciate you letting me know. Now what?"

"No need for us to send anything up to the California State Bar. We're satisfied. You may return to work on Wednesday. The paperwork will be completed by then. You'll get your pay and your vacation days reinstated as soon as HR gets your records updated."

"Sir? What about Longstreet?"

"Unfortunately, Mr. Longstreet has succumbed to his disease. That's all I can say." MacArthur hesitated for a moment.

Succumbed? Longstreet was dead? His mind was blown.

"But when you call your legal assistant," MacArthur

continued, "to give her the good news that you will be back to work, you might ask her a few pointed questions. Congratulations, Williams. Glad to have you back on board."

While mumbling his thank yous, he realized the line was dead.

As was Longstreet. What happened?

He clicked on Selena's phone number.

"Selena. Selena. We did it. I've been cleared."

"Wow, boss. I am so happy. So, when will you be back to work?" Her voice was almost as excited as his.

"Wednesday. Thank you for all you did to get this straightened out."

"I only followed your directions."

"Yeah, well. Not everyone would have bothered. Say, MacArthur just told me Longstreet died. He wouldn't give me any details, but he suggested I ask you."

A long exhale from the other end of the line whooshed through the phone. "He had prostate cancer and died Friday. His secretary, former now I guess, figures he was amassing as much money as possible for his medical bills and his family. But won't the firm make Mrs. Longstreet return it?"

"I don't know. I would expect so. Maybe his life insurance will take care of everything." Nason stilled at the thought of Longstreet stealing for his family's sake. He shook his head. "Well, see you Wednesday."

As he shoved the phone back in his pocket, he felt a catch in his throat. Now he'd never hear Longstreet ask for forgiveness. What now? He needed Longstreet to voice his regret. Didn't he?

Pastor Luke said he had to forgive without it. And Nason had been praying for the grace to do that. But somehow in the back of his mind, he'd been holding on to the eventuality of a meeting with Longstreet in which he asked Nason to pardon him.

Now that possibility was wiped out.

Fiona's voice intruded. *"I need you to ask for forgiveness."* He heard it as clearly as if she were standing next to him. She needed him to say it, just as he needed Longstreet to say it.

I get it now, Fiona. I'm sorry.

He wouldn't hear it from Longstreet, but he could make sure Fiona heard it from him. It was a matter of finding time among all the wedding activities.

Chapter Eighteen

The week since Lottie's wedding had been miserable. Fiona was grateful that the day of the wedding, although overcast and breezy, had been dry. The rest of the week was rainy and cold. She would have been okay with the rain, considering California needed it so badly, if it just hadn't contributed to her misery of missing Lottie.

Selfish. Selfish. Selfish.

She mentally slapped herself and sat up straight as she waited in the rehab center's lobby whose decor did little to buoy her spirits. Too many neutral tones with too few bright accents. It surely didn't help the patients. Or guests, as the staff referred to them. *Silly.* The guests didn't hang out in the lobby. Anyway, it smelled pleasantly of something citrusy.

And she was responsible for her own joy. Well, she needed to rely on the Lord for joy, not someone's taste in decorating.

Despite trying to ramp up her positive attitude, her mouth was dry, anticipating how Maeve's first week had gone and seeing her today. A staff member beckoned her to follow, and Fiona strode after her.

Thankfully, she had a date with Trevor that night. Something to look forward to in a dreary week.

God was good, no matter how their visit went.

Maeve sat in a flower-bedecked easy chair, fiddling with her fingers as her hands lay on her lap. Her mother looked up as Fiona entered and flashed a wan smile.

"*Mamaí*." She bent over to hug her mother. Awkward. She should have waited until they were both sitting or standing. Both of them sitting wouldn't have been any easier. "How are you? You're looking good."

Which wasn't exactly true, but Fiona wasn't about to tell her she looked like day-old oatmeal.

"You don't need to lie, *Iníon*. I know how bad I look."

Busted.

"How's your week been?" Fiona lowered herself into the nearby matching chair and tried to look hopeful. At least, this room was cozier.

"It was terrible." Her voice lacked the usual whine. "But I'm determined to stick it out. No matter how bad it gets." Her eyes held a steely reserve Fiona had rarely seen before.

"That's wonderful. I know you can do it, I'm sure."

They talked about the food and the staff, steering away from the actual treatments.

Fiona leaned forward in the chair. "Mom, what can I do to help?"

"You've already done it, *Iníon*. If you hadn't nagged, I might not be here."

Ugh. Fiona winced. "I don't like the sound of that. Nagging, I mean. I was encouraging you."

Another wan smile from Maeve. "Whatever it was, it helped. Something else helped, too…"

She held her breath, waiting for her mother to elaborate.

"Running into Nason was sort of a wake-up call."

What did that mean? A heaviness pressed in on Fiona. Her mother went on.

"Nason has been nasty to me before. But this time, it was something else. He was so cold, so indifferent. I figured it was because he knew about my...over...incident—"

"He couldn't have known."

"Really? Well, whatever. I knew my only hope was to get sober." Maeve looked at her lap and her fingers that still twitched.

"You...you're not thinking getting sober would bring him back, are you? Because it won't. He's married."

Her mother's head snapped up. "Yes. It will. It has to."

"Mom. No. You have to give up that idea."

"It was the only time I've been happy. Everything up to then had been horrible. My parents were cold, so forbidding. They barely took care of me. But Nason cared. He loved me. How can I get him back? So I can be happy again?"

At last, something within Fiona understood her mother, and her heart broke for her. "*Mamaí*, your happiness isn't up to Nason. It's up to you. And it'll only happen within a relationship with God. With accepting Jesus."

Maeve fidgeted in her chair and avoided Fiona's gaze.

"Mom?" Her mother just had to see this was the only way. Forget about Nason. To admit her sins and look to Jesus. *Please, Lord.*

"Not now, Fiona. Maybe later." Maeve's words were a mere whisper.

Her throat constricted. *Her mother must admit her need.* Probably not today. But what if she didn't see she needed Jesus before it was too late? *Mamaí.* Her heart cried out.

Maeve inhaled deeply and thrust her chin forward. "But know this. Nason *is* your father."

No. Not this again. Fiona felt sick. "We've been through this. The DNA says he's not."

"I don't care what the DNA says." Her voice carried around the room.

Fiona swiveled to see if anyone else was listening. Apparently, everyone was too busy in their own angst because no one looked up.

Did her mother believe her own lie? Or was there something else?

"What makes you so sure?" Fiona leaned in toward her mother.

Maeve looked away again. Her mouth moved, but Fiona couldn't make out the words.

"Mom?"

"Don't hate me." Her mother looked at her, her eyes pleading.

"I couldn't hate you. Tell me."

"I...uh. Well, I was with two men that night."

She almost choked for lack of a good breath while she waited for her mother to go on.

"One was Nason. The other was...was...not by choice. After Nason left, an old friend of mine came to see me. I didn't want him to touch me. I didn't." Maeve dropped her head into her hands and sobbed.

Oh, Lord, not this. Anything but this. Was she that man's daughter? She had to be if the DNA said it wasn't Nason. She clutched her shivering body, her arms shaking. This explained so much about her mom. Her poor mother.

Fiona left her chair and kneeled before her. "It's okay, *Mamaí*. It wasn't your fault. I love you."

The broken woman melted toward her daughter. "Thank you." She added a hiccup. "So, you see. Nason has to be your father. I just can't let it be...him."

How does a daughter respond to her own mother's heartbreak? Especially something of this magnitude. How do you get her to see the awful truth? Or maybe she shouldn't even try. Let her believe what she wants. Whatever gives her peace. But it wasn't fair to Nason. Was it?

"Does Nason know about...the other man?"

Maeve's head snapped up. "No. And he must never know." Her new steely resolve hardened her voice.

———

A cozy fireplace. Great food. And a jaw-dropping gorgeous man for a date. Better than his good looks, he was also the sweetest guy she'd ever known. She should be deliriously happy. Right?

If only she could forget the conversation with her mother earlier in the day. Thinking about it still sickened her. She could be—no, was—the daughter of a beast. Any man who would force themselves on a woman was worse than a beast. He was evil.

She didn't know how to deal with the revelation, and she didn't want to know who the man was, even if Maeve would tell her. Which she probably wouldn't. And now she had no idea how to deal with Nason. Did this absolve him of his desertion? Since he didn't know about the other man, it didn't seem to have any bearing on the case.

Maybe if Nason knew about him, he'd wouldn't blame Maeve as much for the years of subterfuge and her obsession with him. But could she tell Nason? She'd expected her mother to swear her to secrecy. She didn't, so she could tell him without breaking a promise. Breaking her trust was another matter. Perhaps she could convince her mother it was best to tell Nason.

Yeah, and in what century?

Now she had two fathers to cause her pain. To forgive. That tsunami was coming closer. Where could she hide for safety?

The waitperson arrived with their chocolate molten lava cake, setting it between them, handing them two forks.

Trevor held up his fork. "To future non-standing dates."

Fiona clinked forks with him as she laughed. "To future

non-standing dates." How wonderful that he could joke about it.

She should have said yes.

They each took a bite. Trevor moaned with delight at the chocolate concoction in his mouth. Fiona nodded her head.

"What? Don't you like it?" A worried look marred his perfect features.

"No. I love it." She'd better be more enthusiastic and pay attention.

"Is something else going on? You still okay with dating? Non-standing dates, of course."

"Yes—"

"But—"

"Nothing to do with you." She put her fork down and wiped away any chocolate hiding around her mouth. It was also to hide her trembling lips. "I'm sorry. That didn't come out right."

"What's wrong?" His tone was so tender, and his eyes soft and inviting.

Fiona spilled out her story. As she choked back tears, Trevor moved his chair next to hers and wrapped an arm around her shoulders.

"I don't know how to deal with this or what it means about how I deal with Nason." She covered her face with the formerly dry, snowy white napkin.

"I am so very sorry, Fiona. For your mom's experience. For this new information you have to deal with now." He pulled her tighter to him.

She hiccupped into the damp cloth. How she hated it when her body repaid her with hiccups. What must the other diners think of her? "Sorry."

"No need to be sorry. I know this is hard."

"What should I do?"

"You sure you want to hear it?" He pulled away and looked at her intently.

"Y...yes." Did she? She may not like it, but she needed to hear what he had to say. His love of God meant he usually said the right thing.

"Okay. You have to forgive this man who may be your father. Even if you never find out who he is or meet him. In your heart, before God, you have to forgive him."

A knife to the heart. But she wasn't surprised. She expected that would be his answer.

"I haven't even forgiven Nason. Of course, he hasn't asked for it either. Just blames Irina."

"But you have to forgive both men. At least with Nason, you could do it face to face. And, yes, even if he doesn't ask for it."

"What if you were in this situation? You mean you could forgive that easily?"

"I never said it was easy. Just necessary."

"I'm sorry. I know you've been hurt, too, but what if I can't?"

"There's no 'can't' here. God commands you to forgive. He forgave you. Now it's your turn."

The blackness of her own sins shrouded her heart, squeezing it until she thought she couldn't stand it anymore. She used to think she wasn't so bad. After all, she hadn't murdered anyone. Stolen anything. But she discovered all sins were equal. How badly she treated her mother. Her anger at losing out on the promotion. The horrible thoughts she had of getting even with those ex-boyfriends. And her contempt of Nason. Ouch. It was coming full circle.

God had forgiven her all those sins. Now she had to forgive Nason of what he'd done to her.

The tsunami was at her door.

———

Fiona watched Lottie finish packing her personal items from their apartment. Well, her apartment now. She'd scraped enough money together to live solo at least through February. She had no idea what she'd do after that.

And she didn't have the mental energy to think about it.

The screech of the packing tape dispenser curdled Fiona's blood as Lottie sealed the last box.

"Well, that's it." Lottie patted the cardboard box that held her kitchen items. "I hope you don't mind me taking these. Of course, it's not like you do a lot of cooking." Her grin was infectious.

Fiona grinned back. "Like you do?"

"I'm going to have to now. I'm a wife. Think of that. It's hard to believe."

"It's hard to believe you're going to cook."

"Hey." Lottie giggled. "I promised Rex I'd learn."

Fiona's nose burned. She would not cry. She'd been doing enough of that for the last week. Trevor had been doing his best to comfort her, and when Lottie returned, she'd felt a little better.

It hadn't seemed real when Lottie was on her honeymoon, and some of her stuff remained in the apartment. Now it was real. She didn't live here anymore.

Her best friend—former roommate—eased onto the couch beside her. "You'll be all right, you know. It's hard. I get it. But you'll be okay."

Was she talking about herself leaving? Or about Nason? Or *the man*, as she'd taken to labeling him?

Lottie must have read her mind. She continued. "You'll love being alone here. Not having to fight me for the shower. And now you can take down that frilly kitchen curtain you've always hated. I'm surprised you haven't taken it down already."

Fiona glanced at the curtain. "Oh, yeah. I hadn't thought about that."

"Okay. I know. I'm the least of your worries. But you'll be okay when it comes to Nason, too. And *the man*. If you can forgive them. Oh, don't forget Ricky."

That was the problem. The ache inside of her still hurt. A double ache now. But they weren't the same thing. Were they? One helped create her. Through a violent act. Then deserted them. The other nurtured her until he realized he didn't help create her. Then deserted them. In the end, they both left.

Round and round went her thinking. Getting her nowhere.

"Fiona?"

She abandoned her introspection and came back to the present. "Sorry?"

"You're going to find a way to forgive them. Aren't you?" Lottie held Fiona's hand.

When had Lottie taken her hand?

"Fiona?"

"I'm trying. I'm trying. But it hurts too much."

"How much do you suppose it hurt Jesus to die on the cross for you? Thorns on His head. Nails in His hands and feet. Separation from His Heavenly Father. Just so He could forgive you your sins."

Images of crucifixion paintings she'd seen crowded her mind's eye. Flashes from Jesus movies she'd seen seared her thoughts.

She dropped her head toward her lap. The grief of her sin of unforgiveness overwhelmed her. Sobs wracked her body.

Lottie put her arms around her and squeezed tight. "Shh. I know. I know." She rubbed Fiona's back in slow circles.

How could she have been so ungrateful? So callous?

I'm sorry. I'm sorry. Thank you, Lord. Thank you for forgiving me. I forgive them both. Help me remember to not go back.

She prayed silently for a while longer, then wiped her eyes on her sweater. Looking up at Lottie, she smiled, but her lips still trembled.

"I told the Lord I forgave them. I'm worried I'll go back on my word though. But I prayed about that, too."

"Congratulations." Lottie jumped off the couch and bounced around in her version of a happy dance. She twirled and halted. "It's okay if you have to say that prayer every day."

"Really? I thought I'd only have to do it once. I'm kidding. I know."

"Rex and Trevor will be here soon. You'd better wash that face and put on new makeup. You don't want to scare him away, do you? Although I bet he'll be happy to hear your news."

Fiona brightened. "Yes, he will, won't he? He's been praying with me and telling me some of the same things you did. I wonder why it finally got through to me?" She stilled. "I guess it had a lot of sadness and anger to penetrate. And thank you."

"What for?"

"You painted a picture of Jesus' suffering and that reminded me of that movie *The Passion of Christ*. And those scenes of the crucifixion made it seem so real to me. I realized my suffering was nothing like His."

"You're welcome. But the Lord did it. Not me."

"Hey. Now do I have to tell Nason that I forgive him?"

She couldn't do that, could she? Did she have the courage to go that far? Would he throw it back in her face? *Do you fear man or God?*

Lottie tilted her head to the side and planted her fist on a hip. "Seriously? You've done all the hard work. That should be the easy part."

"What if he throws it back in my face?"

"Do you fear God or man?"

Lottie nailed it as if she'd read her mind.

"Okay. Okay. I get it. I'll need to tell my mom, too."

"*When* will you tell them?"

Chapter Nineteen

Christmas lights sparkled throughout Fiona's little apartment, adding to her joy. She wasn't usually one to get carried away with Christmas decorations. In fact, she often made do with only a store-bought wreath on the door.

But this was a special Christmas. She was almost free of the yoke of unforgiveness. And as soon as she could arrange to see Nason, she'd be totally free.

Today, she would celebrate her Savior's birth with extra gladness. One little blip brought that joy down just a notch. She wished her mother had agreed to spend Christmas with her, Trevor, and the Butler family. She declined, saying she wasn't up to being in a large crowd. And the Butlers could be a boisterous family.

Yes, she was a little nervous that Trevor would be at her door any minute, and they were going to visit Maeve. Her mother and Trevor hadn't met yet, but he would charm her. Of that, she was confident. One other little matter niggled at her. She hadn't told her mother about her decision to forgive Nason.

And she couldn't, wouldn't, do it today. Fiona didn't want to spoil anyone's Christmas. Maeve would not understand.

She slipped her new green cashmere sweater over her head and smoothed the silky fibers over her black maxi skirt, a long-time wardrobe staple. Were maxi skirts even in style? She didn't know and didn't really care. She tugged on her new black leather ankle booties.

Examining herself in the full-length mirror, she concluded she'd do. One more thing. She added dangly bell earrings. A new addition to her style. It felt good to wear something besides little diamond studs or her more frequent bare earlobes. Today she was going all out.

Yes, Trevor would charm her mother. But what would Trevor think of her? Despite her growing attachment to Trevor, it wasn't it like they had any kind of an understanding. So it probably didn't matter. She'd be more worried if she anticipated a long-term relationship with him. Or heavens, marriage. She couldn't think that far ahead. Trevor would probably disappear from her life long before that. Just like all the others.

Nevertheless, she worried Maeve would be out of it today and say things that Trevor couldn't understand. She was grateful she'd told Trevor about Nason and *the man*. Fiona didn't need that bouncing up like a Jack in the Box.

Trevor's knock on the front door goaded her to grab a jacket and her tote bag of gifts.

With little traffic on the road, she and Trevor made it to Maeve's Santa Ana facility in record time. Thank goodness, because they would have to travel back the way they'd come to get to the Butler's Laguna home.

She stepped out of Trevor's mustang and shrugged into her jacket. Christmas Day had dawned cloudy, damp, and extra cool. At least for this Southern California gal. The rehab building was always a little chilly, regardless of the outside temps.

A small gift for her mother tucked in the crook of her arm,

Fiona slipped her other arm through Trevor's. She welcomed the heat and the fortification.

Meager decorations appeared randomly placed in the lobby. Couldn't they have done better to bring some cheer? She remembered that the patients seldom saw this space. She had higher hopes for the sitting room.

But her hopes were dashed. Evidence of Christmas was hard to be found in the otherwise cozy sitting room. Maeve perched ramrod straight in her usual chair.

"*Mamaí*, Merry Christmas." Bending down to hug or peck her mother on the cheek was getting easier with practice.

Maeve greeted her with a wan smile. "Hello, pet."

What happened to *Iníon*? No matter.

"Mom." Fiona nudged Trevor forward. "I'd like you to meet my friend Trevor. You remember I told you about him?"

Her mother's face became animated, and she produced a wide smile as she looked at Trevor. "Aren't you a handsome one?" She turned toward Fiona. "Why is he just a friend? He's cute enough to be more than that."

If she could look in a mirror, she was sure to see bright red flaming her cheeks. "Mom."

Trevor chuckled and took her mother's hands in his. "Mrs. Hanlon, I'm delighted to meet you. I'm glad you're looking well. You are by far the loveliest lady in the room."

Her mother giggled. *Giggled*.

She'd better nip this in the bud. "Mom, I brought you a little present." She held out the small, brightly wrapped package.

Maeve eyed the gift for a moment, then snatched it from Fiona's fingers. "Ooh, I haven't had a gift in years."

She hadn't had a gift in years? She gave her a gift at Thanksgiving. Not that they usually did that kind of thing on Thanksgiving, but Fiona wanted to cheer her up.

Her mother picked at the tape, painstakingly lifting each paper flap. Fiona fidgeted.

The wrapping paper removed, Maeve smoothed out the paper, then tossed it away to land haphazardly in the corner. She removed the lid and pulled out a delicate chain and locket.

She held it up, twisting it in the meager sunlight from the window. "It's beautiful, *Iníon*."

"Open it up. It's a locket. See what's inside."

Prying the crevice with the stub of a fingernail, she worked at it until it popped open. "Oh, it's you and me." She turned it so Fiona and Trevor could view the little photo snug inside the heart shape.

"That's lovely, Mrs. Hanlon. Would you like me to fasten it around your neck for you?"

He leaned forward, but Maeve stopped him.

"No. No." She tucked the locket back in the box and slipped the lid back in place. Handing it to Fiona, she said, "You better take this home with you."

"But, Mom, I gave it to you. To remind you I love you."

"Better take it home. For safekeeping, you know." She leaned forward conspiratorially and whispered, "Thieves. Can't trust the lot of 'em."

Fiona hadn't heard of any problems at the facility, but there was no sense arguing with her.

They spoke of the habitual topics, and Fiona asked what was on the menu for Christmas dinner.

"Oh. The usual, I suppose. They don't get too fancy around here."

A bulletin board hung behind Maeve's head. Scattered on its surface were a few notices, including today's menu. Just as she thought. The facility would provide a special Christmas meal.

"But, Mom, you're having," she read the menu aloud, "ham and turkey, mashed potatoes, gravy, cranberry sauce, green bean casserole—your favorite, and crescent rolls. Plus, pumpkin pie."

Trevor took Maeve's hand again. "Sounds pretty fancy to me. You enjoy it, ma'am. You deserve it."

His words warmed Fiona. And from the looks of the smile on Maeve's face, it warmed her mother, too.

"*Iníon*, this charming boy is a keeper. Don't let him get away."

Who was this woman? Where did her mom go? Never had Fiona heard her mother talk like that. But then, Fiona hadn't given her much opportunity. She'd never brought home a boy before. Much less a charming, handsome man.

Should she re-think their steady date status?

Nason's face disturbed her sense of warmth, dampening it as if from a cold shower.

She had to talk to Nason first. And she had to talk to her mother. But today was not the day.

———

Nason threw a quick wave to the Skinners as they headed down the front sidewalk. A sidewalk lined with twinkly Christmas lights he was quite proud of. He'd set them up despite being back to work and playing catch up with his cases.

He slung his arm around Irina, and they turned back toward Rick and Rainbow, who appeared quite cuddly on the couch.

"It won't be long now." Irina almost vibrated with excitement under his arm. "Less than two weeks."

Rainbow's face mirrored the excitement in her future mother-in-law's. Rick looked a little pale. Was he having second thoughts? Probably just pre-wedding jitters, as they say.

If anyone should be pale, it was Nason. He had to pay for most of this shindig. It was a good thing he had a record number of billable hours in the past three weeks and that the firm had reimbursed him for his lost time. He'd be able to pay the remains of the wedding bills.

And he had a huge surprise for Irina. But he'd wait until the kids were gone.

"Rainy, maybe we should get going." Rick pulled at the collar of his button-down shirt. "I have to go to work tomorrow."

"Sure, honey—"

"But I wanted to go over a few wedding details with Rainbow before you leave." Irina's lips formed a pout.

Rainbow looked at Rick, who nodded. But after she turned away, Nason noted the tired lines around Rick's eyes.

The two women chattered as they went off into some other room of the house. Rick gazed at the Christmas tree, but Nason didn't think he was really seeing it. Nor did Nason think Rick could hear the Christmas music coming from the sound system.

"Something on your mind, Son?"

Rick's head snapped up. "No. No. Why would you think that?"

"You look tired, and you've been quieter than usual today." Nason eased into the sectional piece opposite him. "C'mon. What's up?"

"Nothing. Really. Just a little stressed at work."

Nason cocked an eyebrow.

"Well..."

"Wedding jitters? Having second thoughts?"

"No. Absolutely not. Maybe a few jitters. But nothing like having second thoughts. I love Rainbow. I know everyone else thinks she's a little dull—"

"We don't think that. She's just quieter and approaches life with a calmness not seen in the Williams family. Unless she's talking about the wedding. Then she gets quite giddy."

He didn't have the heart to tell his son that he indeed

thought Rainbow a little humdrum. Although she had improved over the last few months.

Or was it his attitude? Life looked a lot brighter since he had been exonerated and was back at work. He'd decided to forgive Longstreet and ask Fiona for forgiveness—even if he hadn't had a chance to do that yet.

An unexpected joy bubbled up. He wanted that for his son, too. But Rick had refused to consider a life in Christ.

Rick sniggered. "I'll say. Just say the word 'wedding,' and she lights up like that Christmas tree. I hope she can handle it after we're married, and there's no wedding to look forward to."

"She'll be going back to school, right? That should keep her busy."

"Yeah, but it's not exciting."

"That's life, son. Maybe she just needs to grow up a little."

"Are you saying she's immature, childish?" Rick huffed.

"No. No. Don't take it wrong. She's been sheltered at home, you know, being homeschooled until she went to college. And she's young. What, barely twenty?"

"Yeah." He relaxed against the cushions again. "You're right. She's young. But she's maturing every day. And I love her."

"I'm sure you do. And I can see she loves you. You've got a good foundation for marriage going." Not that he knew much about that. His short liaison with Maeve hadn't exactly been a solid start for his marriage to Irina.

If only Irina would come to the Lord, too. Didn't the Bible say somewhere that his household would be saved? Mmm, maybe not. Or maybe not in his lifetime. He'd continue to pray for their salvation. But leave it up to God.

Women's chattering voices preceded the actual women into the room.

Rick and Rainbow gathered their coats and gifts, making ready for their exit.

"Thanks, Mom and Dad. Merry Christmas." Rick hugged his mother and gave his father a two-fingered salute.

The door closed behind them. It was time.

"Irina, I have another present for you." While the kids had collected their belongings, Nason had snagged an envelope from his pocket. He held it out toward Irina. "Merry Christmas, babe."

"What's this?" She took the fat white business envelope from Nason's hand.

"Open it and see."

With a decided glee, Irina ran a finger under the flap and pulled out a folded sheaf of paperwork. She unfolded it and squealed.

"We're going on the cruise after all? Oh, Nason." She flung her arms around his neck and kissed him. "Thank you. I'm so surprised. I thought you told me we couldn't afford it since you'd been...on vacation for a while."

"I decided what the heck. We needed a vacation. I can make it up in billable hours when we get back." Legitimate billable hours, he added to himself.

Did he detect "Joy to the World" in the background?

———

Each week Fiona visited her mother and had the same conversations. The weather, the food, fellow guests. They seldom talked about how she was feeling because Maeve didn't want to talk about it.

Last week, on Christmas Day, she'd said she thought she was feeling better. Fiona hoped that meant she was feeling stronger and able to stay clean. That remained to be seen.

Today, as she entered the facility, Fiona trembled. Her mom used to call them the collywobbles. Whatever it was called, she wasn't sure she could make it.

How would her mother take the news? That she had forgiven Nason and *the man?*

Her breaths came too rapidly, and her stomach thought she was on a ship in a storm. No. She would not succumb to a panic attack.

Concentrate on your breathing. Focus.

She halted just inside the door and pawed through her purse. Lavender. She opened the tiny bottle of essential oil and held it to her nose, then dabbed some on her wrists and the back of her neck.

Leaning against a nearby pillar, she rubbed her fingers over it, allowing the nubs and valleys of the carvings to ground her in reality.

Calmed, at least enough not to collapse, she shuffled to the reception desk and checked in.

Her mother probably wouldn't like this one bit. Hopefully, she wouldn't cause a scene because Fiona wouldn't have the energy to cope. Worse? What if the news caused her to relapse? How would Fiona forgive herself for that?

Maeve needed to take responsibility for her own actions.

But it was so hard to remember that.

The inner door opened, and Fiona was summoned to come in. She didn't recognize the staff member who led her down the hall, but she focused on the woman's lopsided gait as she followed.

Breathe in. Breathe out.

Maeve sat up straight in her usual chair in the same sitting room. With the number of people in the room, Fiona was amazed her mother always claimed the same two chairs.

"Hello, Mom." Fiona pecked her on the cheek. She sat in the neighboring chair gripping the padded arms. *Relax.* Her fingers obeyed and splayed out, resting on the flowered fabric. "How are you today?"

"I'm ready to leave. I'm all well now. Can we go?" Her mother looked at her with a hopeful light in her eyes.

Breathe in. Breathe out.

"I'll have to talk to the doctor first. And it's a weekend. Remember. You've only been here a month."

"But I'm ready today." Her voice wavered, and she fidgeted in the chair.

This was not starting out well. How could she tell her mother the news when she was poised for a tantrum already?

She clasped her mother's hands in hers. "You don't want to miss your special Saturday dinner. I promise I'll call the doctor on Monday and see what arrangements can be made. All right?" She prayed her mother would accept the wait.

Maeve's shoulders slumped, but she nodded her assent.

Breathing a sigh of relief, Fiona felt like a mother dealing with a recalcitrant child who had just laid down the pointy stick. But it was nothing new. Hadn't she, Fiona, been the mother in this family since she was twelve? Maybe even before, if she were honest. Putting her mother to bed when she'd had too much to drink. Cleaning house while her mother lay passed out on the couch. Fixing meals for the both of them. Even if the meals were those peanut butter and jelly sandwiches.

"Well, that's settled then." Fiona infused her words with a forced cheerfulness. "How was your Christmas dinner after I left?"

"I wasn't really hungry anyway." Maeve's whine was sneaking its way back into her words.

"You know what? Maybe Lottie's mother will invite us over for dinner later. How would that be?" Thank goodness Lottie's mother was always game to cook dinner for them.

Her mother sat up straight in her chair again. "Really? Would she do that for me?"

"You bet. Say, Mom ..." It was now or never. "I have something to tell you. Please remember that because I'm a Christian, this is something I had to do—"

"What?" Suspicion played over Maeve's features.

"Forgiveness. As a Christian, God forgave me. So I have to do the same—"

"What are you talking about?"

Fiona gulped back the anxiety and forged ahead. "Mom, I forgave Nason for deserting me—"

A strangled cry cut off her words.

But she had to continue. "And I forgave the man who hurt you." If she thought she couldn't breathe before, now she felt faint from lack of oxygen.

"How could you forgive that man?" Each word was clipped. "He was despicable. And you don't even know him. How could you tell him you forgive him?" She nearly spit as she uttered the words.

"I forgave him in my heart."

Her mother glared at her. "And Nason? He doesn't deserve forgiveness either. Have you told him this fantastic secret?"

"Not yet. But as soon as I have a chance." Was that true? She wasn't exactly eager to confront Nason. He'd likely throw it back in her face. But "as soon as I have a chance" didn't confine her to a specific timeline.

Do all things out of love.

Meaning, if she was going to tell him out of love, it would need to be soon. Ricky's wedding was just a week away. Was that the ideal excuse to see him and tell him? Or should she tell him before the wedding?

Chapter Twenty

How could she be so double-minded? The Bible had lots to say about that, didn't it? On the one hand, she was terrified to approach Nason and say what needed to be said. On the other hand, her confidence that it was the right thing to do emboldened her.

So, which was it going to be? Give in to the fear or grab her grit and please God?

Not really a contest, was it?

Fiona lurked in the back of the Crystal Ballroom while a hoard of giggly girls and nervous young men milled around, waiting for the Williams-Skinner wedding rehearsal to start.

Of course, it was her job to be here, to wait in the background in case she was needed.

But she felt as if she were skulking around. Because, in fact, she was lying in wait for Nason, and he and Irina hadn't arrived yet. She shifted from one foot to the other. Again. Then looked at the time on her cell phone.

Ten minutes late already. The Skinners chatted with the pastor, seemingly unconcerned about the lateness of the other parents.

Clunk!

The heavy ballroom door opened noisily, and Nason, with Irina at his side, hurried in. Irina looked straight ahead, but Nason looked around and locked gazes with Fiona.

She lifted a hand in greeting, adding a slight motion with her head. Would he understand?

Moving toward her, he raised his eyebrows.

Her mouth went dry, but she forced out the words. "Nason, can we talk for a few minutes? Maybe after the rehearsal?"

Bad timing trying to do this at the rehearsal. Especially with Irina nearby. To say nothing of all the other family members and wedding party in the room. What was she thinking?

"Yes. That would be a good idea."

He thought it was a good idea? Of all the responses she'd imagined, this wasn't one of them. What did it mean? Was he going to tell her off? Tell her to get lost? Glad he wouldn't have to deal with her again after Saturday?

"Really? Okay..." She should have thought this through better. Where would they meet? How without Irina butting in?

"Irina is taking the girls to the resort's spa right after the rehearsal. I'm supposed to hang out with the men in the game room. Then we'll come back together for the rehearsal dinner tonight." Nason took a breath. "As soon as Irina leaves, I will make an excuse to the guys and find you. Where will you be?"

She had to think for a minute. Where could they meet that was farthest from either group?

"There is a terrace off the Catalina Cafe on the second floor. How about I meet you there?" Her heart continued its odd rhythm.

"Okay. Sure. See you about ten minutes after the rehearsal." He smiled, albeit a bit weakly, and moved off toward the crowd.

Fiona wiped her palms on her linen slacks before she could stop herself. Just what she needed, sweat stains on her new beige pants. She peered down, searching for telltale marks. Nothing. Thank goodness.

She dropped into a nearby chair to do her job, keeping her eye on the rehearsal. But her mind was on the meet up with Nason.

Just as she thought she'd go mad waiting, the pastor shook hands with the bride and groom and each set of parents. The crowd broke up, and Irina and the girls surged toward the door, chattering and giggling.

Fiona trailed the gaggle of girls, staying out of Irina's sight. They turned left, and she turned right and hurried to the stairwell. The stairs exited at the end of a long hallway, the cafe entrance at the other end. Long strides brought her to the cafe's glass-doored lobby. Making her way through the cafe, she came out on the terrace and snagged an out-of-the-way table in the shade of a bright blue umbrella.

She chose a padded wooden chair on the table's far side facing the entrance to watch for Nason. A waitperson approached, asking if she'd like to order.

"Two glasses of water. For now. Thank you." Relaxing in the chair was not working. She wriggled, crossing her legs, uncrossing them.

Doing the right thing should be easy. But then again, it hadn't been so easy when she pushed her mom into rehab. She couldn't argue with the results—at least so far. Maeve hadn't relapsed when Fiona first told her she had forgiven Nason. She would have to trust the Lord that her mom would continue down the path to recovery regardless of Nason and the man.

She needed to do what was right. And this was it.

Nason stepped out onto the terrace, shielding his eyes from the afternoon sun glinting off the ocean. When his gaze finally landed on her, she raised her hand.

Why did he walk so slowly? It was probably a normal speed. It just seemed like he crawled like a tortoise.

As he arrived at her table, the waitperson also arrived with their water.

"Would you like to order now?" He looked from Fiona to Nason and back.

"Water is fine for now." Nason responded quickly, lowering himself to the chair opposite Fiona. "Oh. Unless you'd like to order something?" He raised his eyebrows at Fiona.

"No. This is fine." Fiona flashed her staff badge, a signal she was permitted to sit on the terrace without ordering if she chose. "Thank you."

He nodded and walked away.

Although she was a bit nervous, she'd expected a panic attack. But her breathing was steady, no extra sweat dripping. Even her wriggling in the chair vanished.

Invigorated by the sureness of her task and a courage she didn't know she had, Fiona spoke. Or at least she started to.

"Nason—"

"Let me go first. I know it's not the gentlemanly thing to say, but I'd really like to speak first." He spoke with an earnest confidence.

"Okaaaay."

What was this about? Did he think she was gearing up for another tantrum and planned to cut it off?

"Fiona, I know I gave you a lot of reasons before about why I left." He stilled.

Oh, no. The same old story. Didn't matter. She had forgiven him and had to tell him.

He continued. "It's taken me a long time to admit, but I was wrong in cutting off our relationship. I...I ..."

Wrong? Did he just say he was wrong?

"I'm sorry, Fiona. I would like to ask your forgiveness. I know you may not want to. But I'm asking anyway." Ice cubes tinkled as Nason took a sip of his water. He looked at her over the rim.

Had she heard right?

Lowering the glass, he added, "I became a Christian not too long ago, maybe a year. Two? Maybe two. I've been wrestling with God ever since I ran in to you that first day here at the resort. I'm done fighting with the Lord." Nason let out a long, slow breath.

Say something. He'd become a Christian? The shock had her tongue in knots. Her stomach, however, was the calmest it had been in months.

"Nason, I—"

"You don't want to accept my apology. Forgive. I get it." He turned his head away from her.

"Thank you."

His head whipped back toward hers, his eyes questioning.

"I do forgive you. In fact, that's what I wanted to tell you. That I forgave you." Fiona's eyes watered. Must be that ol' sun.

"You forgave me without me asking you to?"

"I learned recently that I have to forgive regardless of whether you or someone asks. So, yes. I forgive, forgave, you."

"Thank you, Fiona. It must be God's doing." He looked at her, awe shining in his eyes. "Are you a Christian?"

"Yes, I am."

"How long?"

"About two years." Goosebumps prickled the back of her neck. They'd become Christians about the same time. How awesome was that? She finally allowed a smile to pinch her cheeks. "Definitely God's doing."

"Thank you." Nason was smiling now too.

They traded their salvation testimonies and how their families had reacted. Maeve's indifference. Irina and Rick's scorn.

Conversation winded down, each quietly regarding the rolling waves far below the terrace.

One more subject needed to be discussed. This might be

as tough as the actual forgiveness part. Fiona gathered her strength.

"Nason, I don't want you to think you have to go back to being my father. I think it's too late for that. And I'm really fine with it. It doesn't change that I've forgiven you." She stopped talking to see how he reacted to her statement, but he just stared at her. "We can be friends. Or not. I'm not really seeking a relationship with you. Whatever you call it. What do you think?"

Why didn't he say anything? She'd probably just ruined their newfound acceptance of each other.

Finally, he nodded. "You're probably right. We couldn't go back and pick up where we left off. And this—conversation— doesn't mean you have to allow me back into your life."

"It's not that. I know Irina and Rick don't want me back in the family. And, really, I get it. I don't want you to jeopardize your relationship with your family."

"They can't force me to keep you out."

"But you can't force them to let me in. No, I think it's better this way. My mom won't like me acting as if I was part of your family again without her being involved, too, and you know that's not a good idea."

Oh, how she wanted to tell him about *the man*. But she didn't want to betray her mother's trust. And she didn't want Nason to think any worse of her mother than he already did. *I'm sorry, Nason. I wish I could alleviate more of your guilt.* But she couldn't.

"You're right. There are too many complications. Too much time has passed. But how about being friendly acquaintances?"

"Friendly acquaintances?" That was a new one to her.

"Yeah, I don't know if that's a real thing or not. I think I just made it up."

"A smile and a handshake when we see each other? Maybe a card at Christmas?"

"Sure."

They grinned at each other.

Fiona thanked the Lord again and again for His miraculous work in their lives.

———

Lottie and Trevor gaped at her the entire time she related her heart-to-heart talk with Nason earlier in the day. They sat around Fiona's kitchen table—all hers now that Lottie had moved out.

She'd invited Trevor over for takeout Chinese dinner, and Lottie stopped by unexpectedly. Fiona figured she smelled the sweet and sour pork all the way from her new apartment in Irvine.

Now, the table strewn with half-empty cartons, Fiona finished her story.

"Wow. I mean, just 'wow.'" Lottie was the first to find her voice. "What a miracle. Thank you, Jesus."

"Amen." Trevor chimed in.

"It sounds almost too good to be true. Except we know our God is capable of such fantastic things. To think you were both listening to Him ever since you ran into each other."

"To be accurate, Fiona was trying not to listen much of that time." Trevor flashed his signature photogenic smile.

She couldn't help chuckle at the truth in Trevor's statement.

"And," Trevor added, "you're both new Christians. Well, new-ish. God has been working in both of you all this time to get to this point."

"And you're really both good with being 'friendly acquaintances'?" Lottie raised an eyebrow at her. "I thought you were looking to have that father-daughter relationship again."

"I prayed about that a lot, too. I think I'm good without

it." She wrinkled her nose. "Besides, I think it would be weird."

"And what about your mother?" Trevor would have to insert the only stinky note at the end of the day.

She just wanted to go on smelling the violets.

"I'll tell her about it later. When she's out of rehab and stronger. She won't like that I closed the door to any future she might think she had with him."

"When's she getting out? Will she come stay here with you?"

"Not for another month or so. And yes. I've given her apartment manager notice. I can't afford two apartments. I can barely afford one. Besides, she'll need to be where I can encourage her for a while longer."

Lottie stood and gathered the rubbish from the table, dropping it into the trash can. "On that note, I'd better run. Rex will be home from his evening shoot soon. He's trying to get in all the photo work he can before he has to report back to the Army."

Fiona and Trevor stood. Fiona hugged Lottie to comfort her for her soon-to-be separation from Rex, as well as to say goodbye.

"I'm so proud of you. I know the Lord orchestrated it all, but you had to stand on your faith. You had to put on the armor and run to meet a Goliath." Lottie returned the hug, then stepped back, cupping Fiona's shoulders with her hands. "Okay, David didn't wear Saul's armor in the end, so that image sort of falls apart. But you know what I mean."

Lottie waved as she let herself out.

Trevor slipped up to Fiona, filling in the empty spot by her side that her friend had just created. He circled his arms about her and squeezed gently.

"I'm proud of you, too. You were so brave," he whispered in her ear.

"Even if he asked for forgiveness first?"

"Silly. You made the gesture first. You didn't know he was going to do that."

She melted towards his chest.

"I guess you're right."

"Of course I am."

He led her to the couch where they eased down, his hands still cradling hers. "You're really satisfied with the arrangement with Nason?"

Fiona nodded and put her head on his shoulder. "I need to let God be my Father figure. I think that's what I've been looking for all this time anyway."

"You're probably right."

The day had started out with her on the brink of possible disaster, and here she was on the other side of a miracle. Maybe another was taking place within her heart.

"Trevor?"

"Hmmm?"

"You still interested in having a regular date on the calendar, 'Fridays and Saturdays, and maybe Sunday afternoons'?"

She held her breath.

"Do you mean it? Yes. You know I'm more than interested." He let go of her hands and pulled her close. "Maybe we can make it seven days a week." He chuckled. "I'm kidding. Not kidding. Whatever you want."

God surely had been generous with His miracles today.

The End

Author's Note

When I found the quote used at the beginning of the novel, "Forgiveness is the fragrance that the violet sheds on the heel that has crushed it," I was struck by its beautiful image. At first, I saw it was attributed to Mark Twain, but upon further investigation, experts said they could find no reputable evidence of it being from the famous American writer. Rather, they cited multiple references from other authors with similar quotes over many years. Some writers used the generic term "flower;" some used "sandalwood;" all within the same general wording. Whatever its origins, the image of forgiveness being a sweet-smelling balm to the wrong-doer despite his sins reminds me of Christ's sacrifice for a world full of undeserving sinners—you and me.

Paraphrasing that adage, let's wake up and smell the violets. When crushed by someone who has sinned against us, let's return it with forgiveness, applying the sweet smell of violets.

The lack of forgiveness is often the underlying cause for many problems we as humans suffer. While we are under the weight of unforgiveness, bitterness builds, prayers may be blocked, and it impedes our ability to love and accept love.

Most have heard the saying when you harbor bitterness, it's like taking poison and expecting the other person to die. Bitterness sickens us, twists our minds, and leads to unrighteous thoughts and actions. Because God, through the sacrifice of Jesus, forgives us, He mandates we must forgive. When we do not, as with other unrepentant sin, we may find our prayers blocked. When we have unconfessed sin (as in not extending forgiveness), we often don't feel loved and therefore find it difficult to accept love from others.

Fiona struggled with granting forgiveness and battled bitterness and anxiety (I'm not saying all anxiety is due to bitterness or other unconfessed sin.). Because of past failed relationships, she couldn't imagine she'd find love from a good man. In her mind, she was not worthy.

But Fiona was teachable. She sought her mentors and Scripture for guidance.

Nason could not see the problem from the other side. Until his position moved. Then he, too, was teachable.

Setting plays an important role in my novels. *The Fragrance of Violets* takes place in my home area of Orange County, California. Most of the locales mentioned are real except the Princessa del Mar Resort, which is my creation based on several I've visited. I drew on the many similar settings where I've hosted years' worth of conventions and conferences, although I imagined the Princessa swankier than most. As a former convention coordinator, I also interacted with many sales and catering managers like Fiona.

I hope you enjoyed your tour of Orange County, from its beaches to the upscale neighborhood of Coto de Caza, and even to the less than desirable neighborhoods that can be found in Santa Ana and other Orange County cities. (Santa Ana also has its beautiful and historic areas to be enjoyed.)

Orange County and the Princessa del Mar resort will also be settings in my next novel.

Thank you for visiting.

Acknowledgments

A funny thing happened while trying to finish this book. Well, not so funny, really. I tripped and fractured my elbow. My right elbow. I'm right-handed. Typing with one's non-dominant hand is challenging at best, and really, I could not work at all for a time. I praise the Lord for my wonderful friend, Anita Cole, who came to my rescue and acted as my hands. Thank you, Anita.

Another dilemma occurred when my helpful and encouraging critique group suggested Nason's career wasn't really working because I didn't have enough first-hand knowledge or an expert resource. So, at the eleventh hour, thanks to another wonderful friend, Mary Schofield, Esq., attorney-at-law, Nason became an attorney. It turned out Nason's being a lawyer fit the story so much better. Thank you, Mary. By the way, any errors in his portrayal are all mine.

And many grateful thanks to:

My Lord Jesus Christ, who saved me, changed my life in so many ways, and granted me fulfillment of this lifelong dream of being a novelist. I thank you and praise your name.

My husband, a person who normally doesn't read fiction, but who nevertheless reads my books and whose encouragement and teasing motivates me through this journey. I love you.

My children and their spouses, thank you for loving me and being my family. I love you all.

My publisher Celebrate Lit and Sandy Barela, for taking

on this newbie and leading me through the twists and turns of publishing and marketing.

The many other fabulous mentors in addition to Sandy Barela, who have been praying for me and walking beside me, teaching, training, encouraging: Chautona Having; my Serious Scribblers critique group (Cathleen Armstrong, Nancy Brashear, and Kathleen Robison); my prayer team (Denise Bates, Anita Cole, Sharyn Dike, Randi Flynn, Rebecca Kocsis, Sharon Snook, and Susan K. Stewart); my fellow ACFW-OC members; and my WordGirls Group (particularly its knowledgeable and kind leader Kathy Carlton Willis).

My editors who have shown me how to make the story stronger, how to polish the prose, and made this a much better book: Denise Barela along with her Celebrate Lit editing team, Tami Jeffers, and my first readers, the Serious Scribblers critique group.

With a grateful heart,
Susan K. Beatty

About the Author

Susan K. Beatty is passionate about finding courage through faith and grit, particularly through the trials of breast cancer. Her daughter is a metastatic breast cancer thriver and has been an inspiration for her writing. Susan retired from a full-time job in 2017 and is now pursuing a novel-writing career. Her first novel, *Faces of Courage*, is in revision. Susan is the author of *An Introduction to Home Education* manual, was the assistant director of the SoCal Christian Writers' Conference, and is the president of her local ACFW-OC Chapter. She is a professional writer/journalist. Susan is proof you can begin a writing career after age seventy.

facebook.com/SusanKBeattyAuthor

bookbub.com/authors/susan-k-beatty

instagram.com/susankbeattyauthor

Also by Susan K. Beatty

Faces of Courage Series

House of Courage: A Faces of Courage Novelette

Isobel's Mission of Courage: A Faces of Courage Novelette

Courage for Your Everyday Life: A Faces of Courage Flash Fiction
Devotional

Faces of Courage Book One

Carmen's Journey of Courage: A Faces of Courage Novelette

Granny Parsons' Independence Day

THE FRAGRANCE OF VIOLETS BONUS STORY

Susan K. Beatty

Chapter One

Granny Parsons' Independence Day
By Susan K Beatty

When asked, Granny Parsons was often hard pressed to remember her first name wasn't Granny. She'd been Granny for forty years, and she wouldn't have it any other way.

In her opinion, the name Ardith was of no consequence except for legal documents.

She cast a stink eye at the forms lying on the table, the name Ardith shouting at her from the top line.

Ignore it. Maybe it'll go away.

"Who wants a name like Ardith anyway?" Granny mumbled aloud. No one was around to hear, so she could talk to herself all she wanted. Living alone had its good and bad sides.

Granny checked the clock on the microwave. Eleven a.m. Close enough to lunchtime. She slathered peanut butter on some bread.

"Nothing wrong with PB&J sandwiches. They wanted me to eat healthier. Okay. So you got your natural peanut butter, whole grain bread, and low sugar jelly. They still complain."

She arranged the triangles on the plate and added a peach she'd gotten from her backyard tree.

"Almost eighty. Still in my prime, right? But in a place like that, I'll die real quick."

Knock it off, woman.

She wanted to stay on this earth long enough to see great-grandchildren. With ten grandchildren, wouldn't you think one would have children by now? Her son Ned's oldest had been married ten years already. But his response to Granny? He was only forty, and there was plenty of time.

Granny shuffled to the kitchen table with her plate. She set it down and caressed the smooth patina. Gus had made the oak table during their first year of marriage nearly sixty years ago. He'd barely lived to see their first grandchild.

She wanted Ned's oldest to get going already. But, of course, it was their choice. Their freedom to decide.

If only the family would say the same about her.

"It was only one little car accident. Barely registered on the bumper. I'm not senile yet."

She grumbled around her mouthful of sandwich.

They would take her driver's license away over her dead body. A shiver snaked its way down her spine. Better not think about dead bodies.

The family couldn't force her to live in one of those places, could they? Assisted living? More like assisted dying.

The food stuck to the roof of her mouth. What had she done with her iced tea? The glass rested forlornly on the farthest spot possible from her on the kitchen counter.

"Your own fault." She hauled herself up and retrieved her drink, taking a long swallow before sitting down again.

Chimes from the front door caught her mid-chew. Granny shuffled to the front door and spied her granddaughter, Teagan, on the other side of the peep hole. She unlocked the door and threw it open.

"Teagan. I'm so happy to see you, but what brings you here?" Granny drew her into a bearhug. They no longer matched shoulder to shoulder when they hugged. Either Teagan was getting taller, doubtful at twenty, or Granny was shrinking.

"Why was the door locked? You never lock your doors. You okay?"

"Those fool kids of mine think I need to be safer." Why did kids suddenly believe they should tell their parents what to do? Disrespectful. But if she complied with the little things, maybe they'd leave her alone. "Want some tea?"

"Yes, Granny, I'd love some. It's hot out there. Come to think of it, it's not much cooler in here." Teagan went from room to room, turning on the fans. "If you moved, you could have air conditioning."

"Now you just stop that." Granny shook her finger and tried to glare. But she could never really pull it off with Teagan. She was the youngest grandchild and the sweetest. How could a grandmother scold such an angel? "I know they sent you here to do their dirty work."

"No such thing," Teagan said. "Let's go get that tea." She threw her arm around Granny's waist and led her to the kitchen.

Teagan withdrew the jug of iced tea from the refrigerator, filled her glass, and topped off Granny's with the amber liquid.

"Come sit down, angel. So what *does* bring you here?"

"Can't I come visit my favorite grandmother without having a motive?" Teagan wrinkled her brow in mock sternness.

"I'm also your only grandmother at present," Granny said with a chuckle. "How's college then?"

A genuine frown stole across Teagan's forehead. She shook her head, and it vanished. "Just finished finals, so the spring quarter is over. No more classes."

"You have the summer to lollygag then. When do you go back?"

The frown returned. "Not sure." Again, Teagan wiped away the wrinkles and perked up. "So, hey, it's time to finish planning your birthday party and the Fourth of July celebration."

When Granny was a child, she thought everybody celebrated her birthday with parties and fireworks. Once, she loved that she was born on the Fourth of July and the family honored her each year amid flashy lights in the sky. The truth was, she was still proud of sharing her day with the nation's birthday. But this year, getting together would mean the entire clan would bombard her with reasons why she shouldn't live alone.

"Do we have to have a party this year? It's just another birthday."

"Eighty is a milestone. Can't let that pass without celebrating. Besides, I think Dad's got something special up his sleeve." Teagan took a long drink of her tea, emptying the glass.

"What would that be?"

"I've no idea. He's being secretive. Even more than usual."

"I think I'm going to be too tired that day. Or maybe I'll be sick."

"You feeling okay?"

She mentally slapped herself. *Great, now they'll really think I need to go into one of those places.*

"Teagan, sarcasm. Let's get back to the subject of college. Do you need money for registration?"

A tinge of pink washed Teagan's neck as she stared off into the backyard. "Maybe I won't go back in August."

"What are you talking about?"

"I'm thinking of taking some time off and working more. Save some money. You know?"

"No, I don't know. Too many students never go back after

taking time off. Your father, for instance. I don't want that to happen to you."

Tegan flashed a cheeky grin that disappeared as fast as it came.

"Okay, there's something you're not telling me. Spill it."

"It's nothing. I better go. Got a shift at the hotel in an hour." Teagan shot from her chair and hugged Granny. "See you soon."

She fled, the front door clicking behind her. Granny nearly felt the whiplash.

"What's up with that girl? She doesn't usually keep things from me. But there's definitely something going on." She couldn't fathom what it might be.

———

Granny cleaned the kitchen and settled into her recliner for a snooze. Everyone should take a nap after lunch.

The dreamworld took over, and she was running toward her beloved Gus. They were young, just babies, really, teenagers who thought they knew everything. One thing they truly knew was they were deeply, madly in love. When she reached Gus, she clutched him. She would never let him go again.

"How could you leave me, Gus? I've missed you so much."

Gus squeezed back, not saying a word. They stood in each other's embrace, sharing their mutual warmth. Then he opened his mouth, surely ready to say some endearment, when he faded away.

A touch on her shoulder brought her wide awake. Calvin stood over her, his gray mustache twitching. Granny loved her son, and he even looked a little like his father, but right at that moment, she would rather have had Gus in her arms. She pushed her longing down into her soul.

"Calvin. What are you doing here? Want some iced tea?"

She shifted to stand, but Calvin eased her back.

"No tea. Thank you. Your door was unlocked, and here you were asleep. I told you to keep it locked." He settled his six-foot-two frame onto the couch across from her, his navy blue work shirt and pants a contrast to the floral upholstery.

"Stop scolding me like a child. Teagan just left, and she must have left it unlocked." She glanced at the grandfather clock in the corner and realized Teagan had left two hours ago. Oh, well, time was relative.

"Oh? What did Teagan say?"

He was way too nonchalant for her taste. "Why aren't you at work?"

"Just hired a new manager. He really knows his auto parts. Means I can leave the store for a regular lunch." He brought a foot to rest on his opposing knee.

"Glad to hear it. But I still wonder what you're doing *here*." He couldn't fool her. He seldom showed up without a good reason. And she was pretty sure she knew what it was.

"Have you looked at the papers I dropped by? You know, the assisted living ones?"

As if he'd dropped anything else by.

"Teagan says you have a secret."

Calvin's eyes narrowed. "What are you talking about?"

"Something for the Fourth of July?"

His face relaxed. "Oh, yeah. It's gonna be a beaut. A real birthday celebration, too."

If they weren't nagging her about assisted living, they pushed about her birthday.

"I don't need another birthday party. And you know you can't do fireworks in the canyon."

"Who says I'm doing fireworks? You can't continue to live here alone. Between your heart attack and the slip in the bathtub last year. You were lucky Teagan came by and that you didn't break anything. Then that stove fire. And the fender bender. You were lucky to get the fire out so quickly, and the car was just a minor accident." Calvin dropped his foot to the floor and leaned forward. "At least we won't have to worry about you causing another accident."

How could she explain why she didn't want to move? She'd told them already that her house was like one of the family. Fifty years in one home makes you get kind of attached to the place. And she'd lived here with Gus. It would be like losing him again.

No, she couldn't do it. Another vague reason set the back of her mind to itching. But she couldn't scratch it because then she'd have to acknowledge and deal with it.

Fortunately, Calvin sprang from the couch, pulling her from her thoughts. He paced to the fireplace, clutching his fingers behind his back. "Listen. You have to think about this. Everyone in the family works full time. There's no one to come help you long term if something happens to you. Sure, we could get you a part-time caregiver, but what if you need full-time care?"

"Aren't you forgetting something?"

He stopped and raised one brow at her.

"Nothing's wrong with me," Granny said. "I don't need any kind of care. I'm perfectly fine."

"Yes, b-b-but," Calvin sputtered.

"I've been a mother for sixty years. Yours for fifty-five."

"What's that got to do with anything?"

"Mothers know things. I know you tend to get wrought up about something before it's even a possibility."

"It's more than a possibility." He fell back onto the couch, mumbling under his breath.

"Whatz that?" She cupped her hand behind her ear. She wasn't hard of hearing, but that dang boy was muttering, just like when he was a teenager. "For pity's sake! Scram before I lose my temper. You've tried my patience. I am NOT going to move into any old folks' home."

"It's not an old folks' home."

Granny glared at her son. She loved him, but right now, she'd trade him for a bowl of grits. And she disliked grits.

"Now I mean it. Scat. I want to watch the afternoon news."

At the door, Calvin turned for a parting shot. "You *will* have a birthday party."

———

Teagan squeezed her Honda Civic into what little parking space was available on the road fronting the house. Six doors down. And in this country lane with horse properties, it was a good walk. Raucous laughter and the echo of loud voices bombarded Granny and Teagan. From two doors away,

"Sounds like someone is having some fun," Granny said. Crotchety or not, she surveyed with satisfaction her son's home, a cross between a craftsman and a bungalow with a sloped roof, but larger. It never ceased to amaze her that Calvin had designed it himself.

The living room was cool and quiet. A last respite before braving the kitchen and the backyard. Granny and Teagan stepped into the hubbub of food preparation. Platters piled high with corn and biscuits, nestled next to bowls of potato salad and crocks of baked beans filling every bit of counter space.

"Granny. Teagan. You're finally here." Her daughter-in-law Esther broke away from the other women and hugged the newcomers.

"Hi, Mom," Teagan said. "Everything looks wonderful as usual."

Esther put her arm in the crook of Granny's elbow. "Ready to go sit outside on the deck? Cal's been bending over a hot barbecue for hours, grilling your favorite—tri-tip steak. Teagan, why don't you grab your grandmother a cold drink?"

Beneath the umbrella'd tables and tramping feet, hardy

buffalo grass cushioned the ground of the full-acre backyard. Beyond, the ground sloped toward an unused horse paddock and spreading live oak trees, bay laurels, and big leaf maples.

But none of the leaves stirred in the still, heavy air. Not unusual for July. She was glad fireworks had been outlawed in Orange County's fire-prone canyons.

Settled on a shaded lounge chair, Granny accepted hugs and pecks on the cheek from nearly every one of the thirty or so family and friends milling about. Being in the center of the goings-on made her ears throb. But she'd determined to stop being an old biddy today and enjoy her family.

An odd assortment of what she guessed to be electrical equipment covered two tables near the back wall of the house. What in the world? She couldn't even guess what it all meant. Part of Calvin's surprise?

Calvin called, "Steak's ready," and the crowd moved to the over-laden tables. Teagan sat across from her while they ate, not joining in the conversations of her cousins, aunts, and uncles swirling around her. She even ignored her brother Monty's jibes. Maybe she was just hungry. But, no, she only picked at her food.

Concern gnawed at Granny. This was not like Teagan. Not at all. She'd have to keep her eye on this granddaughter of hers.

———

Everyone seemed to have had their fill of the barbecue and sides, and the games ramped into full swing. Just as Granny's heavy lids started to get the best of her, Calvin, her son Ned, and her daughter Cora lugged over a table full of brightly wrapped packages and set it in front of her. Grandkids brought another table, and Teagan set down a three-tiered, lavender-iced cake.

Amidst oohs and aahs, she opened the gifts and accepted a

gigantic piece of white cake with enough of the lavender frosting to spike her blood sugar right good.

Dusk, a color matching the dusty purple icing, spread over the horizon. Granny would be content if it weren't for the fuss they'd made over her. And the concern over Teagan's withdrawn mood.

"Okay, everybody, stand by for a real show." Calvin rubbed his hands together and practically smacked his lips. "Just a few more minutes so the sky can be a little darker."

What was that boy up to?

Calvin, Ned, Monty, and a few of the other grandkids fiddled with the pile of stuff she noticed on the table earlier.

Teagan collapsed into the chair next to Granny, her shoulders slumping.

"What is it?" Granny rested her hand on Teagan's forearm.

"It's nothing. Well, it might be something. But let's talk about it later. Dad's getting his big surprise ready. And I want to enjoy it." She patted her grandmother's hand.

Full darkness was almost upon them. Everyone talked in hushed tones and answered the unspoken call to gather around in lawn chairs. The outdoor lights went dim, and silence washed over the crowd.

The 1812 Overture burst from the speakers, and suddenly the sky was awash with multicolored laser lights crisscrossing each other. Beams of red, white, and blue bounced in time, following the rhythms as the bells pealed and the horns sounded forth. Brass and snare drums punctuated the air and matched the drama in the sky. Heart-stirring cannons exploded and harmonized with the brilliantly colored shafts. The final bells resonated, accompanied by the boasting horns, and the family cheered and applauded. Calvin had indeed outdone himself.

The deck and yard lights popped back on, and Teagan smiled wistfully, so it seemed to Granny.

"Quite a light show. Better than fireworks, even. Always knew Dad had a flare for the dramatic. Are you about ready to get home?"

"Anytime."

Granny grabbed the arms of the lounge and pushed herself up.

Stepping forward, she tangled the toe of her shoe on the hem of her skirt. That old idea of an event happening in slow motion was true. Her inner eye watched her body slowly fall forward. Her hands reflexively reached out to catch her fall.

The slow-mo camera sped ahead, and her arm and body slammed to the deck. Her ears rang with the last sounds of the overture. How was that possible?

Gasps and thudding steps reached through the clanging in her head.

"Granny!"

Calvin's face, inches from hers, came into focus. He threaded one arm under her shoulder and with his free one, grasped her right arm.

"Owww! No, don't touch it." Granny wanted to pretend she was fine. That it didn't hurt. But her body betrayed her.

"I'm sorry." He let go of her arm and eased her shoulders back to the deck. He called out, "Okay, boys, we need to pick Granny up and put her in Esther's van so I can take her to the ER."

She would never live this one down. If the arm was anything other than bruised, they'd use it against her. The screaming pain told her she was not getting off lightly.

"A fractured elbow. Who does that?" Granny fussed as Teagan re-arranged the bed pillows to prop up the sling-encased arm.

"Apparently you do." Teagan smirked. "Oh, I'm sorry. I shouldn't tease you. But you should probably stop wearing long skirts." She tugged the light, woven blanket to cover Granny's lower half.

"That's not the only thing the family is going to make me stop doing. Now they're going to demand I go into assisted living." Granny pressed her lips together to subdue the diatribe building in her head.

"You have to admit your accidents are becoming problematic. Three last year besides that heart attack and two already this year. Now, swallow your pain meds and take a nap." Teagan held a small dish over Granny's outstretched hand and tipped out two oval monsters.

After Granny swallowed, she closed her eyes and waited for the pain to go away and sleep to wash over her. Granny was grateful Teagan had offered to stay with her during recovery. Six to eight weeks. Maybe more.

Ugh.

Perhaps her children wouldn't push her to move while she was recovering. They hadn't mentioned it lately. She could only pray that would continue. She had her doubts.

Speaking of praying, although she'd been doing more of that recently, she determined to increase her petitions to heaven.

Heavenly Father, you know I don't want to leave my home. I want to say "your will be done," but it's too hard—

Granny's eyelids fluttered open. Her gaze found Teagan slumped in the flowery upholstered easy chair next to her bed. Teagan snored softly, and furrows created a bumpy forehead. Her face was pale.

With her own pain and angst crowding her mind, she'd not paid attention to Teagan's body language. With a start, Granny realized Teagan had become even quieter these last two weeks. She'd taken fewer shifts at the hotel, which theoretically should have given Granny plenty of opportunity to observe her.

What a terrible grandmother I am.

For the next hour, she stared at her granddaughter, trying to read her face. It was not like Teagan to nap during the day either.

Finally, Teagan's hands twitched, and she rolled her shoulders back. Eyes still closed. With a mutter, she sat up, fully awake.

"Granny, you're awake. Did I doze off?" She rubbed her eyes and offered a weak smile.

"Try two hours."

"What? Impossible." She stood and clutched her middle.

"What's the matter? You sick?"

"No!" Teagan's voice rose, then a little quieter, she said, "I mean, I'm not sick—exactly." Unshed tears pooled in her eyes, threatening to spill over.

She fled from Granny's bedroom.

That clinched it. Something was terribly wrong. Could she be pregnant? No, impossible. Teagan was the champion of chastity before marriage.

Thirty minutes passed. Where was Teagan?

Granny fetched her tattered Bible from the nightstand and fingered through the tissue-like pages. Colored markers and red and blue inked notes greeted her like old friends. Gus had given her this Bible for their fifth wedding anniversary. When she could barely find room to add notes, she'd bought a new one. It still sat in pristine condition on the little bookshelf nestled on the wall between the window and the corner of the room.

Automatically, the Bible flipped open to the Psalms. Psalm 23. How many hundreds of times had she read this song from David? Verse six was her favorite. "Surely goodness and mercy will follow me all the days of my life." And not just "follow," but pursue.

Thank you, Lord.

She closed her eyes in gratitude for all He had done for her.

"Granny?" Teagan's whisper came from the direction of the doorway.

"Yes, angel." Granny smiled at her granddaughter, even as trouble looked back at her.

"Can I talk to you?" Her voice trembled.

———

Granny patted the bed and Teagan sat next to her. Teagan fluttered her hands up to her hair, then to her clothing to tug and smooth imaginary wrinkles. Granny stretched her blue-veined hands out and stilled Teagan's long, slim fingers.

"It's okay, whatever the problem is. We'll work it out."

Tears spilled out of Teagan's eyes and down her cheeks. She took a shuddering breath. "I'm pregnant."

Granny inhaled sharply. Of all the problems she had imagined for Teagan, this was not one she realistically considered. Her granddaughter had always preached purity to her cousins and friends. How had this happened?

"Oh, my, angel. I'm so sorry. Do you want to tell me about it?"

Teagan sobbed as she hid behind her hands.

Granny, deprived of Teagan's hands, patted her granddaughter's knee and remained silent.

After a few minutes, Teagan wiped her cheeks and lifted her face.

"I let my guard down just one night. Just one night. He wasn't even anyone I'd want to be serious about. Not that it would matter. It would still have been wrong." A hiccup punctuated her words. "I'm sorry. I know I've disappointed you. I've disappointed myself."

Granny clasped Teagan's hands again. "We all make mistakes. Sure, this is a big one for you, but it is forgivable. God will forgive you."

"I've already prayed and asked for His forgiveness. But I'm not feeling it yet."

"Then you are forgiven. Feelings come and go."

"Can you ever forgive me, Granny?"

"It's already done. I assume you haven't told your parents."

Teagan's eyes widened and her face paled more, if that was possible. She moaned. "How will I tell them?"

"They love you and will continue to love you through this."

"But I'll be an embarrassment to them. I overheard one of my college dormmates say her parents threw her out of the house because she'd embarrassed them."

"Well, shame on those parents. Your mom and dad will not think that."

"Really?"

"Look, you have to be prepared that they will be shocked at first, and they're probably not going to be able to hide it. But whatever their initial reaction is, know that they love you no matter what. Just as I do."

"But you didn't act shocked."

"I've been around a lot longer than they have. Not much shocks me. And I knew something was troubling you."

Across the room, a fan rotated and swished in the momentary silence.

Granny whispered, "Have you thought about what you're going to do?"

"Nooooo!" A banshee wail spewed from Teagan's mouth. "I don't know. I don't know." She began sobbing again.

"Cry your little heart out, then we'll talk about your choices."

Teagan sniffed and snapped her head up. "I have choices?"

"Certainly you do, although I'm sure you would never consider abortion."

Teagan shook her head violently.

"But you can give the baby up for adoption or keep it and be a single mother."

Another look of horror gripped her features. "I don't think I could do either of those."

"The good news is you don't have to decide today. You have—how many months along are you?"

"Three."

"So you have about four or five months to think about it. You won't want to wait until the very last minute, of course. You can do some research, and I'll help you. Praying along the way for the Lord to give you wisdom and guidance."

Granny's heart felt shattered in a million pieces. Choices? Yes, Teagan had choices. But what Granny wouldn't tell her was that once that first bad decision had been made, all the decisions that flowed from it were God's second best. Teagan had probably figured that out by now.

Yet God was faithful. He promised to redeem the time, to work all things together for good. But...

What good could come of this unwed pregnancy? Hopefully, a beautiful, precious baby. What else did God have in mind?

Granny shook off her momentary doubts, scooped up the shattered shards of her heart, and handed them to the Holy Spirit.

———

A puff of air ruffled the snapdragons tucked into a bark-covered urn on Granny's patio table. But it was hot, and August air lacked in any comfort, searing the flowers' already drooping petals.

Granny picked up the urn, but her fractured elbow protested. *Oww.* The urn plunked onto the table, teetering with the sudden drop. She steadied it with her good hand.

Four weeks later and her arm, to say nothing of the wrist and hand, felt as if it would never heal. She couldn't shampoo her own hair or tote things around. Good thing it was her left arm and not her right.

And thank goodness for Teagan. She stayed with her most nights and days when she didn't have to work.

A fledgling peace hung over the family now that they'd moved past the initial shock of Teagan's news. Of course, they still weren't averse to expressing their opinions on what she needed to do. Granny supposed her parents had some right to give advice.

She plucked the dying flowers from the vase with her good hand and stepped out back to the compost pile. Tossing them on top, she chuckled, thinking how they brightened up the decaying mound.

"Granny. You out here?" Teagan's weary voice sounded from the back door.

"Coming."

They greeted each other in the open doorway, Teagan hugging Granny gently, keeping to her unharmed side.

"You're here early, aren't you?"

"Fortunately, we were over-staffed today, so I asked to leave early."

They moved into the stuffy kitchen that was no improvement on the heat outside.

"Want some iced tea?"

"Always. But you sit down. I'll get it."

Granny snapped the fan to high and aimed it toward the table. "I wonder how much it would cost to add central air conditioning to this old place. The older I get, the harder it is to handle the heat."

"You could always move—"

"Don't go there. I'm not moving."

Teagan blew out a breath through pursed lips and set the tea glasses on the table. "I'm just sayin'." She put both hands on the table and eased onto the slat-backed kitchen chair.

"You look mighty tired," Granny said, peering at the slump of Teagan's shoulders.

"If I'm this tired at only four months, how will I last another five? Or does it get better?" Her hands cradled the frosty glass.

"What's the doctor say?"

"I'm mostly normal."

"Mostly? What does that mean?" Whatever it meant, it didn't sound good. Or was Granny borrowing trouble?

"I'm a little anemic, so that would account for me being tired. He prescribed me an iron supplement. But I've been taking it for a month. Shouldn't I be feeling better by now?"

"It doesn't help that you're constantly running back and forth to the hotel, your apartment, and here. Taking care of your ol' invalid granny."

"Now stop that. Helping you is not a problem. Your house seems to be the one bright spot where I can relax. And when I'm here, I feel at home."

Home? Here?

The notion ricocheted through Granny's mind. Why hadn't she thought of it before? It could solve both of their problems.

Immediately, an argument waged in Granny's mind. That vague reason of weeks ago finally forced its way to the forefront, begging to be scratched. Okay. She'd admit it. She preferred her independence, living alone. And she didn't like being told what to do. Especially by upstart kids or grand-kids. Why didn't they understand she was still her own person? Someone who could make up her own mind without their interference? An elder whom they should respect?

Would Teagan disrespect her and boss her around?

On the other hand, she was being selfish. Teagan would

need help either with expenses while she was on maternity leave or with the baby if she chose to keep it.

But would Miss Independent Teagan feel like her grandmother was offering her charity? Even so, wasn't that what families, grandmothers, were for? It wasn't charity. It was taking care of each other.

She didn't want Teagan to think she was obligated because her poor, aging grandmother couldn't take care of herself. But it might keep the family off her back in their quest to move her into assisted living.

Could Granny give up some of her independence to help her granddaughter? If so, how could she get Teagan to see the benefits for both of them?

———

Even after a week, the argument warred in Granny's head. She'd lived alone so long, the thought of having someone else in the house full time set her teeth on edge. Even if it was her sweet granddaughter, Teagan.

Sure, they'd gotten along the last few weeks while Teagan spent most of her time in Granny's home. But there were those times when Teagan wouldn't let her lift something Granny knew she could lift. Or when she thought she could have peace and solitude with her morning cup of coffee, and Teagan joined her.

Woman, you're being petty. This girl needs help.

Granny was out of sorts with herself when she and Teagan returned home from church. To add to the internal wrangling, that morning the pastor had preached on I Corinthians 13, reminding the congregation that of faith, hope, and love, the greatest of these is love and that love is not self-seeking. Was that what she was doing? Failing to sacrifice her personal space and making herself a noisy gong?

Granny sucked in a deep breath and pressed ahead.

"Angel, have you considered how you will afford your apartment when you have to stop working?"

"Why would I have to do that?"

"The stories of women having their babies in the field and getting right back to hoeing are greatly exaggerated. You will need to take some time off."

Teagan's eyes widened, then she chortled. "You're too funny. But I see what you mean. So much to think about."

"And God forbid, what if your anemia doesn't get better, and you're forced to quit work early?"

"Thanks for that cheerful thought." Teagan rolled her eyes.

"We have to prepare for all contingencies." Granny took another deep breath. She had to do this for her granddaughter. Direct and to the point was always best with Teagan. "Why don't you give up your apartment and move in with me? You already have your own bedroom and bathroom here. You're here most of the time anyway. Why waste money on rent?"

"Weeeell."

"You and I are independent women. So we can come and go as we like." Granny hoped that was true. No, she didn't just hope, she trusted the Lord.

Teagan tilted her head, her shiny brown hair falling like a waterfall to her right shoulder.

"And maybe it will take a little pressure off the decisions you have to make. You won't have to worry about money. And if you decide to keep the baby, you wouldn't have to move. I could help take care of it."

"I don't think you'd be up to taking care of a newborn."

"My elbow will heal long before that."

"I was thinking more about how you haven't taken care of children since I was little. You know, like twenty years ago."

"I'm not a complete tottering old fool, you know." She punctuated the end of her sentence with a huff.

"Oh, Granny." Teagan's features softened, her blue eyes shining with tears. "I didn't mean that. I'm just concerned about you taking on too much."

"Oh, of course, I know you didn't. But listen. I don't want you to feel obligated, but maybe if you moved in here, the family would leave me alone about that assisted living nonsense." Granny hoped she hadn't pushed Teagan into feeling indebted, despite telling her not to.

"That's a thought anyway."

"Will you think about it?"

"Yes, of course. Now let's fix some dinner. Do you have stuff for a salad?"

It was the right thing to do. Granny told herself that several times, trusting God to show her it was true.

———

Granny put a finger in the book she was reading, then hugged the book to her chest. *Oww.* That rebellious elbow was taking its sweet time to heal. Shouldn't eight weeks be long enough? She dropped the book to her lap, losing her place, then rubbed her arm.

Not even one of her favorite mystery authors or her morning news ritual held her attention today.

Teagan was taking her time deciding whether she wanted to move in, and Granny was getting antsy. Yes, she knew her granddaughter had a lot of matters to consider. But making this decision sooner than later would help make the other decisions. Wouldn't it?

Regardless of Teagan's decision, Granny would not, could not, move into some ratty senior home. And she would not let her kids tell her what to do. Who did they think they were anyway?

Stop thinking like that. You know they're doing it out of love. Yes. But I'm not feeble. I can still make my own decisions.

Somehow, since she'd suggested Teagan move in with her, the idea of losing her independence didn't seem so important. Although she had to remind herself of that from time to time.

Rustling, then footfalls, sounded in the hallway.

"Teagan, that you?"

"No, it's Bradley Cooper."

"Who?"

"Tom Cruise?" Teagan appeared at Granny's side. "You know who that is, right? Or maybe I need to say Clark Gable. Or some other old, old movie star."

"I know who Tom Cruise is." Granny chuckled.

Teagan sank onto the couch, and her face lost its smile, becoming serious. "I've made a decision." She glanced away and peered out the window.

"About what exactly?" Granny held her breath.

"If you still want me to move in here, I would like to."

Joy filled Granny's heart. "Oh, angel, I can't tell you how happy that makes me."

"My lease is up next month, so I'll gradually move the rest of my stuff over. I'll either sell my furniture or put it in storage." Teagan cradled her growing abdomen. "But I still don't know what to do about this."

This being the baby growing inside of her.

"Have you been praying about it?"

"Like all day, every day. But I don't seem to be getting any answers. I don't feel like He's listening."

"Oh, dear one. He's there, and He's listening. He will answer in His timing."

Teagan inhaled deeply and blew it out slowly.

"What are your thoughts?" It wasn't Granny's place to push her one way or the other.

Her granddaughter fell back against the couch. "I checked out the county adoption websites. I can give up the baby and keep it private, or I can choose an open adoption. That would give me contact with the adoptive parents. I also looked at private adoption attorneys. The adoptive parents pay the fees." She closed her eyes and rested her head against the cushion.

"Sounds like you are leaning toward adoption." The joy that was in her heart moments ago evaporated. Wouldn't she get to know her first great-grandchild?

"I don't deserve to keep my baby, do I?"

Granny's breath caught. "Deserve? What do you mean?"

"I sinned, I betrayed the Lord, and I betrayed myself. Me. Preaching to the other kids about chastity. They'll think me a hypocrite."

"Let's not worry about others right now. Forget what you think you deserve. God doesn't sit around waiting to lower the boom on you when you do something wrong. You said you repented and asked for forgiveness, right?"

Teagan nodded.

"Then you're forgiven. But there are natural consequences to our actions. Instead of thinking about what you do or do not deserve, think about what is best for the baby and then what is best for you."

"I don't know which would be harder. Being a single mother or giving my baby away."

"What do you think would be best for the baby?"

Teagan held her grandmother's gaze for several moments. "Children need two parents, don't they? That seems the best. But…wouldn't she think I didn't love her? Wouldn't it be best for her to be with me, her real mother? Besides. Who gives up babies anymore? It seems like everyone just becomes a single mother."

Anguish over Teagan's struggle collected in the back of Granny's throat, strangling her. How could she help her through this? She couldn't decide for her. And what decision would that be anyway? As much as Granny wanted to get to know her first great-grandchild, could she, in good conscience, tell Teagan keeping the child and being a single mother was the best choice?

———

"Thank you, young man," Granny told the person who delivered their steak and garlic mashed potatoes. "Smells delicious."

"This looks amazing." Teagan speared a piece of pink tinged beef. "Thank you for treating me to such a fancy dinner."

"I'm glad you're settled in. We had to celebrate."

Teagan placed her knife and fork on her plate and patted her mouth with the linen napkin. Her bright blue eyes peeked from under her bangs as she gazed at Granny.

"I got the result of my ultrasound today." She paused and gave a Mona Lisa smile. "It's a girl."

"A girl?" Granny was sure her face took on a silly smile.

"And we can celebrate a decision I've made."

Granny's heart sped up. *Lord, help me trust she has allowed you to guide her to the right decision. That it's in your will.* She put down her cutlery and gave her granddaughter every iota of her attention.

"Granny, don't look so worried. I've prayed about this almost nonstop. I'm making the right decision." Teagan's voice softened on the last sentence.

Thank you for that reassurance, Lord. Could she wipe the worried look off her face and encourage Teagan?

"Whatever your decision, I'm here for you."

"I'm giving the baby up for adoption." Teagan's gaze searched her grandmother's, no doubt looking for that reassurance.

Adoption? Would Teagan never get to see or hold her baby? And what about her?

She parked her facial expression in neutral. "You're absolutely sure this is what you want?"

"What I'm absolutely sure I want is a husband, a home, and a baby. In that order. But that's not an option with this baby, no matter how much I already love her. What I want is for this baby is to have a two-parent family. To have the blessings that I had with a loving family."

"Then, angel, you've made the right decision."

"I'm going through a private attorney, and it will be an open adoption of sorts."

"What does 'of sorts' mean?"

"I won't actually know the names of the adoptive parents and won't have contact with them. But I will have access to a sealed file held by the attorney. I can decide to look at it anytime I want."

"Have you signed anything?"

"Only an application, so they can start looking for the right parents. I can't sign any final relinquishment papers until the baby is six weeks old. And then only if I appear to be in a stable emotional place."

Granny searched Teagan's face. She appeared confident, serene even. But she suspected, before all was said and done, Teagan would have a lot more emotional upheaval to work through.

And Granny would be there to love and support her. A good exchange for losing a little independence.

The End

Made in the USA
Las Vegas, NV
12 May 2022

48785598R00162